PRAISE FOR THE WILLIE CUESTA MYSTERY SERIES

"The narratives are consistently straightforward, light and crisp."   —*Publishers Weekly* on *In the War Zone of the Heart*

"The rich and varied characters in this intriguingly twisty tale spring organically from the sandy soil of South Florida. This intelligent, timely novel is sure to win Lantigua new fans."
—*Publishers Weekly* on *Remember My Face*, a 2021 Shamus Awards
Nominee in the Best Original Private Eye Paperback category

"Miami private eye Willie Cuesta is sent to central Florida to track down a missing person. Maybe persons. A heartfelt account of the risks Latinos face in modern America whether or not they're undocumented."
—*Kirkus Reviews* on *Remember My Face*

"This thoroughly entertaining crime novel flirts with a number of the genre's central themes—kidnapping for ransom, drug dealing, betrayal, revenge, the silky seductiveness of a whole lot of money—filtering them through the special sensibility of Miami PI Willie Cuesta. A real find for crime-fiction fans."
—*Booklist* starred review of *On Hallowed Ground*

"The fast-paced action is well matched by concise prose, making this a treat for Elmore Leonard devotees."
—*Publishers Weekly* on *On Hallowed Ground*

IN THE WAR ZONE OF THE HEART

WILLIE CUESTA MYSTERY STORIES

JOHN LANTIGUA

Arte Público Press
Houston, Texas

In the War Zone of the Heart: Willie Cuesta Mystery Stories is published in part with support from the National Endowment for the Arts. We are grateful for its support.

Recovering the past, creating the future

Arte Público Press
University of Houston
4902 Gulf Fwy, Bldg 19, Rm 100
Houston, Texas 77204-2004

Cover design by Mora Designs
Cover art by Grizelle Paz

The story, "The Jungle," first appeared in *And the Dying Is Easy* (Signet, 2001). All the other stories in this collection were first published in *Ellery Queen Mystery Magazine*.

Cataloging-in-Publication (CIP) Data is available.

22 23 24   4 3 2 1

This book is dedicated to Janet Hutchings, Jackie Sherbow and all the other folks at Ellery Queen Mystery Magazine. Thank you for your support.

TABLE OF CONTENTS

INTRODUCTION

Many years ago, I read an article about the writer Dashiell Hammett, who began publishing in the 1920s and is often called the dean of the private eye genre in American literature. Hammett is best known as the author of the classic crime novels *The Maltese Falcon* and *The Thin Man*, but he wrote other novels and shorter works that originally appeared in the old pulp magazines, such as *Black Mask*.

According to the article, Hammett saw the private eye as a modern version of the knights errant of medieval times. They were the warriors who wandered out from their castles on horseback to slay dragons, rescue damsels in distress and deal with the bad guys of the era who were afflicting the general populace. These adventures were known as quests.

In 1998, after publishing three stand-alone crime novels, I decided I wanted to create a private eye of my own. I was living in the Miami area, as I do now. I'm half Cuban and I knew I wanted to make my character a Cuban American and a former cop. I could picture him in my mind's eye, but I didn't know his name. I kicked around some ideas, but nothing sounded quite right. Then I remembered the article I'd read all those years before about Hammett. I wanted my private eye to be a modern knight errant, who went on quests to right wrongs, especially in the Latino communities of Florida. Suddenly, the Spanish surname Cuesta popped into my head. Moments later I heard his first name, and Willie Cuesta was born.

Since then, Willie has starred in five published novels: *Player's Vendetta, The Ultimate Havana, The Lady from Buenos Aires, On Hallowed Ground* and *Remember My Face.* A sixth novel is finished and on the way.

Willie has also plied his trade in numerous short stories. All except one of the stories in this collection were originally published in Ellery Queen Mystery Magazine, one of the very last surviving pulp magazines, now in its eighty-first glorious year.

I think Hammett, if he were still alive, would approve of Willie Cuesta and his quest for justice. I hope you do too.

THE JUNGLE

Willie Cuesta drove over the Intracoastal Waterway and entered Palm Beach at about 10:00 a.m. that Tuesday morning. He had made it from Miami in a little more than an hour and a half. But, of course, there was no way to measure, in either miles or minutes, the distance between his blue collar neighborhood of Little Havana and this posh play ground of America's aristocracy—home to the Vanderbilts, the Kennedys, the Pulitzers and the Posts.

It was his friend Alice Arden, riding shotgun, who put it into words.

"Make sure you don't hit anybody in this town, Willie," she said from behind her sunglasses. "The locals here have lawyers who eat human flesh."

"I'll do my best," Willie assured her.

Willie followed the directions he had received from his old police colleague, Arnie Corcoran. They took him onto Worth Avenue, the main drag, which was no commonplace shopping strip. It featured Saks and Chanel, Ungaro and Armani, lots of galleries and a Gucci instead of a Gap.

Alice's eyebrows arched. "It's Worth Avenue, but I bet it used to be Net Worth Avenue. They shortened it."

They turned and traveled along the oceanfront, but Willie wasn't sure where he was going. So, they stopped and talked to a young man dressed in white linen, just getting out of a lemon-colored Lamborghini. They asked him how to get to the Breakers Hotel, where they were supposed to breakfast with Corcoran.

The man pointed up the road in the direction they were going.

"You go to the estate on the corner that used to belong to Estée Lauder. You turn left, go the length of a good three wood shot, hang a right at that street and you'll see the twin towers." They thanked him, took the dogleg he described, and found the place.

The Breakers was a legendary hotel, hard on the water and also hard on the wallet. They valeted the car in the porte cochere and entered a lobby that looked something like the Palace at Versailles. Lots of columns, tapestries, mythological figures painted on the arched ceiling and large chandeliers out of the Middle Ages. Willie offered Alice his arm and she took it regally, accepting her chance to play Marie Antoinette in sunglasses.

They found Arnie Corcoran in a circular dining room topped with a leaded glass cupola. Arnie was a former patrol lieutenant in Miami who had taken the job of assistant chief in Palm Beach. He was a tall, sandy-haired, red-faced guy, in a summer suit, bright pink shirt and no tie. They ordered breakfast and Arnie addressed the issue at hand.

"It's like I told you on the phone, Willie. We have an extremely old and wealthy man, one of our leading citizens, who has received anonymous messages that his life is in danger. The messages, left on an answering machine, are in Spanish."

"But this gentleman isn't Latino," Willie said.

"No, but his family made its fortune in Latin America. They were officers and principal stockholders in a firm called the Central American Fruit Company, based in Guatemala. Very big banana importers. He worked down there part of the time, running things. His name is Harold Usser."

"He was the big banana."

"Exactly. He said his Spanish was never great because he had managers to actually convey his orders and oversee the native workers, but he understood enough about the messages to comprehend that someone wanted to kill him. The messages are still on the tape. They mention his family and supposedly certain crimes they committed down there."

Willie frowned. "What crimes?"

Arnie shook his head. "Usser insists he doesn't know what the messages mean."

"Does he have any idea who might have left them?"

"No."

"What kind of security does he have?"

"A gardener lives on the property and doubles as a security guard. Usser also has a houseman, a cook who's married to the gardener and a maid. All of them live on the premises."

"Sounds like a big spread."

"You'll see. Anyway, his niece, who lives nearby, feels he's not safe no matter how many servants surround him. She says these threats are the kind that political terrorists in Central America make, maybe because the family took all its money from down there. I don't have anybody on my staff who has ever handled this kind of stuff. But you have, Willie."

Willie shrugged in acknowledgment. Before becoming a private investigator, Willie had worked for years in the Intelligence Unit of the Miami Police Department. He and his colleagues tracked all the political organizations in Miami Cuban commandos, Central American freedom fighters, Colombian guerrillas, Haitian patriots, Israelis, Bosnians, etc. The unit also helped guard visiting diplomats and other dignitaries. It was a busy beat.

Arnie sipped his coffee. "The hotel manager here has very generously given the department use of a suite for the rest of the week, plus access to the health club, golf course, tennis courts, sauna, et cetera. You look into the case, Willie, and tell me what you can, and then you can wile away the rest of the week with Ms. Collins here, on the house."

Willie had a couple of questions, but Alice didn't give him a chance to ask them. She beamed at Arnie. "In the name of Willie Cuesta, I'd like to accept the assignment."

๑๖ ๑๖

A half hour later they had checked in, Alice had been deposited happily at the pool and Willie and Arnie were on their way to the Usser mansion. They followed the oceanfront road south and as they did the mansions seemed to swell. Behind the high walls and the wrought-iron gates guarded by stone lions, Willie saw palaces in different designs—Mediterranean, Spanish Colonial and some in a style that could only be called Classical Gaudy. Arnie noticed Willie's wide-eyed gaze.

"A lot of these were built before there was an income tax. They had some extra change to spend."

"So I noticed."

A minute later they pulled up to a pair of those tall gates. A gold plaque embedded in the wall announced that this particular bungalow was called LA SELVA. In Spanish that meant "The Jungle." The white stucco wall was about twelve feet high and vines crawled over it from the other side.

Arnie spoke into an intercom and the gates swung open automatically. A long, winding stone drive, at least a quarter mile long, led them through a lush tropical garden, a few acres across, which explained the name on the plaque. There had to be a hundred varieties of palm trees in there, not to mention banyan trees, *flamboyanes,* air plants, and several peacocks strutting about.

The road emerged from the trees and became a driveway that swept up to the front door of a two-story, Spanish Colonial fortress. It was about a block long, complete with bell tower. The roof was red-tiled, the walls white stucco, the railings and window grilles black wrought iron. All that architecture seemed to be held together by leafy green vines that had almost consumed the construction. The jungle indeed.

They were met at the marble front stairs by a short, stocky, serious Latin man about forty, dressed in a camouflage shirt and cap, with a rake in his hand and a pistol on his hip. He introduced himself as Juan, the gardener and security guard.

Then the houseman appeared at the door. His name was Carlos, a slender and slightly older man with salt and pepper hair, who wore a crisp white shirt, and pants and bow tie that were both black. He led them into a dark foyer as big as the lobbies of some hotels; then through a high-ceilinged drawing room large enough for a national dance contest and so dank it felt as if a torrential rain would fall inside at any moment; and, finally, into a cluttered study that smelled of books rotting from humidity. Each room was crowded with pre-Columbian ceramics, old paintings and studded Spanish Colonial furniture, so that you might have been in a minor and badly lighted museum south of the border. In between those artifacts stood potted banana plants, lots of them, maybe to remind visitors where the money had come from to buy everything.

The man they had come to see also resembled a museum piece. Harold Usser sat in a high-backed red chair and a beam of light fell through the arched window right on him, although he looked exactly like the physical type who shouldn't be in the sun. He was a heavy-set, red-faced man, with a bald dome, who had to be at least eighty years old. It looked as if he were dressed to match the banana plants, in a green silk robe and green slippers. His expression was disgruntled, maybe because of what he was seeing on a nearby television screen, where stock prices crawled by. His yellowed teeth were bared in a growl. A cigar burned in an ashtray next to him, clouding the room.

Near him stood a slender, middle-aged woman, expensively dressed, who Willie figured had to be the niece. He was right. Her name was Nadine Usser.

After introductions were made, Ms. Usser simply pushed the message button on the answering machine next to her uncle. A man's voice was heard, speaking somber Spanish.

"This is a warning that Señor Harold Usser has very few days left to live. The crimes committed by him and his family in the past will be the cause of his death. His sins have finally caught up with him."

That message ended and then another came on, the same voice, but recorded several days later, according to the dates given by the machine. It was basically the same warning, but it ended differently.

"Now you are even closer to your undoing, Señor Usser. The spirits of the past will put you in your grave soon. Very soon! You know your crimes and you know why you will die." That was it.

Arnie asked to hear them again. Willie listened as he glanced around the room. The walls were decorated with old, framed photographs, some of them sepia tint, most of them taken in the tropics, particularly on banana plantations. They depicted lush stands of banana plants; a few large, white-faced men, some in sun helmets; and lots of small, dark local workers. Other photos depicted fancy social occasions where the white people were dressed more formally and the local workers, dressed in white, helped serve the food and refreshments. Those workers all had the same dazzled look on their faces that peasants seemed to get before cameras—like deer caught in the headlights.

The messages finished playing and Willie sat down before the old man.

"Mr. Usser, you've said before that you don't know what these messages mean—the reference to crimes. Is that still true?"

The old man fixed him with rheumy eyes and that bitter expression, as if he'd just bitten into an unripe banana. He spoke loudly, the way people do who don't hear well.

"I said I didn't," he shouted in a gravelly voice and turned back to the television.

His voice indicated he had smoked too many cigars, his belly reflected too many bananas, and his face was fissured not only with time, but with rum and maybe other drink. Mr. Usser had not only been a producer of bananas, but a consumer of "the good life." Although it appeared he didn't have much good life left. He looked like a very unhealthy man.

"And you have no idea who issued these warnings?"

The old man erupted then. "I just told you, didn't I! Do what you're paid for and leave me alone! All of you, get away from me! Get away from me now!" He waved his hand irritatedly, as if to strike at Willie, and turned back to the stock ticker on the television screen, as if it were his own heart line on a hospital monitor.

The niece rolled her eyes and then she, Arnie and Willie left Harold Usser to keep track of his largesse. They went into the drawing room and Nadine Usser apologized.

"Excuse my uncle. He doesn't sleep well. He's been under the weather."

Willie suspected that Harold Usser's climate had always been somewhat unpleasant.

"I take it you also have no idea what those messages mean," Willie said.

She shrugged. "For years I've heard what everyone in my family has heard. That the company always paid off politicians down there, that we controlled a corner of Guatemala, that if the family had trouble, labor trouble, it just hired the army to go in and take care of it. I've heard that people were killed in those disputes. Now some say those were crimes the company committed. My uncle insists it was a jungle and that's the way business was done back then in the jungle. He says he has committed no crimes. Period."

As the niece spoke, Willie noticed a maid in a black uniform dusting a table just outside the room, her back to them. He nodded in her direction.

"I've seen three of your servants and noticed they're all Latin. I imagine they all speak Spanish."

She nodded. "All the servants are from Guatemala. My uncle has always had people from there working for him."

"Do you think any of them might know who's behind these threats?"

She shook her head. "I can't imagine it. These are good people, Mr. Cuesta, not terrorists. And they've all been with him for a while. The truth is my uncle can be unpleasant, as you've seen, and he has had trouble keeping servants. But this group has been very steady, very loyal. In fact, lately one or more of them has been staying up at night to make sure he is safe."

The maid was still dusting that same small table just outside the door. She was within earshot and had been for a while. Of course, servants would always be curious about strangers in the house, such as Willie. He turned back to the niece.

"Does this house have room for a guest?"

"Of course."

"Then, I think I'll spend the night."

❧ ❧

Arrangements were made. Arnie went back to the hotel to pick up Willie's toiletries and a change of clothes and Willie called Alice. She had just come in from the sauna.

"A lot of ladies only in towels, Willie. You would have liked it. I've been invited to play croquet on the back lawn later and drink martinis. We'll miss you." Willie told her it was good that at least someone was enjoying his vacation and that he would see her the next day. He hung up then and headed outside.

First, he wandered into the extensive garden, drifting around, then examining some orchids, until he felt eyes on him. It was Juan, the somber gardener, watching him through the vegetation. He was replanting a small palm next to a fern-lined pond when Willie approached. Willie spoke to him in Spanish, complimented him on his green thumb, and they exchanged pleasantries.

"How long have you worked here?" Willie asked finally.

"Two years now, Señor," he said, still working his shovel.

"I understand your wife is the cook."

"That's right, Señor. Her name is Naomi."

"Did you come to work here together?"

"First I came and then my wife, after the other cook left."

"I understand quite a few servants have left over the years."

Juan shrugged and plunged the shovel into the rich earth.

"I don't know about that, Señor."

"And how was it you found these jobs? You just got lucky?"

Juan glanced at him from under the brim of his camouflage cap as if he were peeking at him from behind a bush. He was a watchful, wary fellow, which maybe was fitting since he was the security guard.

"No, we came because I knew Carlos, the houseman. He helped get us the jobs."

"So, Carlos has been here some time."

"Yes, Señor."

"Is he the one who has been here the longest?"

Juan nodded. "Yes, sir."

He seemed increasingly uncomfortable at the questions and now he put down his shovel.

"Excuse me, but I need to bring more soil." He turned and disappeared into the dense foliage.

Willie waited a few minutes for him, but Juan didn't return. The soil must have been far away. Willie then found his way back to the house and went looking for a glass of water to fend off the afternoon heat. He found it in the kitchen, a dusky, high-ceilinged cavern full of ovens and cupboards, at the rear of the house, where he also found Juan's wife, Naomi. A small, dark woman of about forty, she had a stocky build like Juan. But unlike her husband, she was friendly and smiling. She wore a long apron with black and white cows imprinted on it.

Willie gulped his water. "Do you like working here, Naomi?"

She nodded enthusiastically. "Oh, yes, Señor. I like it here very much. It is a very beautiful place."

"But I understand that Mr. Usser is sometimes difficult, unkind. That he has driven many servants out of here over the years."

As Willie might have expected, the woman didn't want to discuss the disposition of her employer. One could lose his or her job that way. She simply shrugged and smiled enigmatically.

"I guess you and the other servants who work here now are just more understanding than the others were," Willie said.

She nodded. "Maybe, Señor."

"I'm told you and your husband came to work here at about the same time. Did you come directly from Guatemala?"

"Oh, no, Señor. First we worked in the sugar cane fields near here. Then Don Harold—Señor Usser—he hired us."

"I see."

The western side of Palm Beach County was dedicated to agriculture, much of it owned by sugar companies. The work was hot and backbreaking and was performed almost exclusively by Latin and Caribbean immigrant cane cutters. The arrangement made for radically different populations from one side of the county to the other. The cane cutters on the west and the Social Register types in the east, right on the ocean. Willie imagined that it also made for a handy supply of servants who would be more than willing to move across the county and live in mansions.

Willie sipped his water. "I understand that Carlos, the houseman, helped you find this work. Did you know him from the cane fields?"

Naomi nodded and the smile remained in place. but behind her eyes Willie suddenly saw the same wariness he had seen in her husband. He sensed someone behind him, and when he turned, he found Juan standing in the doorway watching them. He didn't have his rake, but his gun was still on his hip. Naomi reached for her coin purse.

"Juan has to take me to the store now, Señor. I need to buy shrimp for dinner. Don Harold, he only wants it fresh." They excused themselves and hurried out about as fast as they could go.

Willie drained his water and went looking for Carlos, the houseman. But he didn't find him. Harold Usser was napping in that same red chair and apparently Carlos had snuck out.

But Willie did find the maid, the same one he had seen earlier in a black uniform. She was cleaning the guest room, or at least she was pretending to, when Willie went to freshen up. When he walked in she was looking into the closet where his clothes hung.

As he opened the door, she whirled around as if she'd been caught at something. Earlier, Willie had only seen her from behind. Now he saw that she was an older woman, about sixty. Her skin was extremely creased by age and by the sun and across her right cheek was a scar, light pink amid the dark lines, where she had once been badly cut.

"Were you looking for something?"

"I was just making sure your clothes were hung up correctly, Señor."

She closed the closet door and they introduced themselves. Her name was Beatrice. Willie encouraged her to finish her dusting and sat down on the edge of the bed.

"How long have you been here, Beatrice?"

"About three years, Señor."

She didn't look at him as she dusted. Maybe it was out of Latin deference. Maybe she was shy, or maybe it was behavior that came with that scar.

Willie watched her work. "So, you've been here a bit longer than Juan and Naomi."

"That's right, Señor."

"Did Carlos, the houseman, also help you get this job?"

She passed her dust cloth over the dresser, which already looked clean.

"Yes, Señor. Carlos helped all of us. He's a good man."

Willie was afraid she would skip out on him as the other two had, so he got right down to the nitty-gritty.

"Do you know anyone who might have reason to threaten Señor Usser? You must have heard about the phone calls."

She was shaking her head before he concluded the question. "I don't know anyone who would want to hurt Don Harold."

"Even though Don Harold is sometimes a very unpleasant person?"

"I don't know what you mean, Señor."

"You must have heard the accusations against him and his family. You're from Guatemala, aren't you? His was a very well-known company down there."

"I know nothing of such things, Señor. I'm just a simple servant."

She made for the door then. Willie stood up and blocked her way. For several moments they stood in silence just inches apart. He wanted to ask her how she had gotten the scar on her face, but he couldn't bring himself to do it.

"What is it, Señor?" she asked him.

"I understand that the servants have been staying up at night guarding Señor Usser. Is that right?"

"Yes, Carlos and Juan have done that."

"I guess you're all very worried about him."

Willie looked into her eyes, and she hesitated before she spoke. "Yes, that's true. We are very worried," she said. "Is that all, Señor?"

Willie nodded. "Yes, that's all." He stepped out of her way. She turned the scar away from him and hurried down the hall.

Dinner was served promptly at eight o'clock in the formal dining room. The only two people at the table were Harold Usser, who sat at the head, and Willie, right next to him: The table had to be twenty feet long, and was covered in a bright white linen tablecloth, held in place by antique silver candle sticks that looked Mexican in design.

Carlos was the principal dinner servant. Willie hadn't seen him all afternoon, until he came to the table wearing a short, white waistcoat and carrying the wine.

Usser and Willie ate in almost total silence. Willie tried a few conversational gambits, but the old man didn't respond. He ate very little, grumbled about the food, and tired before the last course was served. He was helped into a wheelchair and was taken up in the elevator to the second-floor bedrooms to retire for the evening. Willie ate his dessert alone, caramelized bananas with vanilla ice cream. They were delicious.

Right after dinner it got dark. Night fell over the sea and the shaded grounds like a shroud. Willie smoked a cigar on the patio facing the ocean and watched the last daylight disappear. Then he went looking for the servants, figuring to ask a few more questions or at least have someone to talk to.

But he couldn't find any of them. First, he tried the kitchen, but Naomi had decamped and no one else was there. Then he roamed the gloomy house, first floor and second. Old man Usser was asleep in a four-poster bed in the master bedroom. But no one else was to be found.

The servants' quarters were in a separate structure across the driveway from the main house. That building was also finished in white stucco and consisted of a central corridor with four rooms leading off it, two on each side, like a dormitory. The hallway was decorated with more old photographs of the banana plantations in Guatemala, maybe to make the servants feel at home. Willie knocked on each door, but received no reply. The place was abandoned.

The garage stood right next to that building and it appeared all the vehicles were there, including a relatively new Rolls Royce, a vintage Rolls and a pickup truck for the servants.

The only place left to look was in that sprawling garden, or the Jungle as it was called. Willie began to walk the trails that wound through the vegetation. There was a moon and it provided him with just enough light to navigate the narrow paths. The night insects made quite a racket. The garden was as dense as a jungle and Willie wondered what other kinds of creatures—snakes, in particular— might also be found there. But he kept going.

Then he heard voices. Quietly, he made the last bend in the trail and saw the servants, all four of them, plus a fifth man who was younger and wore a full beard. He was dressed in black.

They all stood in the shadow of the outer wall of the estate and next to an open wrought-iron door that said SERVANTS ENTRANCE. Over the door burned a light bulb that illuminated them. As Willie approached, the fifth person, the bearded one, was speaking excitedly. Willie heard only a few words.

"¡. . . que le matemos!" That we kill him!

Carlos answered him excitedly, but Willie didn't hear what he said.

Then, suddenly, they all saw him. As Willie stepped into the light of the bulb, the bearded man bolted through the open gate. Willie tried to get to him, but both Carlos and Juan clogged the doorway and Willie couldn't grab him. By the time Willie squeezed through them, the bearded man had run down the road. He soon disappeared into the darkness.

Willie turned and confronted them all. "Who was that guy?"

It was Carlos, still in his white waistcoat, who answered. "He's a young man who used to work here as a chauffeur. He came by just to say hello."

"What's his name?"

"Ramón."

"And why did he run away?"

Carlos shrugged. "Because he isn't supposed to be here. Those are the rules that Señor Usser made for former employees. But Ramón just came for a harmless visit."

Willie's eyes narrowed into a squint.

"Harmless? That's why he was recommending that you kill Harold Usser?"

Carlos feigned surprise. "No, Señor. He did not say that. He wasn't speaking of Señor Usser at all."

"I heard it."

Carlos shook his head, his intelligent eyes delving Willie's face. "You misunderstood, Señor. You see we have a cat that has come on the property and tried to kill the peacocks. He was speaking of that. No one here would ever think of killing Don Harold. That's preposterous."

He glanced at the others, and they all shook their heads.

Willie wasn't believing any of it.

"There's something going on here and you people know what it is."

Carlos closed the gate, secured a padlock and turned to Willie. "We don't know what you're speaking of, Señor Cuesta. Believe me, none of us wants to see Señor Usser hurt. Now, it's late. We need to rest."

Before Willie could say anything else, the servants all headed back toward the house. They disappeared into their quarters. Willie watched them go and then hurried into the house.

He decided right then not to take any chances. He went up the stairs to the master bedroom, entered quietly and found old man Usser asleep. He was breathing shallowly, but breathing nonetheless. Willie plopped down in an armchair in the corner and lighted the lamp there. He kicked off his shoes and reached into a bookcase next to the lamp for an old mystery novel. Harold Usser wasn't going to die on Willie's watch, even if it meant staying up all night.

Over the next several hours he heard all kinds of noises. Usser issued a couple of weak cries, as if he were having nightmares. Other noises came from the sea, but lots of them came from that old creaking mansion. At one point he was sure he heard voices outside the window. He had his gun on his hip when he looked out. He thought he had heard a voice speaking urgently, like the young, bearded man had earlier. But he saw nothing. Maybe he imagined it. Maybe it was the winds off the sea, whispering through the house. Whatever those noises were, they didn't come any closer. Not then and not all night.

It was just after dawn, 6:30 a.m., when Beatrice, in uniform, opened the door and entered to attend to the old man. She was surprised to find Willie there. Then she looked down at Harold Usser. The old man's mouth was open, and his eyes were closed. She bent down close, as if to wake him, and Willie saw concern cross her face. She reached out, put her hand on Usser's cheek and pulled it away as if she had been burned. She whirled toward Willie.

"He's dead."

Willie jumped from the chair. He took Usser's limp wrist but found no pulse. He too touched the old man's cheek and found it as chilly as marble. Usser had been dead for hours.

Willie stared at the only door. He hadn't fallen asleep. No one had come through it. He was sure. Usser and he had been served from the same wine bottle and same serving dishes the night before, so he couldn't have been poisoned at dinner.

Usser's doctor was called right away and then his niece. Willie left a message at the station for Arnie, asking him to come. The servants were all clustered in the hallway when the doctor arrived.

He did a quick examination of the corpse and said it appeared that Usser had died of natural causes. "He was dying for a long time. He ate too much, drank too much and screamed too much." But he said an autopsy would be performed nonetheless because of the recent death threats.

Willie left them all gathered in the room and the hallway and walked outside. Looking over his shoulder, he made sure no one was watching and entered the servants' quarters. He opened the first door and slipped in, closing the door behind him. He saw right away that it was Carlos' room. An old, framed, black and white photo sat on a night table. It was of a man who looked much like Carlos, with his arm around a young boy of about five. It looked like it had been taken in Guatemala, maybe fifty years before.

Willie opened the one small closet, found nothing of interest, then inspected the dresser. In the bottom drawer, under some clothes, he found Carlos' immigration papers. His last name was Castillo, and he was fifty-five years old.

Willie also found a bound sheath of old, yellowed newspaper clippings in Spanish from the 1950s. The headlines spoke of turmoil, demonstrations, land disputes, army offensives, battles, people killed. They were the events Usser's niece had spoken of. The name of Usser's company appeared many times and even a photo of Usser, as a much younger, healthier and flint-eyed businessman. He had been the most powerful man in one corner of that small country.

The last clipping carried the headline "LABOR ORGANIZER ASSASSINATED!" A photo depicted a lifeless body lying face-up on a muddy rural street. The dead man was named Carlos Castillo. Willie looked at the photo in the paper and the one on the dresser. It was the same man.

Willie was still studying the clipping when the door opened behind him. It was Carlos. He looked at Willie, at the clippings and back at Willie. His face was flush with both surprise and fear.

Willie held up the last clipping. "This was your father, wasn't it?"

Carlos nodded cautiously but said nothing.

"He was a union organizer who went against the banana company, Usser's company, and they killed him. That's what these clippings say."

Carlos nodded. "And those clippings are correct."

The other three servants had appeared in the doorway behind him. They entered and closed the door.

"And the rest of you?" Willie asked.

Carlos answered. "Juan and Naomi, their families both had their land taken away from them by Usser. Their parents were forced to work the rest of their lives on the plantations, and they all died young."

"And Beatrice?"

"Beatrice was the most beautiful girl on the plantation until she said no to one of Usser's managers, then he cut her with a machete. She went and showed Usser, but he did nothing, because the manager was a favorite of his. He produced a lot of bananas. There was no recourse. Usser was a law unto himself in that part of the jungle. He was an evil man."

"And you all wanted revenge?"

Carlos nodded solemnly. "Wouldn't you?"

Willie said nothing and Carlos continued. "We worked this out over several years, waiting for openings, arranging who would take the jobs, making sure that everyone who worked for the old man thought the same way. That we were all from that same corner of our country, all had suffered at his hands and we all wanted him dead."

"And Ramón, the young chauffeur?"

"Him too."

"So why didn't you kill Usser, like Ramón wanted last night?"

"Because we saw that Usser was dying of his own evil. Not just of old age. He never knew that I was the son of a man he had ordered to be killed, but in these last years he would tell me that I reminded him of someone, of a man who had been killed. To Beatrice he used to say that she reminded him of a girl he had once known in Guatemala. Juan and Naomi made him remember all the people whose land he had stolen and who he enslaved. He was haunted by all those faces. Hardly anyone came here to see him because he was such a terrible old man. We were the only ones who surrounded him, and we gave him nightmares. If he didn't speak about those old days himself, then we would ask him, remind him of those who had died. He was dying of those nightmares, stewing in his own juices, because our faces forced him to remember his own savagery."

"But Ramón wanted to kill him.

"Yes, Ramón also comes from a poor plantation family from our part of the country. He wanted to poison Usser, shoot him, anything. He had young angry friends who wanted to help him. But we told them no. In fact, we kept Ramón from killing Usser."

Willie frowned. "What do you mean?"

"Exactly what I said. We not only didn't kill Harold Usser, Mr. Cuesta. We saved his life. You yourself heard it last night. And that's why we kept watch these nights. But we did so only so that Usser would die from the nightmares of his own making. That was justice enough."

"So, when the autopsy comes back, it won't say he was slowly poisoned, or any other act of murder."

Carlos shook his head. "All the autopsy will say is that an old man—a bad old man—died of his own bad habits, his own evil."

Willie looked at the clippings in his hand again, considered what had just been told and then finally put them down. He glanced at the servants and left that room, knowing he would never say a word to anyone. What was there to say?

He went back to the guest room, packed his things and got out of that tropical haunted house as quickly as he could. Alice was waiting next to the pool.

THE JAGUAR AT SUNSET

Willie Cuesta popped the cap on a Sierra Nevada, poured it into one of his best Irish beer glasses, fell into his favorite chair and poked the remote. Moments later, the baseball game graced the screen. His hometown heroes were already in the fourth inning, but Willie knew exactly what had happened so far. He had listened to the first three innings on the car radio while parked diagonally across from a motel in Little Havana doing a bit of divorce work. The middle-aged, cheating spouse he was tracking was apparently not a big baseball fan. He was, instead, a very big fan of his twenty-something secretary with whom he had rented the room. They had been in there a good two and a half hours.

Willie had snapped them going in and coming out and then headed home, which was nearby. He didn't like divorce work much at all, although it did pay the bills some days, and it did give him a chance to listen to the ball game while on the job. Now he could watch the rest of the game and wait until morning to write his report on the motel meet-up.

He propped his bare feet on the coffee table, crossed his ankles, took a satisfying sip of his beer, and then his cell phone sounded. He checked the screen, expecting to see the number of either his mother or his brother, Tommy, both of whom lived nearby, but it was neither. It was a number he didn't recognize, potentially a paying customer.

"Cuesta Investigations," he cooed into the phone.

"Is this Mr. Cuesta?" The voice on the other end was male and on the young side.

"Yes, it is. After-hours calls come directly to me." The fact was, Willie had no secretary, receptionist or even an answering service,

19

and all calls, no matter what time of day, came directly to him. But the fellow on the other end of the line didn't need to know that.

"How can I help you?"

"My name is Ira Deal. I was referred to you by Betty Costa and I need your help."

Betty Costa was a local lady who sponsored political debates and town hall meetings with public figures. She had hired Willie and his operatives on occasion to supply security just in case the differences of opinion got nasty.

"What kind of help can I give you?" Willie asked.

"I need you to act as a bodyguard for someone, someone very important to me."

The voice was full of emotion. In fact, it was full of fear.

"Who is this person you want to protect?"

"I'd prefer to meet with you and explain it all. Tonight, if possible."

Willie grimaced. He had just gotten comfortable, and the game was close. But business was business.

"Where do you want to meet?"

"There is a Brazilian restaurant in North Miami Beach called Rio."

"Yes, I know it."

"Can you meet me there in a half hour?"

"Okay, I'm on my way. How will I recognize you?"

"I'm six foot seven, I have red hair and I'm wearing a shirt with bright blue flowers on it. It shouldn't be hard to spot me."

"Gotcha."

ᥫᩣ ᥫᩣ

Willie listened to the ball game on the radio as he made his way from Little Havana to North Miami Beach. It was tied two-two in the sixth when he pulled up and parked across the street from the restaurant. It was on a busy commercial stretch of Collins Avenue, just a block from the beach.

He walked into the restaurant and spotted a TV above the bar. But true to its Brazilian roots, it was tuned to soccer, not baseball. Willie scanned the place for his prospective client and found him at a table at the rear near the kitchen. Ira Deal stood up as Willie approached and substantiated that he was all of six-seven. He was about twenty-five, gangly, sunburnt, and his red hair was shaggy. Apart from the flowered shirt, he wore jeans and sandals.

"Thank you for coming out at this hour," he said as they shook hands.

Willie sat and scanned the place. He had been by it but never in it before. It featured lots of large, leafy potted plants and, on the walls, colorful oil paintings of Brazil. Most were of familiar scenes: a roaring river flowing through an Amazon jungle; brightly feathered toucans in treetops; the towering statue of Jesus Christ overlooking the city of Rio. When he had been on the Miami PD, Willie had gone to Brazil once on an extradition case and had seen the statue in person. He was there to slap a Brazilian guy in shackles and throw him into prison in the US and Willie wasn't sure if Jesus, staring down at him, was happy with him or not.

A moment later, the kitchen door flapped open, and a waitress emerged with a steaming plate that smelled of cooked fish and coconut milk. Willie hadn't had dinner and suddenly realized how hungry he was. But he had business to discuss first.

"So, Mr. Deal, who is it you want me to protect?"

The youngster reached into his shirt pocket and fetched a color photograph that he handed to Willie. It pictured himself, smiling, with his arm around a much shorter, much darker, pretty young woman with indigenous features and long, flowing hair like a black waterfall. They were standing against a backdrop of thick foliage. She was not smiling.

"Where was this taken?" Willie asked.

"In Brazil, in a town deep in the Amazon jungle."

"And the girl shown here with you, who is she?"

"Her name in Constancia Mattos. I call her Connie."

"And why is it she needs protecting?"

In answer to that, Ira Deal reached into his pocket again and extracted another photograph. This depicted a middle-aged, dark-skinned, rural couple posed in front of a modest cinder-block house, also against a jungle backdrop.

"Those are Connie's parents, Oscar and Maria Mattos. They were murdered last year not far from the house pictured there. They had just left it and were walking into town when they were gunned down by someone hiding in the jungle."

Willie frowned. "Who killed them and why?"

"The names of the man or men who actually shot them to death are not known. No one else was around and assassins are a dime a dozen these days in the Amazon jungles. As for why it was done, everyone knows the answer to that. Connie's parents were leaders in a movement to stop ranchers, timber lords and miners from destroying the forests that surrounded their small village. Oscar and Maria were descendants of a native tribe that has been there for many hundreds of years with minimal contact with the outside world. But in recent years business interests from outside the Amazon have decided fortunes are to be made there. They've invaded the region with chainsaws, bulldozers and armed thugs. Several local leaders who spoke out against them were gunned down. As for Connie's parents, first the assassins came and torched their only truck. Then they poisoned their dogs and set their outbuildings ablaze. When that didn't work, they moved in and finished the job."

"And your friend Connie was able to escape."

"Connie wasn't there. She is oldest of four children and her parents had sent her to study in a larger town nearby. After her folks were murdered, she went back home and sent her younger siblings away to live with relatives. Then she addressed the Brazilian media, denounced the national government for turning a blind eye to the killings, accused the provincial police chief of being in the pay of the land grabbers and also named a local wealthy landholder as the one who had paid the assassins and signed the death warrants of her parents."

Willie grimaced. "That didn't make her too popular with the powers that be, I imagine."

The boy shook his head. "Right away she began receiving death threats. That's when I met her and convinced her she could do more by leaving that region and telling her story to as many people outside Brazil as will listen to it."

"And just what were you doing in Brazil?"

He shrugged. "I studied environmental sciences in college, and I was there because Brazil is in the front lines in the war to save the planet."

If Willie had ever met someone who seemed ill equipped to be in the front lines of a real shooting war, it was probably this kid. He was all idealism, and on top of that he was six-seven, had that bright red hair and would stick out in a place like Brazil like a metal duck in a shooting gallery.

"So, you convinced Connie to come here."

"Yes. It wasn't easy, but I did."

Willie shrugged. "So why are you worried? You really think those goons from the Amazon will come after her here? Killing her here would draw exactly the kind of attention that they won't want. The US government would raise hell and the Brazilian authorities would have to go after them."

He nodded. "Exactly, and that's why they won't send someone from land-owning clans or someone who can be easily connected to them."

"Who will they send?"

He took a deep breath, squirmed in his seat, leaned his long upper body across the table toward Willie and dropped his voice.

"When Connie and I met, we fell in love. But she already had a boyfriend in the town where she had been studying. His name is Gaspar. He wasn't very happy that an American had come along and taken his girlfriend from him. In fact, he threatened her, which was another argument I used to get her out of there. But then Connie and I received information from a friend in that town that the people who killed Connie's parents had contacted Gaspar. They were telling him that a man didn't let anyone come along and steal his woman. They told him they could arrange for him to take his revenge against Connie."

Willie was squinting at him. "In other words, Connie would end up dead, but it wouldn't be for political reasons. It would be for reasons of unrequited love and that would be the end of it."

"Exactly."

"But he didn't manage to kill Connie before she left Brazil. Do you really think he would come all the way here to cause her harm?"

Ira Deal's eyes opened wide with fear. "Oh yes, Mr. Cuesta, I do believe that could happen. First of all, you have to understand that a young woman like Connie speaking out against the powerful in her region has enraged those local bosses. And many officials in the government in Brazil are in the pockets of the bad guys. For Gaspar to get a passport under a false name would be extremely easy. For him to be given the money he needs to come here and kill her would also be no problem. And they would probably offer him extra, enough for a nest egg, if he makes it back to Brazil. And he is the kind of angry, vengeful, hopeless person who would do it."

Willie didn't argue with him. He could recall incidents in the past when powerful people in Latin America had sent assassins to kill enemies of theirs who had escaped to the US. It had happened more than once, and, presumably, it could happen again.

"But he still has to be able to find her," Willie said. "This is a large country. It isn't very difficult to hide her."

Ira Deal nodded once. "Yes, that would be true if Connie were willing to hide, but she isn't. As I told you, she insists on speaking out about the killings of her parents and other persons who have been murdered in Brazil trying to protect the land. She was invited to speak at a United Nations hearing in New York, but first she is going to speak at a rally here."

"When is that and where?"

"Tomorrow afternoon, and it will be to a group of environmentalists in Everglades National Park, at a place called the Shark Valley."

Willie was acquainted with the place. Everglades National Park had several entrances and Shark Valley was the closest to Miami. In fact, if you took Southwest Eighth Street, the main drag of Little Havana where Willie lived, and you followed it thirty miles west, you left all the strip malls and housing developments behind, you entered the wilds of the Everglades and ran right into Shark Valley.

"It's pretty far from the center of Miami, but it's still part of Miami-Dade County," Willie said. "If you're worried something could happen to your friend Connie, why don't you notify the county police? They can provide protection."

Ira shook his head. "I tried that. The detective I talked to said a national park is federal land and not their jurisdiction. He also said that even if it had been on their beat they don't supply personal bodyguards. I talked to a national parks ranger too, but he told me that their job is to protect the wildlife and they don't have the manpower for what I was proposing. He said if I was so afraid something would happen to Connie that we simply shouldn't go. But he doesn't know Connie. She's determined to do what she promised to do. At that point a friend in the environmental community here referred me to Betty Costa, and she recommended you."

He was glad Betty had recommended him, although he would have preferred that it not be as complicated an assignment.

First there was the site itself. Shark Valley featured a visitor center near the road and an observation tower farther into the wilderness, the two sites linked by a long, narrow bike path. It was all carved out of the Everglades vegetation. Anybody could use the cover of that surrounding undergrowth to get pretty close to whoever they were stalking anywhere on the premises—especially if the would-be assassin was a native of the junglish Amazon region. And being the closest park entrance to the city, the Shark Valley site was usually pretty busy. Both locals and tourists could be found out there on any given day. A guy stalking Connie Mattos could count on a certain amount of crowd cover as well.

"How many people are expected at her presentation?"

"Oh, Connie's case is very well known among environmental activists, including many Brazilians living here. I'm expecting a hundred people at the very least."

Willie winced. That would just add to the multitude among which a killer could hide—if there was a killer.

"Do you have a photo of the suspected assassin?"

Ira Deal shook his head.

"No, Connie left any photos of him behind because he acted so badly when she broke up with him. We tried to find a photo of him through other means, but we weren't able."

Willie was left with his mouth open.

"How exactly do you expect me to find this guy in a crowd of people? Will he have a neon sign on him saying 'I'm a killer'?"

Ira Deal looked pained. "I think you'll just have to stay very, very close to Connie. Can you tell me how much it will cost?"

Willie told him his day rate, plus the rates for at least two other operatives who would be posted around the site during the rally to keep their eyes peeled for a suspicious character. Ira Deal stopped him before he finished.

"We can't afford all of those people. The truth is, we can't even really afford you, but I'll scrape up the money somehow. Since you'll only be working a few hours, do you offer a half-day rate?"

Willie squinted hard and told him he didn't work half days. Ira Deal didn't argue.

"Okay, I'll find the money."

"That's good," Willie said. "Now, since I'm going to be very, very close to your girlfriend at that rally, close enough to get shot myself, maybe I should meet her."

Ira Deal dug into his pocket to pay for the Pepsi he'd drunk. "We're staying at a small hotel not far from here. I'm not letting Connie go out on the street, so I'll take you there."

Just then the kitchen door flapped open again and Willie caught the tantalizing aroma of coconut. He grabbed the waiter by the sleeve as he went by, and he stopped.

"What is that?" Willie asked, pointing at the steaming platter on the tray.

"Camarão no coco," the waiter pronounced in Brazilian Portuguese. It was just close enough to Spanish that Willie knew he was talking about shrimp cooked in coconut milk. He could see the little critters swimming in their aromatic white bath. They looked luscious, but Willie would have to come back later. He and Ira headed for the hotel.

They walked down Collins Avenue a couple of blocks. This wasn't South Beach, which had been redeveloped over the years and drew a big-spending party crowd from around the globe. This was North Beach, five miles up the coast. It was an old, low-to-the-ground, sun-bleached, beachside neighborhood that was populated by Latin immigrants as well as tourists. It featured small hotels, cheap restaurants, travel agencies, shops where you could buy cut-rate calling cards for foreign lands, as well as storefront immigration attorneys who could help you apply for legal residence if you decided you wanted to stay.

At a corner was an Argentine restaurant where they turned right toward the water. There they entered an aging, two-story, blue stucco structure, with blue-and-white-striped awnings, called the Lido Hotel. The lobby was low-ceilinged, paved in dark blue Cuban tile, and three ceiling fans churned the humid air. The stucco walls were white and hung with framed color photographs of the beach and ocean. The front desk was crammed diagonally into the far corner, its façade encrusted with shards of seashell, probably scavenged right off the nearby sand. Behind it hung an old-fashioned wooden grid that held room keys, with each pigeonhole numbered. Next to it a bright red sign advised that checkout time was ten a.m. Walking into that lobby, Willie felt he'd traveled back in time to the 1950s.

He followed Ira Deal across the lobby and up the tiled stairs to the second floor. The narrow hallway was carpeted with a well-worn, fake-Persian runner. At the end of the hall, closest to the water, was Room 212. Deal stopped there, knocked, and a moment later a woman's voice from inside asked who it was.

"It's Ira."

Willie could hear a chain being removed, the door opened halfway, and they slipped in. The room was painted a faded aquamarine color and more photographs of beach scenes hung from the walls. The blond furniture was past its prime and an old-fashioned box air conditioner hummed in the window overlooking the street.

The door closed behind them, and Willie turned to see Connie Mattos. She was even more beautiful than in the photograph Ira had showed him. Short, no more than five-two, slim, with that same cascade of shining black hair that fell to her waist. Her skin was unblemished, the color of the finest mahogany. Her eyes were not just dark, but almost black, and she was fixed on Willie as if she had just encountered him on a trail in the deepest Amazon and wasn't sure if he was dangerous. Even without her dramatic personal story, Willie understood what attracted Ira, as well as the other man who was in love with her. She was a natural Brazilian beauty.

Ira introduced Willie and they shook hands, but she still didn't smile. She and Ira sat on the bed and Willie took the one wicker chair near the window. Willie's pidgin Portuguese was not good enough to conduct an interview and Connie didn't speak English. But she had studied Spanish at school and knew just enough so that she and Willie understood each other.

"Ira has told me about what happened to your parents, and I want you to know how sorry I am," Willie began. "He has also told me about a man who may be trying to harm you. A man by the name of Gaspar. I need to know everything you can tell me about him, beginning with what he looks like, how big he is."

She squinted and thought about that a few moments, as if she were seeing him in her mind.

"He isn't tall like Ira. He is smaller, about ten centimeters shorter than you."

Willie was six feet even, which meant Gaspar was about five-eight or five-nine.

"Is he thin, heavy, in between?"

"He is average. Not fat or very skinny, but he is very strong."

"Dark skin? Light skin?"

"Not as dark as me, but darker than you."

"So, it's in-between. How about his hair?"

"It's straight and it's black."

Willie winced. So far Gaspar sounded like a Brazilian everyman.

"Does he have any distinguishing marks?"

She thought that over for a couple of beats and then tapped a spot above her left breast.

"Right here he has a small tattoo. It is the head of a jaguar."

Of course, Gaspar would most likely be wearing a shirt, so that wouldn't help much at all.

"What else can you tell me about him?"

That one made her think even more, but she finally found a couple of facts she thought might be relevant.

"In Brazil, in the Amazon, he made his living as a hunter. He is an expert shot with a rifle and he has won competitions with the bow and arrow."

Willie flicked his eyebrows. "You don't say."

The task at hand was sounding worse every minute. The man he was being hired to find was of average appearance, at least for a Brazilian. On top of that, he was a crack shot in the jungle, and the landscape where Willie would probably have to find him was as close to a jungle as it got in Florida.

"Anything else you think I should know?"

They stared blankly back at him. At that point he was tempted to hit the road, but they were such helpless children he couldn't bring himself to do it.

"I'll do what I can," he said finally.

He arranged with Ira to collect half his fee early the next day. Then he left the two young lovers and headed back toward the restaurant. The streets of North Beach were almost empty now. He passed a real-estate office and stopped momentarily to check out the prices on the local properties pictured in the window. He noticed that a man had been walking behind him, maybe a half-block back, and that he too stopped to peruse something in a window. He wore a baseball-styled cap and dark sweatsuit. That was all Willie could distinguish in the meager street light. Willie started to walk again, went about thirty yards, stopped again and glanced back. The man behind him was gone. Willie looked across the street, then back down the block, but the stranger had disappeared. As absurd as it sounded, in that urban setting he found himself wondering what it would be like to be stalked by a guy with a bow and arrow. Nerves, he told himself. Nothing but nerves.

He set off again for the restaurant. On the way he checked his phone and learned that the Miami Marlins had fallen 3-2 on an error in the ninth. On the other hand, when he reached the restaurant, it was still open and they had one serving left of shrimp swimming in coconut milk. Something was something.

ꕔ ꕔ

Willie collected half his fee from Ira at ten a.m. the next morning at the same Rio Restaurant. While he was at it he tucked away a Brazilian breakfast—crusty hot bread with guava jelly, fresh sliced papaya and a big glass of passion-fruit juice. The tastes of the tropics.

With his stomach full and money in his pocket, Willie headed for the Everglades. The rally wasn't scheduled until that afternoon, but he wanted to get the lay of the land well ahead of time. He crossed Biscayne Bay from Miami Beach to the mainland, headed south then west on a series of highways, until he turned onto the narrow, two-lane ribbon of road that ran into the Glades. Soon that road was bordered on both sides by a carpet of reeds, never taller than about five feet, growing in shallow, slowly flowing water and stretching to the horizon in all directions. That was the essential landscape of the Everglades.

Here and there were clumps of bushes and stunted trees that amounted to islands in that sea of grass. For some reason, in Florida those spits of land were called hammocks, maybe because they were the only places where a person might actually hang a hammock. But in general, the vegetation hugged the earth and that made the sky above seem immense. The powerful Florida sun helped evaporate Everglades water, creating large, fulminating clouds that drew a driver's attention to the heavens. A friend of Willie's had once referred to those clouds as the mountains of Miami. They were the only ones for hundreds of miles.

With all the visitors attracted to Everglades National Park, tourism entrepreneurs had also made their way out there. On the sides of the road you passed two typical roadside attractions. One was airboat rides. The Miccosukee Indians were the local Native American residents and several of the families were in the airboat game. They would take you skimming over that water, weaving through those hammocks at high speeds, making hairpin turns that sent towering sheets of water into the air and made the marsh birds take to the skies in beautiful, arcing flight.

The other roadside enterprise frequently seen in the Glades was alligator wrestling. A Miccosukee wearing traditional dress would go one-on-one with a full-sized gator. The matches weren't exactly on the up and up, given that the alligators were very old and had been fed just before the show so that they weren't hungry and just wanted to go to sleep. To make sure they followed the script, they were also drugged to the gills. That said, when the human wrestler pried open the beast's mouth and you saw the gaping jaws full of large, triangular, jagged teeth—like thick white arrowheads—a tremor ran through you.

About twenty-five miles down that narrow road he saw the sign for Shark Valley. He turned in and immediately stopped at the guard shack. A small, thin, gray-haired lady in a park ranger uniform advised him it would be ten dollars to gain access. Willie paid and posed a question.

"Some local environmentalists are meeting here later today. Can you tell me where they're meeting?"

She pointed back over her shoulder. "On the green next to the observation tower."

"Can I drive to the tower?"

Her tone turned stern. "No, you cannot. No cars past the parking lot. You can take a tram tour or rent a bicycle."

Willie gazed into the distance. "I've been here before, but I forget. Just how far is it from the parking lot to the observation tower?"

"Seven miles."

Willie winced. He sure hoped there was a tram scheduled to leave soon. But when he reached the visitor center, he found that a tram had just left and the next wouldn't be departing for more than two hours. He gazed at a rack full of old-fashioned, single-gear bikes just outside the window.

"How much do you charge for one of those honeys?" he asked the clerk.

"Eight dollars per hour."

Willie glanced at his watch, knew he didn't want to lose two hours waiting, and handed over his credit card. Minutes later he had bought a bottle of water from a vending machine and was mounted on a lady's bicycle—the only kind they had left—pedaling up the paved path that wound through Shark Valley. It was wide enough for a car and in the old days, when he was a police officer, he could have gotten permission to drive in. No more. Now he pedaled.

For the next forty minutes he pumped away. The winding path took him through a landscape that was no different than the waterlogged countryside he had just driven through. Lots of shallow water on either side, clogged with reeds and lily pads, with just enough hammocks and smaller clumps of bushes to hide behind if you wanted to ambush someone driving or pedaling by. Frogs, snakes and tadpoles made ripples on the surface of the water. Alligators were also in attendance, although they made no ripples. Instead, they lay in the reeds, just their eyes and a bit of snout showing above the water, waiting for some giddy bicyclist to veer off the path and provide them with lunch. Willie could do without gators. But he recalled what he'd been told about Gaspar and his hunting prowess in the jungle. Any experienced woodsman could pull off to the side of the narrow Glades road and drop a small canoe or kayak in the water. For a guy born and raised in the Amazon, the Everglades was more like a neighborhood park, probably not all that difficult to navigate, gators or no gators.

As for birdlife, along the path it was mostly Everglades buzzards, who seemed to be waiting for one of those same cyclists to have a heart attack and keel over on the path. They hung out on the highest branches of the bushes, occasionally taking wing to scope out other dining possibilities. Willie hoped they weren't some sort of omen about his assignment.

He pedaled as the sun rose in a clouded sky. Along the way, he crossed paths with a couple of groups that had gotten an early start and were already on their way back to the visitor center. You could also take the entire loop around, which was longer, and that's what the trams did. But hardly anyone else wanted to be out there in the noonday sun. At one point he turned to look back and saw only one other bicycle going in the same direction he was, but a good half-mile behind him.

He made a bend in the road, saw the observation tower and a few minutes later arrived. It was a lonely structure that featured a sweeping concrete ramp that took visitors up about thirty feet. That left you at the base of a bell tower, which rose another twenty feet into the sky. Willie walked up the ramp and then climbed the metal rungs of the ladder to the top of the tower. From there he could easily see all the way to the main road, every bend in between. He could also see all the Everglades grass on either side of the bike path that would afford cover for an assailant. Not good. In the far distance to the east, through the haze, he made out the Miami skyline.

The green where Connie Mattos was to speak was just beneath the tower. A slightly raised platform had been built there and a podium had been propped on it. Anyone standing there would make a very easy target from just about anywhere in the surrounding vegetation. Not good at all.

He was sweating from the seven-mile ride out and now he had to return. The person pedaling behind him had never arrived. Maybe he, or she, had simply turned back, or maybe they had turned off onto one of the sandy side trails. Willie eyed each of those paths warily on the way back, but he saw no one.

He reached the visitor center, returned the bike, headed back home, but stopped at the first airboat concession he encountered not far down the road. It was a place run by a Miccosukee Indian named Otis Tiger. Otis was one of the elders of his tribe and Willie had met him while collaborating on a case on the reservation during his days as a cop. At the front counter he found a young girl in traditional tribal dress—blouse and full-length skirt embroidered with blue herons. Her name was Naomi Tiger.

"I know your grandfather," Willie told her and before long he was speaking by cell phone with Otis. Within a few minutes he had explained the situation to his old friend. The Miccosukees were indigenous to South Florida and the fact that the girl in trouble was a member of an indigenous tribe down in Brazil was all that Otis needed to hear. He agreed to help.

By the time Willie arrived back home in Little Havana it was early afternoon, and he was drenched. Before he jumped in the shower, he called Dino Nuñez. Willie was head of security for his brother Tommy's nightclub Caliente—Hot—the best salsa club in the city, and Dino was his chief bouncer. He was a black Cuban, about six-five, all muscle, with a shaved, bullet-shaped head. If he asked you to leave the club, you left quick. He had worked until five a.m. the night before and he was not happy about being woken up.

"Willie? What the hell you want at this hour?"

"I need you to help me with an assignment I'm on."

"When?"

"Now."

Dino grumbled, but Willie could tell he was sitting up to get out of bed.

"Where is this job?"

"The Everglades."

"The Everglades!" A stream of choice words reached Willie. "You gotta be kiddin' me, brother."

Dino usually worked in beautifully cut suits over silk shirts, with a bit of bling around the neck. He was a large lounge lizard, not a nature lover.

"I'm not kidding, *compadre*."

"And how much are you paying me for this?"

"You'll get half my day rate."

"Half a day?"

He started on another string of epithets, but Willie told him he'd pick him up in a half hour.

"And bring your gun."

꩜ ꩜

To transport Connie and Ira to the Glades Willie borrowed his brother Tommy's black SUV with the tinted windows. Dino was waiting for Willie on the curb in front of his house. He had donned white linen pants, an off-white *guayabera* shirt with gold embroidery, white shoes and wraparound shades with gold-colored frames. This evidently was his Everglades outfit.

Twenty minutes later they pulled up in front of the Lido Hotel. Ira and Connie were waiting in the lobby, both of them wearing very long faces. Ira held a large FedEx envelope in his hand.

"This arrived just a few minutes ago, addressed to Connie."

Willie opened it, removed a small bundle wrapped in toilet paper and found a small, electric-green parrot, the kind that commonly flew wild in parts of Miami. Stuck right through its breast was the broken shaft of an arrow, the small arrowhead bathed in blood. The body hadn't deteriorated that much, and Willie figured the bird hadn't been dead more than a day. The envelope was marked overnight delivery, the sender was identified as Carlos Diaz—surely a pseudonym.

Willie rewrapped the bird and returned it to the envelope. He knew what both Ira and Connie knew: Gaspar was close and was announcing his intentions. The abandoned boyfriend also wanted to make sure that they were both as scared as he could make them and he had apparently achieved that goal as well.

Willie fixed on Connie. "You shouldn't do this, you know."

She shook her head. "I won't let them stop me. I am going to speak."

Ira Deal looked disconsolate but said nothing. He knew he could not dissuade her. Willie had the couple wait in the lobby of the hotel while he checked out the beachfront street. It was only a block or two from there that he'd seen the suspicious individual who had disappeared into the shadows the night before. But now the only people visible were in bathing suits, with no place to hide weapons. Willie hustled Ira and Connie into the back seat of the SUV. With Dino at the wheel, they took off for Shark Valley.

Willie kept a sharp eye on every vehicle that came close to them for the next forty-five minutes, on the highways and on the two-lane road that sliced through the Everglades. But no one bothered them.

They turned into Shark Valley and were waved through the ranger checkpoint. Dozens of local environmental activists had already arrived and were piling onto trams to be transported to the observation tower. Still in the SUV, Willie told Connie to study the people gathered there and to make sure Gaspar was not concealed among them. She did as asked and shook her head.

"No, he's not there." Only then did they emerge.

The lady park ranger he had met that morning was still on duty, helping herd the visitors into the open-air trams. According to her nameplate, she was Sergeant Platt. She recognized Willie and he pulled her aside to explain to her his concerns about Connie. Her expression grew grave.

"You're sure about this?"

He had brought with him the FedEx envelope with the dead parrot in it and showed it to her. She stared at it, obviously appalled at the macabre message and whoever had sent it. She told Willie to wait a minute, disappeared into the park office and emerged with a holstered handgun around her small waist.

"Let's go."

Willie now had triangulation, always an advantage in a protection scheme, something he had learned during his days on the Miami-Dade PD guarding foreign dignitaries. Sergeant Platt planted herself right next to Connie in the tram and Dino sat shoulder-to-shoulder with Ira. Willie stood on the running board next to the driver, which gave him a clearer view to both sides of the narrow road.

The tram followed the paved trail. Willie carefully assessed each wall of reeds, each clump of bushes they passed, each tangle of underbrush. He saw a few alligators lounging in the shallow waters, closer to the path this time, but they were the only dangerous characters encountered during the trip.

About a half-mile before the observation tower, Willie spotted Otis Tiger's airboat. He asked the tram driver to stop, hopped off, nodded to Dino and Sergeant Platt, and the tram took off again. Otis sat in the bow of the airboat, which was being piloted from a raised seat by one of his countless male offspring. The younger man pulled the craft right to the fringe of grass off the paved trail and Willie hopped aboard. There was no more than about five inches of water right there, but that was more than enough for the airboat. A moment later the motor roared, the big fan in the back hit high gear, the nose of the craft lifted out of the water, and they were speeding through the liquid landscape.

Otis was dressed in a hand-woven Miccosukee shirt consisting of white lightning bolts against a crimson background. His hair was white, and he wore it in braided pigtails down to his shoulders, topped by a Panama hat with an eagle feather stuck in the brown band. He was one stylish Miccosukee. Willie shook his hand and the old man told him it was his grandson, Carson Tiger, at the controls.

"He's the best of his generation," Otis boasted.

They wove through the occasional clumps of bushes and soon caught up with the tram that was just arriving at the observation tower. Carson throttled down, until the boat hardly made a sound, and they drifted through the reeds, about two hundred feet away from the tower where the crowd had gathered in front of the podium. Willie had no trouble spotting Ira and Dino, who were both a half-foot taller than the people around them. He couldn't see Connie, but he knew she was between them.

Willie also glanced up at the tower and saw Sergeant Platt at the very top, exactly where he had asked her to be, to keep watch.

The airboat stayed in low gear and drifted slowly, as inconspicuously as possible, offshore. The thicker and taller vegetation was found on the west side of the tower. Willie and Otis figured any attack would probably come from there, so they stayed on that side, searching every clump of cover for a sign of a canoe or kayak and, possibly, the would-be assassin. The sun was low in the sky and the bushes cast shadows on the water. Willie kept seeing people where there were no people—only shadows.

From there they heard the introductory remarks and Willie saw Connie standing next to the podium. Dino was on one side of her, scanning the surroundings. Ira stood to the other, ready to do the translating when she spoke and providing whatever protection he could, which wasn't much. Between the airboat and the tower were several clumps of bushes. Willie saw Otis studying them through his old, squinting eyes. Willie leaned toward him.

"Don't you think we should get between those bushes and the girl?" he whispered. "He can get a clean shot at her this way."

Otis held up a hand.

"Be patient," he said. "Let me do the hunting here."

His people had lived there for centuries, so Willie, despite his concerns, didn't argue.

Moments later, he heard Connie introduced, followed by a wave of applause, and then watched her take a step up to the podium, putting her in clear view. He turned to look at Otis, but the old man was squinting at a specific clump of bushes about fifty yards away.

"What is it?" Willie whispered.

Otis pointed at clumps of bushes nearer them. "You see the birds in these bushes," he whispered

Willie looked up and noticed crows which had settled in the highest branches of the hammocks right around them. He nodded.

Otis pointed at the clump farther from them. "No birds are there. Why?"

Willie looked and saw that he was right. Those bushes were free of birds.

Otis turned and gestured to his grandson Carson, whispered something in the Miccosukee language, and the airboat began to circle around the back of that hammock on low throttle. When you had hunted from airboats for years, you knew how to move them without making noise. But again, their positioning worried Willie.

"We need to get between those bushes and the girl."

Otis simply held up his hand. In the background Willie heard Connie. She was speaking about her parents, how they had been killed and why. Of course, the crowd before her had no idea that, even as she spoke, an assassin might be taking aim at her. Willie heard her young, vulnerable girl's voice and it made his heart race.

Within seconds they had glided all the way around to the west so they could now see the back of the clump of bush indicated by Otis. They were maybe one hundred twenty feet from it. Otis tensed, squinting in that direction. That was when Willie saw the green nose of a canoe sticking out from under a curtain of branches. He also saw a human form, a man, apparently lying flat on his stomach on the sandy hammock. From there he had a clear shot at Connie.

It took every ounce of restraint Willie had to keep from screaming out. He turned to Otis, who already had his hand up as the airboat
slowly drifted into position. Then suddenly Otis called out in a loud
voice, making a sound like a very large marsh bird.

"Ayeeee."

Gaspar turned, saw the airboat and jumped to his feet in the
knee-high water. He was holding a rifle and he raised it to fire. But
now he was facing the setting sun, which was directly behind the airboat. He squinted but obviously he couldn't see. The blazing sunlight painted his face and made clear his confusion. He pulled off a
shot, but it passed well over the airboat. By that point Otis had raised
his rifle to his shoulder. He squinted down the barrel, pulled off one
shot that hit Gaspar in the middle of his forehead and knocked him
over backwards into the water like a falling tree. He hit with a splash,
trembled for several moments, and then stopped moving.

Willie heard Connie's voice hesitate, but only briefly. No one
would be able to see Willie and Otis clearly—nor Gaspar—through
the vegetation. Moments later, Connie went on with her speech.

Willie turned to Otis. The old man nodded once.

"Hunting in the Amazon with all those jungles and tall trees is
one thing. Hunting here is something else."

The two shots had apparently awakened a couple of nearby
gators, who came out from under cover and headed toward the dead
man. Otis had Carson close in, which scared the gators off, and they
dragged the body aboard. Gaspar was dead, his eyes wide now, no
longer squinting as if he were taking aim. Willie pulled down the
collar of his shirt and there was the jaguar just above his heart. It was
already starting to pale.

IN THE TIME OF THE VOODOO

Willie Cuesta walked into Clarke's Pub on South Beach at noon. He was there to meet Alice Arden, immigration attorney extraordinaire, for their monthly high-cholesterol lunch. Clarke's made the best burger in South Florida, and maybe the best anywhere. The patty, constructed of Angus beef, was two inches thick, oozing with juice, replete with blue cheese, sautéed mushrooms and sinfully good bacon. Alice skipped the bacon; Willie didn't.

Willie claimed their normal table in the far corner and stared at Sports Center screening silently on the TV above the bar. Two minutes later, Alice walked in, her mid-length blond hair swinging, wearing a blue business suit over a hibiscus-red blouse, and showing just enough gorgeously tanned thigh to make every guy in the place pause in mid bite of his burger. Alice was an excellent attorney, one of the best, something Willie had to remind himself of almost every time he looked at her.

They had been meeting for this monthly lunch for several years. Alice regularly threw Willie work, so they saw each other often. The lunches were meant to be purely social occasions during which they would catch up on personal and family matters. Willie had always wished that they could get even more personal, but it wasn't to be. Alice adhered to strict rules about not mixing work with that sort of play.

Unlike most of their lunch meetings, this day she strode in with a super-serious expression on her lovely face. She fell into the chair across from him, chucked her handbag onto the floor, and propped her silken arms on the table.

"We have to talk."

"About what, amiga?"

"I just got a call from Clotilde St. Jean. She's scared out of her wits."

Willie frowned. He knew Clotilde quite well. She was born in Haiti, but later had become a US citizen and Alice had helped her bring her children to live with her in America. In fact, it was Willie who had traveled to Haiti, collected the two children, and taken them to the US consulate so that their blood could be drawn for DNA testing. That blood had matched their mother's and they had eventually been allowed to come, but it hadn't been easy.

Just then the waitress brought both their drinks. Neither of them was a daytime drinker, so that meant unsweetened iced tea for Alice and lemonade for Willie. They had been going there so long the servers knew what to bring them without asking. They sipped their respective refreshments.

"What's the problem with Clotilde?" Willie asked.

Alice leaned farther forward and dropped her voice.

"When Clotilde was just a child—about five years old, I believe—her father was murdered."

Willie's eyebrows elevated. "Murdered? She never told me."

"It's not something she likes talking about, but his death was a homicide. His throat was slashed one night on a dark street in the city of St. Marc where they lived, and he was abandoned there to bleed to death. He was found the next day at dawn."

Willie winced. "Did they ever get who did it?"

Alice rolled her baby-blue eyes. "There was never any doubt who did it. It was the Tonton Macoute."

Willie whistled. "Really."

"Yes, really."

During his time in the Intelligence Unit of the Miami-Dade Police Department Willie had heard of the Macoutes. In Haiti, they had been plainclothes, government-sponsored assassins who operated out of the presidential palace and who for decades created a reign of terror throughout the country—robbing, raping and murdering. Their main job was to terrorize the people and make sure they didn't cause any trouble for the big shots. The government armed them—with guns, knives and machetes—but they looked nothing like police or soldiers. Instead, they wore sporty civilian clothes, often topped off with rakish Panama hats and menacing black sunglasses. The casual-killer look.

But they also brought another dimension to their badness. Many of them had been recruited from ranks of voodoo practitioners, which made them extra frightening. They were hobgoblins. One moment they might be sacrificing a chicken to the voodoo deities, and the next they were slicing the throat of a human being in the middle of the night. Sometimes those victims were political opponents of the government, but other times people were killed randomly and left hanging from trees, or in the middle of the street, for no other cause than to create terror. Such killings were a warning: "If you are even thinking of questioning the powers that be, you will end up just like this."

Willie sipped his lemonade. "Her father was murdered by a Macoute, but if it happened when Clotilde was a child that has to be thirty years ago or more."

"Correct. But here's the thing, boyo. Clotilde and other family members knew which of the Macoutes had murdered her dad. The killer's name was Marcel Metellius. He had been a kind of bogus voodoo priest and was a well-known ghoul in the neighborhood where they lived. Two days ago, she walked out of the shop she owns right here Miami, in Little Haiti, and she saw him. What's even worse is that he saw her." Alice punctuated the statement with a flick of her fine eyebrows.

Willie considered her words. He knew that after the old Haitian regime was overthrown in the 1980s, it was rumored that some Macoutes, trying to escape retribution from the relatives of their victims, made for Miami. If that was true, Willie had never run into any of them. They apparently lived quietly off the proceeds they had looted from Haiti and as long they kept their noses clean in Miami, neither Willie nor other cops had grounds to move against them.

But later the laws changed. These days anyone arriving in the US had to check a box on the immigration form and swear that they have never been accused of a human rights violation. If you lied in answer to that question, you committed a crime. All former Macoutes were considered major human rights violators and were no longer allowed in. And if he got caught and deported back to Haiti this Metellius could easily end up dead. Many people back there hated the Macoutes.

Willie leaned forward. "So, is he one of the Macoutes who came all those years ago legally, or did he somehow sneak in later?"

Alice shook her head. "Nobody by his name was allowed in legally. I already checked that with a friend of mine at Immigration. He must have come in later and almost certainly he did so by using a made-up name. In fact, Clotilde thinks she knows exactly when he came and how. You can ask her."

"And you say he recognized her too? How can that be if she was just a little girl when he killed her father?"

"It isn't that he recognized her, but she said her eyes went so big when she saw him that he noticed. Maybe he realizes that she knows who he is."

"She's afraid he's going to come after her to keep her quiet."

Alice shook her head. "Not just that. Do you know what the name Tonton Macoute comes from in Haitian folklore?"

Willie shook his head. "I have no idea."

"The Macoute is an evil spirit who walks around with a big sack and steals children. Do you understand? Clotilde is afraid he's going to hurt not only her but her kids."

Just then the burgers arrived. They dug in but given what they'd just been talking about neither of them had his or her usual appetite for the Angus. About halfway through, Alice shoved her plate aside.

"I'm worried about this, Willie. We worked too hard to help Clotilde and bring those kids here to have anything happen to them."

"I'm with you," Willie said.

"You're the only person who can help me on this. You're already acquainted with them and you know Little Haiti from your days on the force."

Willie was nodding but not saying anything now. He sensed that Alice was setting him up for something.

"You're my boy on this. You're my hero."

Willie winced. "This means Clotilde doesn't have money so I'm not going to get paid, right?"

It had happened before on other cases, and he had never refused her. Alice knew that he didn't like thugs any more than she did. She

fixed on him with those soulful eyes of hers and uttered the words
she had uttered in the past at such moments.

"We'll get paid in heaven, Willie."

Willie just hoped he didn't arrive in heaven sooner than scheduled.

ॐ ॐ

He left South Beach, drove across Biscayne Bay to the mainland
and turned onto Biscayne Boulevard. About three miles north of
downtown he headed west and within a few blocks was in the heart
of Little Haiti. Willie had begun his police career as a patrolman on
the Miami PD and had spent quite a few nights in the neighborhood.
Back in those days the duty had mostly involved investigating break-
ins, other minor economic crimes and domestic disputes. Little Haiti
produced little serious violence. The people who had emigrated from
Haiti, the poorest place in all the Americas, had already experienced
enough trouble back home and they weren't looking for more.

Then came the era when the older, established street gangs,
headquartered in the neighborhoods to the north, began descending
on Little Haiti to deal drugs, commit armed robberies and rough up
anybody who crossed their paths. In time, the Haitian kids formed
their own gangs to protect themselves. You got shootouts and
killings and suddenly what had been a fairly peaceful haven became
perilous. By that time, Willie had been promoted to detective,
assigned to the intelligence unit and spent time investigating the
gangs. Police cracked down and in time that wave of violence
calmed. Little Haiti these days was more like it had been—poor but
relatively peaceful.

Willie drove down the main drag of the neighborhood, Second
Avenue Northeast. No one would ever mistake it for Rodeo Drive in
Beverly Hills, but attempts had been made over the years to spruce
it up. The stunted storefronts had all been painted in pastel colors
and new signs were painted to introduce each business. Little Haiti
featured an unusual number of churches, music stores and hole-in-
the-wall operations where you could wire money home. They
reflected the linchpins of Haitian culture—God, rhythmic Caribbean
music and family. Bakeries, restaurants and groceries featuring Hait-

ian food products were also well represented, all stuffed into a stretch of city only a few blocks long. Near the end of that strip, on the east side of the street, stood Clotilde's Religious Articles and Caribbean Gifts. A sign in the window said "Closed," although it was early afternoon. That was bad for business, Willie told himself.

He drove two more blocks, turned left and located the bright pink stucco house Alice had described to him. It was Clotilde's cousin's place, where she and her children were holed up because she was afraid to go home.

Willie pulled into the driveway. Clotilde emerged and met him on the screened front porch. As always, she was dressed simply but beautifully—in a tight, blue, knee-length skirt, a white blouse embroidered with large red roses and a matching red silk scarf tied into a turban around her head. The red turban was a signature with Clotilde, a way to pick her out of a crowd. She gestured Willie into a chair.

"We'll talk out here, Willie. I kept the kids home from school. I told them we're staying here for a few days with their cousins because work is being done on our house. I don't want them to know what is really going on. I don't want them as worried as I am."

She met Willie's gaze. Clotilde was a woman who had been through a lot in life and didn't scare easily, but this moment was clearly an exception. For the first time ever he saw real fear in her beautiful ebony eyes.

"Tell me about this man," Willie said.

She looked into the distance and slowly shook her head as if struggling to find the words.

"He was a Macoute, but even more of a monster than most Macoutes. He not only murdered my father, but he killed many people over the years. The Macoutes, they all wanted you to be afraid of them. Some of them used that fear to get money from people, or to get women to sleep with them. But there were some who took a personal pleasure in killing. They wanted people to think of them as demons and Marcel Metellius was one of those. He walked around always with big dark glasses so you couldn't tell who he was looking at. But then he would stare at a person and his lips would twist into an evil smile and that person would think: 'I am the next one he will kill.'

A shiver ran through her, and she fell silent. Willie gave her a moment to tame those scary memories.

"I'm told you saw him here a couple of days ago."

She nodded. "It was about six-thirty in the evening, and I left my shop to buy a soda at the corner. A man was coming out of that same store. I was maybe twenty feet away from him when I saw his face. He must be close to sixty years old now and his hair is gray. His face was always thin and it's even thinner now, with sunken cheeks. But beneath those years it looked just like him. I stopped and stared as if I had seen a ghost."

She was fixed on Willie but was staring not at him but through him.

"And then what happened?"

"He looked up at me and frowned. I'm not sure what he thought in those seconds. Maybe he just saw a woman staring at him for no real reason. But maybe he realized that I recognized him."

"What did he do?"

"He didn't do anything at first. It was me who turned around and headed back to my store, as if I had forgotten something. I locked the door, put the Closed sign in the window. Then I sneaked out the back way and started to walk home. But when I reached the corner just down from my shop he was standing there, a few feet away, staring at me. He smiled at me just as Metellius used to do to frighten people—a twisted, evil smile. It was only for a moment, but in that moment I knew for sure it was him."

Willie nodded in commiseration, picturing the frightening face-to-face meeting after so many years. Incidents like that happened in Miami, a city that was a refuge for so many people from Latin America and the Caribbean, including people who, back in their home countries, had been hunter and prey.

"He didn't follow you home, did he?"

"No, I made sure he didn't do that. I hurried home, told the kids to pack, and we came here."

"And have you seen him since?"

She shook her head. "No, I haven't seen him exactly, but I believe he's been watching me. Strange things have happened."

"What kind of things?"

She gazed in the direction of her shop. "Yesterday, I opened up as usual. This is Easter week and it's always busy for me. I can't afford to abandon my business, but I kept an eye out for Metellius all day. I didn't see him, but when I was walking back here just after dark, I thought I heard someone walking behind me. I turned, but no one was there. I kept going, but a minute later I heard something again. When I turned, I saw someone step into the shadows. I called out, but the person didn't respond. Instead, I heard a noise—the noise a rattle makes."

"A rattle? Like a kid's rattle?"

"Yes, that is the sound. But in Haiti a rattle is also used in rituals by voodoo priests. The tradition is that the rattle is filled with bones taken from the spines of snakes."

Willie's eyebrows elevated. "Snake bones. Spooky stuff. Whoever it was in the shadows was trying to scare you."

Clotilde nodded. "I'm not a believer in voodoo, but that sound did scare me. I still wasn't sure who it was. I figured maybe it was some kid having fun. I yelled into the dark and told him to just go home. Whoever it was didn't follow me any farther, or at least I didn't see anyone. I made it home and locked the door. But this morning when I got to my shop I found this lying in front of my door."

She reached into her handbag, pulled out a red bandana and unwrapped it, revealing a small, carved, black figurine that fit in her hand—a smiling skeleton wearing a black top hat and a long frock coat.

"This is the spirit of the dead in Haitian voodoo," she said. "His name is Baron Samedi and his image is used by people to work black magic."

Willie gave it the once-over. "Nasty looking."

Clotilde nodded. "Nasty looking like the one who left it. I picked it up, stepped back out into the street and almost two blocks away, on the corner, I saw a man staring at me. It was Metellius and I could tell he was smiling at me again, laughing at me. Then he turned, walked around that corner and disappeared." She was looking at Willie now. "He's trying to scare me, trying to make me leave here because he knows I've recognized him. In Haiti, that's what he would do—terrorize a woman to get what he wants—and that is what he's trying to do here."

Willie remembered during his days in Miami PD sometimes going into Haitian homes and seeing small altars to the voodoo saints. Often it was only a clear glass of water and a lighted candle, which was a way to protect the household from evil spirits. Other times the altars were more elaborate, with many carved figurines and skulls, plus flowers, food and bottles of liquor that constituted offerings to the saints. Willie understood the power that the voodoo cult had among some Haitians and how someone like Clotilde, who wasn't a believer, could still get plenty scared when she was targeted by it.

"If he's here, he must have come in illegally," Willie said. "Macoutes are now persona non grata here. I assume he came in using a false name and Alice tells me you may know when that was."

Clotilde nodded nervously. "After the earthquake in Haiti a couple of years back, people who were badly hurt were brought to Miami for medical care."

"Yes, I remember."

"A rumor ran here that some people who weren't hurt at all had their heads and bodies wrapped in bloody bandages, so that nobody knew who they were, and they were smuggled onto the medical planes. They were brought to hospitals here and then just disappeared." She snapped her fingers. "Just like that they vanished. Everybody said the men who did that were old Macoutes."

Willie had never heard that one before. But he could see how such a story could gain traction among the Haitians. The image of notorious killers disguised as mummies made for an irresistible horror story. Truth was, people were smuggled from Haiti by sea with some regularity. Many were caught and sent back but others made it to shore and melted into the population. An old Macoute might arrive that way too.

"So why don't you report all of this to the police?" Willie asked.

Clotilde just shook her head.

"The police around here have heard too many stories like this. People accuse others of plans to hurt them. They find chickens with their throats cut on their property and they report their enemies are using voodoo or Santeria against them. If I tell the police I have seen a Macoute they will think I'm seeing ghosts. They'll do nothing."

Willie knew she was probably right.

"So, what is it you want me to do? I don't know where he lives, what identity he's using and I've never seen him."

"Oh, you'll know him when you find him, Willie. You'll sense the pure evil in him."

Willie wasn't sure that his "pure evil" detection apparatus was as fine-tuned as Clotilde thought it was. How did someone go about searching for a goblin?

Just then the front door opened, and her two children emerged, stationing themselves to either side of her. The girl, Georgette, was about twelve; the boy, Terrence, had to be ten. They both had a lot of Clotilde in them and were beautiful kids.

"I told you to stay in the house," Clotilde scolded. "Say hello to Mr. Cuesta and go back. Don't make me angry." They did as told.

"They're growing up to be healthy, gorgeous children," Willie said.

She nodded. "And I want them to stay healthy and gorgeous. Please, help us, Willie."

"I'll do what I can," he said, although at the moment he had no idea what that would be.

He left, climbed in his car, drove back to Second Street, pulled to the side of the road and mulled it over for a while. He was glad Clotilde had so much confidence in him, especially since he had no idea where to start.

He was parked directly across the street from Clotilde's Religious Articles and Caribbean Gifts. On one side of the front door the show window featured bright blouses made from Caribbean textiles, wooden wind chimes made to sound in a warm breeze, paintings of village scenes done in the colorful primitive style native to Haiti. The other side was filled with a whole choir of Catholic saints, plaster statues in different colors and sizes, for her very religious Haitian clientele. One image was of the Virgin Mary, and it was life-sized, the kind of effigy people in Miami bought when they had prayed for a cure of a sick loved one and their prayers had been answered. It was a way of saying thank you to a saint, moving him or her into your household.

Given the season, Clotilde had also laid in a supply of Easter bunnies and baskets, propped here and there in the window. No, it was not a good time for her to be closed.

Half a block from where Willie was parked, an older Haitian lady named Odette ran a sugar-cane press where she made cane juice. She had been there for years and during his days on patrol he had often stopped there for a drink. Right then he needed a dose of energy and he got out, walked up there and ordered. Odette recognized him and made small talk as she picked a piece of cane from a stack, fed it into the press, cranked the handle and filled a plastic cup with the frothy juice. Willie paid her, climbed back into his car and sipped, listened to a Haitian tune playing from the closest music store, and tried to decide what to do.

Occasional pedestrians passed on both sides of the street. Among them was a slim man of middle height in a gray fedora who appeared to be in his fifties, maybe sixty. Willie paid him no more attention than he did the other passersby. But a minute later, while Willie was still sipping his juice, the same man passed again in the other direction, paused in front of Clotilde's shop, went to the door and peered in. Willie watched him. After several moments the man turned very deliberately, walked to the edge of the sidewalk, looked right at Willie, lifted his hat, revealing a head of short gray hair and issued a loud, mocking peal of laughter. Willie froze for a moment. The man cackling at him appeared to be unhinged, crazy. The look, the laugh, they were precisely what Clotilde had described. Willie knew it could be no one but Metellius.

He put down his drink, threw open the car door and jumped out, but by that time the other man had scampered to the corner and disappeared around it. Willie sprinted after him and entered the side street. He didn't see Metellius, nor anyone else. Alleyways ran behind the stores in both directions and beyond that the street was lined with brightly colored houses surrounded by foliage. Willie tried the alleyway to the south and then to the north. Nothing. He then ran down the street looking into yards but saw no sign of him. He searched for a good fifteen minutes and then gave up. Metellius had dematerialized, or at least disappeared. Like a demon.

Willie walked back to his car and climbed back in. Propped on the dashboard, where a small statue of St. Christopher might have stood, was a black figurine just like the one Clotilde had found out-side her store. The spirit of death.

Willie picked it up, craned around in all directions, but of course the other man was gone. He stared at the voodoo figure. Metellius had doubled around and duped him. He had also accomplished what he wanted. Willie was afraid, not for himself, but for Clotilde and her children. Maybe Metellius had seen Willie sitting there in the car and assumed he was guarding the shop. But maybe the old Macoute had somehow found out where Clotilde was hiding. Little Haiti was like a small town, and it wouldn't have been hard to discover who Clotilde's family members were. Maybe he had staked out the cousin's house, seen Willie there and followed him. That was one explanation. Believers might say the old voodoo priest just had a sixth sense about who was hunting him. Willie wasn't a believer, but the thought entered his head.

He dialed Clotilde's number and she answered right away.

"I want you to find someplace where you and the kids can stay outside of Little Haiti," Willie told her.

He had just left her, and this new proposal clearly surprised her.

"Why do you want us to do that?"

Willie did not want to tell her what had just happened. That would only scare her more than she already was.

"It's a precaution, Clotilde. Go stay with someone who lives in some other neighborhood. That way both of us won't have to worry about the children."

Silence ensued on the other end. She probably suspected that Willie wasn't telling her the whole truth, but in the end, she chose not to ask any questions. Getting the kids even farther away from Metellius couldn't be argued with.

"I have a cousin up in the North Miami neighborhood and we can go there."

"Perfect. Promise me you'll pack up right now and go."

"I will. Don't worry."

꩜ ꩜

Willie hung up. He sat there for a while, keeping an eye out for Metellius, but the ghoul was long gone. So, he headed for Alice

Arden's office downtown on Brickell Avenue. She had a client with her when he arrived, but a few minutes later he was sitting in her office with a view of Biscayne Bay.

Alice swiveled from her computer and afforded him her full attention.

"Okay, shoot, Sherlock. Give me the lowdown."

Willie told her of his conversation with Clotilde, from start to finish. She had heard some of the tale already, but not all the details. Then he took out his new dashboard doll, propped it on her desk and told her how he had come into possession of it.

Alice squinted at it. "I don't like that at all."

"Me either, mamita. To tell you the truth, when I went to meet with Clotilde I had my doubts that this guy she saw was really the goon who had murdered her father—this Marcel Metellius. It's been thirty years since she saw him and maybe she was imagining things. She's obviously haunted by her father's death and Metellius has always been in the back of her mind. Maybe this wasn't the same man. Maybe this was just some crazy old coot who had taken a liking to her and was acting the fool."

Alice picked up the figurine and ran her long fingers over it.

"Clotilde is not some schoolgirl who frightens easily, Willie. She's always been a very level-headed lady. If she says she recognized this guy my gut tells me to believe her."

Willie held up a hand. "Don't worry, after my run-in with him, I'm now a believer."

"The question is why Metellius is acting this way? For a guy who's a fugitive from justice, that is certainly strange behavior."

Willie leaned back and crossed a leg. "On the way over here I hashed that out. It's my experience that men who at any point in their lives have had the power to frighten people, to terrorize them, become addicted to that power. Intimidation was how they influenced the world around them, how they made themselves felt, and it's hard to give that up. Clotilde spotted Metellius and was obviously afraid of him. Maybe that old feeling of power is pulling at Metellius, making him want to drive Clotilde out of her wits. And he wants me to know he isn't afraid of me either."

Alice shook her head as if trying to rid it of a thought. "Crazy. Just crazy."

"He probably is. All those years of evil affected his mind. He certainly looks crazy and that makes him extra dangerous. That's why we can't let him get close to Clotilde again and risk her getting hurt."

"So, what do we do?"

"If we had a photo of him we could circulate it all over Little Haiti, but we don't have one. And I can't sit and just wait for him to appear again. I'm doing this pro bono and don't have the luxury of waiting him out. But maybe we can use his craziness to our advantage. We need to bring him out of the shadows on our schedule, not his own. We want Marcel Metellius to show up at Clotilde's shop, or somewhere else he thinks she will be, and I'll be waiting for him."

Alice Arden cocked her head.

"Does this mean you're going to use Clotilde as bait? Doesn't that sound just a bit dangerous?"

Willie shook his head. "Don't worry. I won't let anything happen to her. It isn't foolproof, but if we do lure him, I can detain him and call the cops. Then we can establish if he really is Metellius, and he can be imprisoned as an international human rights criminal."

"And just how do you propose luring him, as you put it?"

"I don't have the answer to that at the moment. That's the main reason I made my way here. You've always been extremely seductive. I figured I'd leave that bit to you."

Alice Arden rolled her eyes. "Believe me, I've never seduced a Macoute. Not my type."

She started to swivel again as she thought out the problem, and they sat in silence for several minutes. Alice had lots of Haitian clients, had spent a lot more time in Little Haiti than Willie had lately and had a much better chance of coming up with a solution. Willie stared out the window at the clouds drifting in off the ocean and over the bay as if an answer lay in them. Alice Arden suddenly stopped swiveling.

"I know what we'll do. We'll go see Wilfred Vidal."

Willie frowned. "And just who is that?"

"Wilfred runs Radio Creole. It operates right out of Little Haiti and everybody, I mean everybody who's Haitian, listens to the Radio Creole for a good part of the day. He plays Haitian music, and it is the only place for people to get the latest news from Haiti. You can't be in Little Haiti without hearing it everywhere you go, day and night. We'll get Wilfred to help us lure him."

"You think he'll do that?"

Alice Arden was already up out of her chair and grabbing her purse.

"I got his grandmother permission to come here years back when the feds were giving her trouble. He'll do it."

Alice was already out the door and Willie hustled to catch up.

The "studios" of Radio Creole were about a half block off Second Avenue on what was—except for the radio—a residential street in Little Haiti. Wilfred Vidal lived there with his wife and kids in a weathered white-stucco house. Behind the house, in the backyard, he had built a smaller house out of unfinished cinder blocks and topped it with a corrugated aluminum roof. From that roof protruded an antenna about fifteen feet high, the top of which just cleared the papaya and banana trees bordering the property. Except for the antenna and a small air-conditioning unit in the front wall, a person might have mistaken the structure for a somewhat spacious toolshed.

On the metal door of the shack hung a poster hand-printed in red: "Quiet!" From inside, Willie could hear the muted strains of Haitian pop music, all twangy strings, organ and steel-drum percussion. Alice Arden scraped her nails against the aluminum and someone inside called: "*Antre.*"

The one-room space they entered was low ceilinged, had no windows and was lighted mostly by three dim bulbs hanging from a cord that sagged from one end of the room to the other. The rest of the light in the dusky space was distributed by a couple of computer screens. Right in between the screens was a control panel to modulate sound and two microphones. Also crammed into the room were a telephone, various tuners, sound speakers both large and small, several turntables, a pair of CD players, shelves that contained hundreds of vinyl records and CDs and, in the far corner, a stunted refrigerator with a hot plate propped on top of it.

Wires ran every which way and an attempt had been made to soundproof the aluminum roof by gluing cardboard egg cartons to the inside surface. It was certainly ingenious, but Willie wondered how effective it was when it poured rain.

Sitting behind the control board was Wilfred Vidal, whom Alice had described as DJ, newscaster, reporter, technician, janitor and owner of Radio Creole. Wilfred was a small, stocky man with very dark, almost black skin, and the light from the computer screens made it look dark blue. He wore a red Miami Heat basketball jersey and was bobbing to the music, a Haitian combo that seemed to be channeling Bob Marley. He looked up and smiled at Alice Arden.

Moments later the music ended, and Wilfred spoke in mile-a-minute Creole, a mixture of French and an African dialect. Then he poked one of the CD players and another tune started. Wilfred turned off his microphone, got up and gave Alice a large hug. She introduced Willie and he invited them to sit.

"What brings the best immigration attorney in Miami to Radio Creole?" he asked in his elegantly accented English.

"We need your help with a very serious matter," Alice said.

Wilfred opened his arms. "Whatever you need, you know I will help if I can."

"You know Clotilde St. Jean, don't you?'

"Yes, of course. A beautiful lady and she has advertised her business on the station."

Alice went into the account Clotilde had given to Willie. When she reached the fact that the man menacing Clotilde was a former Tonton Macoute, Wilfred's face stormed over.

"A Macoute!"

Alice Arden nodded. "That's right. His name is Marcel Metellius. Have you ever heard of him?"

Wilfred pondered the question and shook his head. "No, but I'm not from Saint Marc the way Clotilde is. I'm from Port-au-Prince and we had our own monsters there." He looked from Alice to Willie and back. "What is it that you want me to do?"

"We want you to make announcements over the air. Sunday is Easter and Clotilde has lots of gifts and religious articles on sale. We want you to announce that Clotilde will be keeping her shop open late tomorrow night, Saturday, to accommodate last-minute customers. She will be open until ten p.m."

Wilfred worked that over in his mind.

"So, you're going to try to trick him. You think he will hear that, maybe wait for her to leave and try to do something to her."

Willie shrugged. "We know his past, we know he wants to scare Clotilde and maybe harm her. Maybe he won't hear it, and if he does maybe he will do nothing. Maybe he is sane enough to sense a trap. But just maybe we can tempt him to show himself. Then we can corner him."

Wilfred nodded. "Oh, I'll make sure he hears it. I'll tell people about Clotilde's shop all day long today and tomorrow. It will be free advertising for my friend Clotilde and maybe, just maybe, we catch a Macoute."

꥞ ꥞

Alice and Willie headed back to her office on Brickell. While driving they devised an intricate plan of action to go along with the announcements on the radio. Later, Willie would realize that all the additional planning and scheming made no difference in the end because they were dealing with a madman. Trying to lure him would turn out to be a good idea, but anticipating what he might do after that was totally useless. By definition, criminally insane people didn't fit into anybody's neat plans. But Alice and Willie weren't thinking that way, so they built their trap.

Alice agreed to call Clotilde and fill her in. One part of the plan would require the help of a female security operative, and she would have to be black. That was Willie's responsibility. Once he got back home to Little Havana, he dialed the number of Muriel Neville. Muriel was a former Miami PD policewoman who had worked some of the roughest parts of the city before retiring. These days she helped Willie with security assignments from time to time. Muriel was a tough cookie and the perfect person for this particular job. She was happy to hear from him.

"What's up, Willie? You have work for me?"

"Yes, I do, Muriel, although the question is if you want to do it. It's a bit dicey."

She chuckled. "You know me, Willie. I do dicey."

Willie described Clotilde's problem and what he and Alice had devised. Then he told her he was working pro bono and that was when he was afraid she might bail. But the fact that a woman was being menaced by a ghoul like Metellius was all Muriel needed to hear. It awakened the old bloodhound in her, just as he'd hoped it would.

"Don't worry, Willie. I'm in."

Willie gave her details on what she would need to do.

"Be at the shop tomorrow at nine-thirty p.m. Bring your old service revolver just in case."

"I'll be there, brother."

Willie hung up, turned on the radio and listened to some Haitian music while he poured himself a beer. When the tune ended, he heard a DJ speaking in Creole and soon made out the words "Clotilde's Caribbean Gifts." Wilfred was good to his word.

By the time he went to sleep that night he felt he had matters in hand. He was as wrong as could be.

৩৯ ৩৯

The next morning Clotilde arrived at the shop with two cousins who would work with her during the day. That was part of the plan. One of them was a big guy named Granville who would double as salesclerk and bodyguard. Willie didn't think Metellius would make a move before dark, if at all, but having Granville there afforded security just in case. Willie took advantage of that time to run down folks who owed him money from previous assignments. He managed to squeeze a partial payment out of one Puerto Rican lady for whom he'd done divorce work. Somethin' was somethin'.

At a few minutes before eight that night he drove into Little Haiti, parked on a side street a couple of blocks from Clotilde's shop, walked down Second Avenue on the opposite side of the street and checked out the situation. Clotilde had moved a couple of her life-sized statues out onto the sidewalk on opposite sides of the door—the Virgin Mary and St. Joseph. Willie wasn't sure if she'd done that as a marketing ploy or as a way of dissuading Metellius from approaching her place of business. They were high-powered security personnel.

Several customers were in Clotilde's place taking advantage of the extended hours. Clotilde and Granville were waiting on them. Clotilde was dressed in black, but still wearing her signature red turban.

Willie looked up and down the dusky street. The other store-fronts on that strip were already dark, except for the corner store at the far end. Willie had passed a restaurant on the previous block that was open, and he could see another one on the next block where a couple of cars were parked in front, but they wouldn't be open for long. That patch of Little Haiti tended to roll up the sidewalks early. If people were out, they were at nightclubs in other parts of the city. A few pedestrians were around, but they all seemed to be headed somewhere and didn't look at all suspicious.

Willie waited until no one was near and tucked himself into a very narrow alleyway that ran between two buildings on Second Avenue. From there he had a clear view into Clotilde's shop, but nobody could see him. Families lived on the second floor above that alley and the aroma of Haitian goat stew—griot—wafted down to him accompanied by Haitian dance music. Willie leaned against the wall and waited.

Right at eight o'clock, Granville finished his shift and left Clotilde to work the late clientele by herself. That was also as arranged. Granville was not happy about that aspect of the plan, but Willie had convinced him leaving Clotilde on her own was the best way to bring Metellius out of the shadows. Willie promised to take good care of his cousin. For the next hour he watched that entrance and the two big plaster saints stared back as if they could see him. A couple of other customers arrived, bought Easter baskets and left. An occasional car drove by and a few more pedestrians passed, but both kinds of traffic petered out as the night progressed.

Just after nine-thirty his cell phone buzzed. It was Muriel.

"I'm here, Willie boy."

Muriel had been instructed to park behind the shop.

"Any sign of anyone back there?" Willie asked.

"Not a soul."

"Good girl. Get in there."

Two minutes later Clotilde disappeared into a stockroom in the back of the store. She appeared again moments later, except it wasn't Clotilde, it was Muriel. She was also dressed in black and had simply taken the red turban, put it on and sent Clotilde home out the back way. The plan—that whole pointless plan—was working perfectly.

For the next half-hour Muriel made like a shopkeeper, straightening stock, sweeping a bit, checking her watch for closing time. Nobody went into the shop or even walked by.

At ten o'clock sharp she came out, wheeled the Virgin inside, followed by St. Joseph. She adjusted the red turban, retrieved her handbag and hung it from her shoulder, flipped the sign in the front window to Closed, turned out the lights, emerged, locked up and headed down the street in the direction of Clotilde's cousin's house. She was steady as a rock, Muriel, a real pro.

She walked resolutely down the empty street, vaguely in rhythm to the music seeping from the second floor above Willie. He watched her head north, saw no one try to follow her, stepped out from his hiding place and fell in a block behind her, but on the opposite side of the street. The Haitian music and the smell of the griot stayed with him.

As planned, Muriel walked another two blocks on Second Avenue. She left the commercial strip, entered a much more run-down stretch of the street, featuring a ramshackle Haitian church, older storefronts, some of which had been boarded up and an empty lot where a Haitian outdoor market operated during the day. Willie watched closely, wary that Metellius would emerge from the shadows. But he didn't. Muriel kept walking, but no one appeared, neither benign nor dangerous.

A block later, Muriel crossed the road, glanced momentarily in Willie's direction and disappeared down a residential side street heading west. Willie saw no one follow her, but walked faster just so he wouldn't lose sight of her for too long.

That side street was much narrower and darker, lined with houses, partially obscured by shade trees. It was devoid of people, at least outside. Television light sifted through the blinds and shades of some houses. Haitian music seeped from a couple. Thick foliage in the yards, as well as cars and pickups in driveways, offered convenient cover for anyone wanting to get the drop on her and again Willie fixed on possible hiding places as Muriel passed them. But she made it to the next corner with no interference. Willie was starting to think that the attempt to lure Metellius had been a waste of everyone's time.

He watched Muriel make the next corner and turn north. He reached that same street, was about to fall in behind her again when he heard a noise behind him. It was the sound of a snake rattle.

Willie whirled around, but saw no one. Muriel had obviously not heard it and kept walking. Willie let her go and crept slowly, cautiously south on that same dimly lit side street in the direction he had heard the rattle. The sound had stopped now and Willie paused, staring into the shadows.

Moments later it sounded again, several shakes of the bones, this time coming from somewhere behind the dark houses. Willie knew that now it was he being lured. Metellius had lost interest in Clotilde—or Muriel—and now it was Willie who was in his evil sights.

He pulled his gun, edged forward and found himself at the mouth of an alleyway that passed between the backyards of the homes. Standing in the darkness about halfway up that pathway was a person. Willie couldn't distinguish who it was, but a moment later the rattle sounded again, and then a crazed cackling.

Willie headed toward him and the dark figure turned and dashed up the alleyway, the rattle sounding as he ran. Willie sprinted after him, past darkened backyards. In one, a dog burst out barking ferociously. Metellius crossed the next side street and continued up the alleyway, with Willie gaining on him. About halfway up that next block, the Macoute turned left off the paved path and disappeared from view.

Willie ran to that spot and stopped. A metal gate was open, leading into the overgrown backyard of a small, dilapidated wooden house. No lights were on in it or in the houses to either side. This was a decaying block of inner city and the structures all seemed abandoned. Willie could see the back door of the house wide open and through that darkened door he now heard the snake rattle.

Willie hesitated. The house was a trap, and he was being tempted to enter it. But what could he do otherwise? He could call the police, but what would he say? What had Metellius actually done besides smile at Clotilde, shake a rattle at her, leave a voodoo doll outside her door? Maybe he could be charged with stalking, but Saturday nights were busy and that would not be enough to attract the attention of the authorities. No, Willie was on his own.

He eased through the gate, ran to the wall next to the door and pressed himself against it. The sound of the rattle stopped for about ten seconds but then it started again. He also heard a man's voice chanting in the Creole language.

Willie peeked around the doorjamb, saw nobody in the short passageway, entered with his side pressed against the near wall, both hands holding the gun. The house was dank, smelled of rotting wood, the air thick with dust and mold. He felt a light switch pressing against his back, tripped it, but nothing happened. The house had no electricity.

He could still hear the rattle and the chanting just feet away and called out:

"Metellius."

The only answer he received was the sound of the snakes' bones and murmured words.

Willie edged his way up that hall. Right in front of him a piece of the plasterboard ceiling had broken, probably from a leak in the roof, and hung down blocking his path. In the ceiling he could hear rats running around. He moved to the other wall, slid past the obstruction and came to another doorway. Willie reached into his pocket, pulled out his cell phone and turned on the flashlight. A narrow beam of light bounced off the rotting floor. He pointed it into the small room right next to him and saw a soiled mattress on the floor, partially covered with an equally soiled sheet and also a ratty, uncovered pillow. The mattress was surrounded with pools of wax where candles had expired. If this was where and how Metellius was living, he obviously had very little to lose.

Willie edged forward. Dim candlelight flickered on the far wall of the next room. He peeked around that doorway and swept the beam from his phone across what had been the living room of the house. The windows had been boarded over. Sodden, rotting furniture was strewn about, including a stuffed chair that looked partially devoured by rats. Here too Willie could hear the rats scurrying above him and worried about them falling on him from above. He had to get out of there fast.

He took one more step, swept the flashlight to the far corner of the room and there he saw Metellius. The Macoute was standing in front of a voodoo altar that had been created on a square wooden table. It featured one small burning candle, dead flowers, empty liquor bottles, what looked to be rotting fruit and two skulls that stared at Willie from their vacant eye sockets and wore the eternal smile of the dead.

As for Metellius, he wore a black top hat and a long frock coat, just like the voodoo spirit of death, Baron Samedi. He smiled the same toothy, frozen smile as the skulls. With his left hand he shook the rattle. In his right he held a large hunting knife very close to his neck.

"Drop the knife," Willie said.

Metellius's eyes blazed as if he were in ecstasy. For a moment Willie thought the madman would come at him, but he didn't. He cackled one last time, chanted something unintelligible in Creole and then slowly, expertly pulled the blade of the knife across his own throat. Blood poured from the wound instantly, but for several seconds the smile stayed frozen exactly where it had been, aimed right at Willie. He made one last effort to laugh, but all that emerged from him was a bubbling sound. Then his rabid eyes rolled toward the back of his head—toward eternity. He crumbled, buckling back against the altar, collapsing it and then slumping to the floor where he lay surrounded by the dead flowers, broken bottles and the skulls.

Willie didn't move. He knew there was no sense trying to save him. A guy with Metellius's history knew how to kill. He had stewed in his own evil juices for so long he had become insane. His head was now askew but the grin was still glued in place.

A shiver ran through Willie. He didn't believe in any of it, but it still gave him the willies. He punched 911 into his phone, stepped over a stray skull, got out from under the agitated rats in the roof and made for the door as quickly as he could to wait outside for the cops.

He'd had enough of the voodoo.

THE AVENGING ANGEL

Willie Cuesta sat in a Cuban restaurant in Little Havana speaking with his old colleague Bernardo Cruz. Bernie was pushing seventy now and had retired several years back from the Miami-Dade Police Department. Willie, almost thirty years younger, had also left the force to open his own private-investigations firm. In the old days, he and Bernie had worked together in the Intelligence Unit, tracking down a variety of foreign criminals who had set up shop in Miami. Some were representatives of outlawed political organizations, from Latin America and elsewhere, who liked Miami as a warm place to hide out and launder money. Others were common criminals who saw Florida as a place to open branches of their usual illegal businesses—drug dealing, arms vending, human trafficking, et cetera.

At the moment, Willie and Bernie were recalling the operations they had run to roust elements of the Russian mafia, who had shown up in Miami after the fall of the Soviet Union. They had both spent a lot of time undercover in Russian bathhouses and high-end Russian restaurants, which wasn't a hard way to make a living.

"I never seen so many pinky rings in one place," Bernie was recalling.

"Only on the ones who still had pinkies," Willie said, scissoring the fingers of his right hand as if lopping off a digit. "Those guys could get rough."

They were still sipping their coffees and discussing the quality of the herring in the different Russian eateries when Willie's cell phone sounded. He glanced at the screen, saw a local number he didn't recognize and answered.

"Cuesta Investigations."

"Is this Mr. Cuesta I'm speaking to?" a young man asked in Spanish.

"Yes, it is," Willie said, switching languages.

"You are the one who works as a bodyguard?"

Willie shrugged. "Well, that's one service I offer. How can I help you?"

"I need your protection right away. A man who has arrived here in Miami wants to murder me."

That made Willie wince. The kid sounded overexcited, and Willie wondered if he might be exaggerating just a bit.

"Who is this man and why does he want to harm you?"

Across the table, Bernie frowned at what he was hearing.

"I will tell you that when we meet," said the young man.

"Where do you want to do that?"

"It will have to be here where I live. I can't risk going out on the street."

Again the young man sounded over the top. It made Willie hesitate and the fellow on the other end picked that up.

"You'll understand better after we talk."

"Where is it you live?"

The kid gave him an address in East Little Havana, maybe twenty blocks from where he and Bernie were sharing a bite. Willie then told him his day rate.

"And I require two days up front, in cash."

He expected his prospective client to bail at that point, but it didn't happen.

"That's fine. I can pay you when you get here."

"Okay. I'll be there in a half-hour. By the way, what's your name?"

"Carlos. Carlos Miranda."

⌾ ⌾

Willie finished his coffee with Bernie and headed for the address. East Little Havana had been for many decades a neighborhood where refugee groups had established their homes. Starting in the 1930s it had been settled by Jews fleeing the Nazis and their allies in Europe. By the 1960s, most of the Jews had moved on to

better neighborhoods, just in time for Cubans fleeing the Castro government to fill the ramshackle homes. The Cubans also prospered
and dispersed around South Florida. These days it was home to
many Central Americans who had fled to Florida in the 1970s and
80s escaping the guerrilla wars in their countries. The neighborhood
was made up largely of old boardinghouses and small, weathered
apartment complexes, because that's where newly arrived refugees
could afford to live, often with more than one nuclear family crowded into single-family accommodations. The walls of those living
quarters were suffused with aromas of the various cuisines that had
been cooked there over the decades—and also with some of the fears
that all those fleeing families had brought with them.

Lately, however, development in nearby downtown Miami had
spread into the fringes of the neighborhood, resulting in some of
those older buildings being torn down and replaced by taller, more
modern structures. Willie found Carlos Miranda's address, a five-
story building with lots of windows and wide verandas, right on the
edge of that new development. It was a nice enough place, although
it was surrounded by old, worn, sun-blistered, water-stained East
Little Havana housing, so that the views from those new verandas
weren't exactly Venice.

Willie took the elevator to the fourth floor, knocked on the door
of number 407 and heard locks being unbolted. It was not Carlos
Miranda who came to the door. A young woman stood there—in her
mid-twenties approximately, small and thin, with extremely white
skin which was set off by her long, straight black hair and deep-set,
coffee-colored eyes. She wore tight white jeans and a cream-colored
blouse. If she hadn't looked so wary, she would have been extremely
nice to look at.

"I'm here to meet with Carlos Miranda," Willie said in Spanish.
"Am I at the right apartment?"

The young woman nodded but said nothing. She let Willie in,
locked the door behind him, gestured toward a stuffed chair and then
called toward the bedroom.

"Carlos, he's here."

Willie glanced around the apartment. It was functionally decorated, with some supermarket art on the walls and, as far as he could

see, no family photographs or other personal touches. In fact, it looked like it had come furnished.

"He's just getting out of the shower," she said. "Can I offer you something to drink?"

Willie said he was fine, and she sat down on the sofa across from him to wait for Carlos. The young lady was quiet but not shy. She studied Willie up and down without expression as if she were measuring him for a new outfit. Or maybe she was trying to see where he carried his gun. Lots of people did that the first time they met a private investigator.

"I didn't catch your name," Willie said.

"My name is Nina."

"Can you give me an idea what this is about?"

She thought that over for a few moments and then answered as if she were a bit embarrassed.

"Carlos and I, we grew up in the same neighborhood in El Salvador and have loved each other since we were children. Several years back he joined a gang and over time he became a local leader. But every day gang members around him were being killed in the wars with other gangs, more and more all the time. He knew that eventually it would be him. He decided to come here, and I followed him."

"I understand."

Willie had read about the savage gang violence in El Salvador in recent years and could easily comprehend her fears. Whole cities in Central America had fallen under the control of criminal street gangs that had become major vendors of drugs and guns in their countries. In many cases, young men could only be admitted to a gang if they committed a murder. In some instances, they were required to kill a complete stranger selected at random on the street. The region was running with blood and entire families were trying to escape north.

"But now you are here," Willie said. "What is there to be afraid of?"

"The top gang leaders do not simply let you leave the organization. The only way to quit one of those gangs is to be killed. They tell you that when you join. 'The only former members are those who no longer draw breath.' Because he broke that rule, they have sent someone to kill Carlos. Through a friend we have learned who that killer is and the fact that he's already here."

Willie was about to ask who that was when Carlos Miranda stepped into the room. That stopped him cold.

Fresh from the shower, he wore only narrow black gym shorts and no shirt. He was in his twenties, mid-sized, swarthy, with the muscular body of a boy who had spent time lifting weights. And almost every square inch of that fine body, including his face, was embroidered with tattoos.

Carlos Miranda was apparently accustomed to being stared at, studied by people who were seeing him for the first time. He stood still for a few moments and allowed Willie to take in the gaudy gallery of designs all over his body. Across his forehead, in dark blue, flowing cursive, was the name of his gang—M-18. Like anyone who had worked in law enforcement, Willie was acquainted with M-18, which had become in recent years one of the largest, most brutal criminal organizations in the world. On each of Carlos' cheeks were tattooed about a dozen tiny crosses, a miniature cemetery just below his muddy brown eyes. Willie had to wonder if those crosses represented fallen comrades, enemies he had himself murdered or a combination of both.

From Carlos' chin, the head of a rattlesnake stared out at Willie. His neck had been turned into the diamond-patterned body of the snake and the rest of it was coiled on his chest. Tattoo artists had turned his legs into braided vines, like those found in the most tropical jungles of Central America. His arms were covered with women's faces, dollar signs, more crosses, a small Virgin Mary and, on the back of his right forearm, a swastika. Willie wondered if this kid had any real idea what a swastika represented in modern history. If he didn't, that was bad; if he did, it was even worse.

He shuffled into the room, shook Willie's hand limply and sat on the sofa next to Nina. At first glance, he looked like a world-class young thug. But his gaze was anything but aggressive or fierce. It was tense, somber, much the same as his girlfriend's. In the boy's case, given his gang background, Willie wondered if he had seen so much violence and death that he had aged prematurely. The eyes looked like they had been transplanted from a much older individual.

"Your girlfriend has told me about your past and how you left the gang," Willie said.

Miranda shrugged. "I was going to end up dead—and not of old age."

"How long have you been here?"

"About twenty days. Nina came a week ago."

"I understand you are afraid that your fellow gang members may have sent someone here to harm you."

Carlos shook his head. "It isn't maybe. I've received a warning from an old friend in the gang. I know for sure that the killer is here. That's why I don't go out, especially during the day, and why I asked you to come here." He raised his tattooed hands to his tattooed cheeks. Carlos Miranda wasn't someone who would blend easily into a crowd. That was for sure.

"I want to get rid of these tattoos, but I can't even risk looking for someone to do it," he said. "I'm sure he'll be monitoring all the tattoo artists who can do such a job. In fact, he probably has them paid off to keep an eye out for me."

Again, he sounded paranoid, but when you were dealing with an organization like M-18, there was no such thing as paranoia.

"Who is he, this killer?" Willie asked.

"My source told me the passport he used to come here is under the name Rafael Suárez."

"So that's not his real name?"

Miranda shook his head. "The assassins who track down individuals like me, they use many names. And there is something else you should know about them."

Willie cocked his head and waited to be enlightened.

Carlos again tapped his tattooed face. "You can't expect him to look like me. No, amigo, the assassins sent to hunt down guys who leave the gang don't look like the rest of us. Years back, the founders of the gangs figured out that not everyone in the organization could look like a goblin. There had to be members who could move about without attracting attention—special operatives who would have no tattoos, who could blend into the business world, who could be used to move large amounts of money across borders and also hunt down the ones they considered traitors to the tribe. This guy you'll be looking for, he is one who specializes in killing people like me and he was chosen and trained when he was very young. You will see no tattoos and he will look nothing like a gangster. Because of that, and what his job is, in the gang he is known as an avenging angel."

Willie's eyes narrowed and he studied those words. He had never heard of that special breed of assassin, but he had never spoken before with a former leader of a gang as large and lethal as M-18. He figured few "civilians" ever had.

"What else can you tell me about this avenging angel?"

Carlos shook his head.

"Nothing. The angels never have attributes that can be easily described."

Willie thought of angels he had seen portrayed in religious paintings. They were always on the young side, handsome, but sexless. They all looked alike. He looked down at his notebook where he had written the name Rafael Suárez. One of the famous angels of the Bible had been named Rafael, or Raphael in English. Maybe this guy was an assassin who had read the Scriptures. Who knew, but at least Willie had that as a lead.

"About payment for my services," he said.

The young woman got up, retrieved a purse and counted out two days' pay into the palm of his hand. Willie wrote out a receipt on notebook paper and stood up.

"Keep those tattoos indoors until I tell you it's safe," he told Carlos.

He bid them goodbye—the goblin and his gorgeous girlfriend, Beauty and the Beast—and headed back home.

ᔆ᠊ ᔆ᠊

Willie's apartment, in a duplex just off Calle Ocho—8th Street—in Little Havana, also served as his office. He arrived home, looked up a number on his laptop and called.

Art Yeager was head of security for the Miami Visitors and Convention Bureau. He was a former county detective and Willie had known him since they were both on the force.

"Hey, Willie. How's the boy?"

He sounded happy, but why wouldn't he be? He had landed a cushy job in Miami's largest industry—tourism.

"I need a bit of help with a case I'm on, Art."

"What can I do to help you, Willie?"

"I'm searching for a visitor to our fair county who is going by the name Rafael Suárez. Can you tell me if anyone is registered at a local hotel under that name?"

Willie knew a guy in Yeager's position had the police powers to request the names of registered guests at the county's hotels and motels on any given day, although he needed good reason.

"I can't do this if it's just a missing-person case, Willie. Sometimes people don't want to be found and it's no crime."

"I'm with you, Art. But this is the case of a foreign citizen who I'm told may be here to seriously injure a client of mine. I wouldn't ask you if it wasn't serious and I would never divulge where I got the tip."

"Gotcha. I'll send out an urgent e-mail to all our members. I'll get back to you."

Willie nibbled on the remains of a Cuban sandwich he found in the refrigerator from the previous day. A half-hour later his cell phone sounded and Art was on the line.

"A Mr. Rafael Suárez is registered at a small motel on the edge of Brickell neighborhood, called the Stardust. He's in Room 212."

Willie jotted it down. The Brickell area lay on the edge of Biscayne Bay, not far from East Little Havana, where many Salvadorans lived—including Carlos Miranda. If you were hunting for one of those Salvadorans—with plans to kill him—that was a strategic place to stay.

Willie thanked Art for his assistance.

"Just don't do anything I wouldn't do, Willie."

Willie said he wouldn't, although he wasn't sure that was true. Fifteen minutes later he was parked diagonally across the street from the Stardust Motel, with a clear view of a unit on the second floor—Room 212. It was a white Art Deco structure with doors, window sashes and outdoor stairs painted bright orange, which made it appear like an imitation Howard Johnson's. It had probably been built in the 1950s or so.

Willie sat watching and listening to talk shows on the radio for more than three hours. He was learning a lot about the world, but very little about the man he was searching for. Finally, a few minutes before seven p.m., the door to Room 212 opened and a young man emerged. Like Carlos, he looked to be in his mid-twenties. He was café au lait in color, with short black hair and glasses with thick black rims. He wore an off-white, long-sleeved *guayabera* shirt, matching slacks and light brown shoes. Dressed in white like an angel, an avenging angel, Willie thought to himself.

Suárez closed the door, headed down the orange stairs, looked both ways down the street and then walked in the direction of the bay. Willie waited a few moments, climbed out of his car and trailed him, but on the opposite side of the street. Pedestrian traffic was light, with most local workers having gotten off a couple of hours before and already home. But as Mr. Suárez neared the Brickell business district the byways grew busier with after-work diners and drinkers.

About three blocks from the motel, Suárez made a right, crossing in front of Willie, headed down a street lined with restaurants and bars and stopped outside a well-known watering hole named Huey's. Willie stopped as well, maybe a hundred feet behind him and across the street. He watched as Suárez looked around, spotted a small, wrought-iron table on the sidewalk right next to the street and sat down. If you were hunting someone you wanted to kill, that vantage point would give you a clear view of the passing parade.

Willie lingered where he was, watched the man order from the waiter and considered just how he might approach a professional assassin. You had to expect that a pro in the killing game would always carry the tool of his trade—most likely a gun—so you had to be careful about trying to get close to him. Then again, about a half block beyond Huey's Willie saw a Miami PD patrol car parked and two uniformed men leaning against it shooting the breeze. They provided a measure of deterrence against anyone thinking of causing trouble, including an assassin. And after all, Willie wasn't being paid just to watch this guy from down the block.

Of the half-dozen tables on the sidewalk, one was empty. Willie waited a few minutes until two people sat at the table, then he crossed the street, made a show of looking for a place to sit and approached the man in question.

"Do you mind if I share your table?" he asked in Spanish.

Suárez glanced up at him, but Willie didn't give him a real opportunity to say no. He pulled out a chair and settled into it. The other man frowned.

"Be my guest," he muttered, barely audible.

Willie waved down a waiter and ordered a glass of red wine.

"Can I offer you a drink in exchange for your hospitality?" he said to his table mate.

Suárez, who had a half-full glass of beer before him, shook his head.

"No, thank you. I have all I need."

Willie figured if you were searching for the person you'd been sent to kill, you probably wanted to be careful you didn't consume too much alcohol. It wouldn't be beneficial for your aim.

Willie made a show of gazing around, all the time sneaking glances at Suárez, trying to spot the hint of a gun under his shoulder or at his waistband. He didn't see what he was looking for, but the hood could have been carrying a holster against the small of his back. That was where Willie had tucked his Browning.

Willie's wine arrived, he lifted it, smiled as a group of young ladies passed and toasted.

"Here's to Miami and its beautiful women," Willie said.

The other man raised his glass perfunctorily and sipped.

"Are you new here?" Willie asked.

Suárez nodded. "That's right."

"From where?"

He thought that over a moment.

"Central America."

Willie brightened. "Where in Central America?"

That made the other man fidget with his beer glass.

"I've lived in different countries."

Willie sipped his wine.

"What were you doing there?"

The man across from him was losing whatever good humor he'd had. Willie could see it in his eyes.

"I did many different things. What is it that you do, if you don't mind my asking?"

Willie glanced down the block at the two patrolmen, who were still there, not a hundred feet away. He decided that the crowd, and especially those two cops, offered him enough protection that he could risk provoking his prey. He leaned forward and whispered.

"I'm a private investigator and I am being paid to determine who you are."

Willie's own right hand had moved toward his back holster just in case. He expected the man next to him might also reach for a weapon, but he didn't. Instead, he put his hands on the armrests of his chair and started to rise as if he would run. Willie reached out and grabbed his wrist.

"Don't do that," Willie said sternly, but not raising his voice. "If you try to run I'll call those men right down there."

With his free hand he gestured toward the two cops. The other man glanced at them, then back at Willie. His eyes were full of fear.

"What do you want with me?" he whispered. "Why are you doing this?"

Willie fixed on him. He figured Suárez had arrived at the conclusion Willie hoped he would—that doing anything to provoke the two policemen down the block was a bad idea. And maybe he figured he could bluff his way through. Willie wasn't going to let him do that. He leaned in close, tightening his grip.

"I know who you are, Rafael. I know what you are doing here. I know you are an avenging angel."

The other man put on a show of being baffled. "What are you talking about? What about an avenging angel? I have no idea what you mean."

A woman at the next table had suddenly taken an interest in them—one guy grasping the wrist of another guy who looked distressed, scared. Willie let go, feigned interest in the street traffic and the woman turned away. Then Willie leaned over as if he'd dropped something and as quickly and discreetly as possible reached around Suárez's back and felt for a weapon. Nothing.

"What are you doing?" the other man demanded in a whisper.

"I'm going to pay the bill and you're coming with me. If you try to run, I call those cops. I don't think you want to talk to those cops, do you?"

Suárez gazed down the street, back at Willie and shook his head nervously.

Willie reached to the small of his own back, clutched his Browning and held it beneath the table so Suárez could see it. The other man glanced at it and froze.

"You will do what I tell you," Willie whispered. "If you are genuinely not who I think you are, you will go free."

The other man had the look of a trapped animal. He didn't argue. Minutes later Willie had paid, and they headed back the way they had come. Willie kept Suárez just in front of him, with his right hand on his gun in his pocket. When they reached the car, Willie used the remote to unlock it.

"Get in."

Suárez did as told, and Willie climbed in the driver's side. He had pulled out his Browning, held it in his lap with his left hand, pointed at Suárez and started the car with his right.

"Don't do anything to make me nervous," he said.

Suárez glanced at the gun, eyes full of dread and said nothing. Willie pulled out, drove about ten blocks west, turned off onto a quiet side street and parked. He shifted the handgun to his right hand and kept it against his thigh, pointed at the other man. He turned on the interior light so that Suárez would be sure to see it.

"Let's go back to what brings you to Miami. You are an M-18 assassin. You're here to hunt down and kill a member who left the gang."

The other man's mouth fell open and he scowled.

"You're crazy and you have everything backwards. I was once in M-18 and quit the gang. I am not hunting anyone. I am running for my life."

Willie squinted at him hard. Suárez's sleeves were buttoned tight around his wrists. On the back of his right hand the skin was discolored. Suárez realized what Willie was studying, reached to his wrists, unbuttoned the cuffs of both sleeves and rolled them up all the way past his elbows.

Tattoos—garish tattoos—stared at Willie from both forearms. On the left a naked woman stared at him with the Roman numerals XVIII—18—across her breasts. On the right was the depiction of a brooding devil with 666 across his cape. Again, the numerals totaled 18. Suárez unbuttoned his shirt from his neck to his navel. Across his chest M-18 was stenciled and beneath it a face of Jesus Christ with tattooed tears falling from his eyes.

Suárez reached up with both hands and touched his face just below his eyes. "I used to have tears like those tattooed here but had them removed. Look closely."

In the interior light Willie could see the discolorations. Suárez held out his fists, upside down.

"I had tattoos on the backs of my hands too and had them erased." Again Willie could see scars, probably left by acid. More sophisticated practitioners used lasers to remove tattoos, but Suárez had apparently resorted to whatever he could.

Willie stared at the evidence before his eyes. He was not looking at an avenging angel, not by the definition he had heard from Carlos.

"There is another former gang member here who believes you were sent to execute him."

Suárez glowered back. "If someone has come here to execute him, then the assassin has probably been sent to kill me as well."

Willie was fixed on him, as if truth became visible if you stared hard enough. He had questioned a lot of people over the years, as a police detective and now in private practice. If he had to guess—and he did—he would bet the guy before him was telling the truth.

Willie kept his gun in his right hand, pulled out his cell phone and dialed Carlos Miranda, who answered after a pair of rings.

"It's Cuesta. I have Rafael Suárez sitting in front of me. He's not the right man. He's not the assassin, not the avenging angel."

At first there was only stunned silence on the other end.

"What do you mean it's not him?"

"He's unarmed and covered in tattoos—M-18 tattoos. Does that sound like the angel you are afraid of?"

"Where are you? I want to see him. I want to talk to him."

Willie told Miranda to wait, put his hand over the phone, told Suárez who Carlos Miranda was and what he was requesting. The other man froze.

"Is his name known to you?" Willie asked. "Do you know Miranda?"

Suárez shook his head. "There are thousands of members in M-18. We don't know each other."

But he was terrified of him anyway. If he was telling the truth, Suárez had run thousands of miles to get away from M-18. Now he was being asked to meet with another veteran of the mayhem, someone who, like himself, had probably committed countless violent crimes, including murder. Willie could smell the fear emanating from his skin.

They sat in silence for several moments. Willie had completed his assignment. He had located and debriefed the suspected killer and done it quickly. He had earned his money and wanted only to prove that to his client.

"I will make sure my client is not armed when you meet," Willie said to Suárez. "It will be as brief as possible, and I will ensure that he doesn't know where you live. If you do what I ask I will protect you and then never bother you again."

Of course, the implication was that if Suárez didn't do as he was being asked Willie would bother him again. An undocumented person—which Suárez was—would certainly see it that way. After a few moments, he nodded.

"Okay, I'll go. But it has to be someplace safe."

Willie worked that over in his mind. During his days in the Miami PD patrol unit he had driven just about every street in the city, including those in East Little Havana. The perfect place popped into his head, and he spoke into the phone.

"Carlos?"

"Yes?"

"About five blocks from where you live, down the same street, there is a small park, right on the Miami River. Do you know the place I mean?"

"Yes, I know it."

"Meet me there in a half-hour. The man I'm bringing is unarmed and you must be unarmed as well. I will ensure your safety. Is that understood?"

⁘ ⁘

Ten minutes later Willie and Suárez pulled up to the park in question. It was a small space, maybe fifty yards wide, well lighted, with several park benches facing the narrow river. About a hundred feet downstream some boats were docked—a small tug and a few fishing craft. No one appeared to be aboard any of those vessels. Across the water, darkened warehouses lined the far bank, also abandoned, and nobody sat on any of the park benches. The spot would provide the privacy Willie wanted to conduct the meeting.

They got out of the car. Willie scouted bushes on either side of the open space, led Suárez to a spot right next to the riverbank and told him to stay still. He could not be seen there, and he could also not escape from that spot unless he jumped into the dark river. Once he had Suárez tucked away, Willie leaned against a street lamp and waited.

Ten minutes later a car approached. It rolled slowly along the last half block leading to the park, pulled in next to Willie's car and the lights were doused. Carlos emerged and crossed the grass toward Willie. The two of them stood isolated in the pool of light.

Carlos wore long pants, a long-sleeved dark shirt and a brimmed baseball cap, in an attempt to cover his tattoos. Willie quickly frisked him. He found nothing and called for Suárez to come out of hiding. The other man emerged from behind the bushes and crossed slowly, cautiously, toward them. When he reached the pool of light, he stopped.

"Show him," Willie said.

Suárez rolled up his sleeves, exposing the tattoos on his arms. He then unbuttoned his shirt and showed Carlos that artwork as well. He tapped below his right eye.

"I used to have teardrops here," he said. "You can see the scars. I am no avenging angel."

Carlos stared at him, the irrefutable evidence before his eyes. He nodded slowly.

"Yes, I see."

Just then Suárez turned, stared past Willie and his mouth fell open. Willie whirled and found Nina standing at the edge of the pool of light. She wore white pants and a white tank top with a diaphanous white blouse unbuttoned over it. She gripped a gun in both hands, expertly, steadily, the gaze in her eyes as cold as lead— the gaze of an avenging angel. In that split second, she pulled off one shot that hit Carlos in the side of head, killing him before he hit the ground. She swiveled toward Suárez, but Willie threw a body block that knocked Suárez from her trajectory. The shot she fired clipped Willie's left bicep, just as he pulled his Browning from his back holster. Nina had not taken her eyes from her prey, Suárez, and pulled off another shot. Suárez's scream filled Willie's ears just as he pulled the trigger of his own gun. The shot he fired hit Nina in the middle of the forehead, and she fell straight back to the grass, where she lay with arms and legs splayed. She trembled once. After that, she didn't move at all.

ꙅ꙰ ꙅ꙰

The shots had been heard by residents on either side of the park. Police cars and Fire Rescue ambulances arrived within minutes. Carlos and Nina were dead. Suárez, hit in his heavily tattooed right arm, was rushed to the hospital but would live. Willie's wound was nothing more than grazed flesh and he had the EMT techs bandage him right there. The moment they finished, homicide detectives were waiting to debrief him. They weren't happy that he had arranged the meeting of undocumented gangsters on his own, without their knowledge. But it was too late now.

Willie explained to them that Carlos and Suárez were both runaway M-18 members and Nina was the assassin assigned to gun them both down. The detectives stared down at the dead girl, obviously dubious.

Willie's eyes narrowed. In the glare of the headlights he noticed a minor detail on the body and he crouched down. The girl's head had fallen to one side and her long dark hair lay splayed on the grass, exposing the nape of her neck, which in life had always been concealed. There he saw a tiny, deep-blue tattoo no more than a quarter-inch high.

It was an angel.

THE HARDER THEY FALL

W illie Cuesta stood in his local toy store staring at an aisle full of Barbies. They all stared back with their beady, plastic, mostly blue eyes.

That week was the birthday of his five-year-old niece Sofia, youngest child of his brother Tommy. According to his sister-in-law, Connie, who always guided his gift buying for her girls, a Barbie was still the best idea. But, of course, he couldn't buy just one. Sofia's seven-year-old sister, Victoria, would be very upset if Uncle Willie didn't show up with something for her as well. Every birthday was a windfall for both of them. At such tender ages, they already knew how to work him.

Connie would not like the Barbies to wear skirts that were too short or be too sexy. In the end, he bought two that were fully clothed, one with a dog and the other with a pony. He was heading for his car in the parking lot when his cell phone sounded. He saw a local number that was not familiar to him.

"Cuesta Investigations."

"Is this Mr. Cuesta I'm speaking to?" The voice was male, young, speaking English with a distinctive Caribbean lilt.

"Yes, it is."

"You do private detective work?"

"Exactly." At the moment he was carrying two Barbies, so he didn't look much like it, but that's what he did for a living.

"Emil Jones told me to call you."

Emil Jones was a Jamaican who ran a restaurant in the Overtown area of Miami, one of the major black neighborhoods in the city. When Willie had worked in the Patrol Division of the Miami PD he and his partners had sometimes stopped there to eat. It wasn't fancy, but the food was tasty and cheap. On good days, Emil picked up the check.

The accent on the other end of the line sounded Jamaican too, which explained the reference

"I've known Emil a long, long time," Willie said. "What is it I can do for you?"

"It's tricky business, brother," the young man said. "I don't want to talk too much over the phone. Can you meet me at Emil's place in half an hour?"

Willie could do that, but first he quoted his day rate. He would hold a brief initial meeting for free, but after that the meter started running.

"That's fine, brother," the other man said. "I'll be there."

"What's your name?" Willie blurted before the other hung up.

"Neville is my name. Neville Spear."

ʘ) ʘ)

Willie drove east and north from Little Havana where he lived and about twenty minutes later crossed into Overtown. It was a neighborhood settled many decades ago by blacks from both the Deep South and the Caribbean, and you still heard both accents on its rough-and-tumble streets. It had been a high-poverty area for decades, and most Miami residents made it a point to stay away. Willie, being a former patrol cop, had no such qualms. He had treated people right and, so far at least, he'd had no trouble during his occasional appearances in the neighborhood as a private operative.

Emil's Cafe sat on a potholed street lined with struggling businesses and older stucco residences in pastel colors, most of which needed repairs and fresh coats of paint. Emil's joint was the exception. Willie saw it from two blocks away: its red-tile roof, its walls an electric lime green, with bright purple palm trees stenciled on either side of the front door. Emil had been turning a profit for thirty years or so and he spent part of that on a regular, spiffy paint job.

It wasn't quite lunchtime, and Willie found parking right out in front. He walked into a large dining room furnished with rustic hand-carved wooden tables and chairs, knotholes and all, imported from the islands. Reggae music sounded from speakers in every corner of the room. On the wall right in front of Willie hung a large poster of the late Jamaican musician Bob Marley. If there existed a Jamaican restaurant or nightclub anywhere that didn't feature an image of the great Bob, Willie had never seen it.

The dining room was empty, and Willie took a seat at the back facing the door. The menu on the table featured a photograph of a mouth-watering roasted chicken with two flags crossed in the foreground—the American on one side, the black-and-yellow Jamaican banner on the other. Willie knew that Emil was seriously loyal to two things—the American entrepreneurial spirit and his secret recipe for Jamaican jerked chicken. The smell of it wafted from the kitchen now—a rub made of brown sugar, onion powder, garlic, cayenne pepper, and God only knew what else. It was delicious.

Also delicious was the young waitress who came to Willie's table—an island girl with a sea-blue sarong tied around her hips and a matching halter top. For the moment he ordered only an unsweetened iced tea.

"Is Emil around?" Willie asked.

"Not right now. He be back later," she said in her lovely island intonation.

Willie sipped his tea, keeping an eye on the doorway for Neville Spear. Minutes later, the waitress appeared at his side again.

"You waitin' to meet with someone here? A guy who go by Neville? If it's you, he out back."

Willie picked up his tea and followed her through a rear door to a small patio next to the kitchen shaded with banana trees. It was a cramped dining area where the kitchen help ate, with a tall wooden back gate leading to the street. Standing there, he found a young man—black, tall, slim, but well-muscled. He wore a flowered shirt, with dreadlocks that hung to his shoulders and jeans that hung way down on his hips. He held out a hand and, despite his obvious strength, shook hands limply. He motioned Willie into a chair and they sat either side of a tin table emblazoned with an ad for Red Stripe beer, a Jamaican brew.

"Better out here, brother," Neville Spear said. "I don't need nobody noticing us together."

The waitress took his order, and a minute later Neville was gripping a Red Stripe. He also ordered a plate of curried goat, a specialty of the house. He sipped his beer.

"Anybody tell you anything about me?" he asked.

Willie shook his head. "No, but that's because I haven't asked anybody. What would they tell me if I did?"

The kid thought about that for a moment then leaned forward and dropped his voice.

"People, they'll tell you that I belong to the Rain Posse."

Willie was about to sip his tea but that stopped him in mid motion. In the United States, especially in Wild West lore, a posse was a group of law-abiding citizens who were deputized to pursue fugitive criminals. But in Jamaica the term had taken on a different meaning. In fact, it was just the opposite. On the island, a posse was a criminal enterprise, known, in particular, for drug smuggling and illegal trade in weapons. Some of those gangs had branches in Miami. The largest and most fierce of them was the Rain Posse. Nobody knew exactly why it was called that. The best guess Willie had heard was that the gang had become so much a part of the life on the island that it was as natural as the rain.

Willie now gazed at Neville Spear in a different light. He wondered if the kid was packing a gun under that flowered shirt. Most posse members did, mainly to be ready for run-ins with other gangs. But there was something in the kid's tone that made Willie wonder.

"That's what people say about you, but is it true? Are you a member of the Rain Posse?"

Neville Spear shrugged. "I am . . . and I'm not."

"What the hell does that mean?"

Neville looked over his shoulder and leaned farther forward.

"Two years ago, my half-brother, Malcolm Jones, he gets shot dead by a member of the Rain Posse. They was in an argument over some girl. The gangster just shoots him in the head. My brother, he was older than me. He lived here in Miami and he die here too. I was livin' with my mama back in Jamaica, in a city they call Port Antonio, across the island from Kingston, the capital."

Willie nodded. He had vacationed in Jamaica with his ex-wife and he knew the layout. Neville sipped his beer.

"My mama, she cried hard when she heard Malcolm, he dead. I got a different father and a different last name, but I loved my brother. Me, I was mad. I wanted to find out who did it. In Port Antonio, a detective for the Jamaican Constabulary Force, he knows my family. His name is Raymond Knowles. He comes to me and asks, 'You want to get revenge for Malcolm?' I say, 'Yes, dude, definitely I do.'"

Willie's brows went up.

"How did he propose you do that?"

"He say to me, 'People in Kingston don't know Malcolm was your brother. I want you to go undercover in the Rain Posse. Find out who killed Raymond, who killed other people, here on the island and in Miami. Then we take them all to prison. Then your mother she can stop cryin'.'"

Willie's gaze narrowed.

"And how did he propose you infiltrate the Rain Posse?"

"He tells me that the posse is always looking for new business. In Port Antonio, we got boats comin' from all over the islands and from down Venezuela and Colombia too. Sometime they carry cocaine, heroin." He flicked his eyebrows wickedly to punctuate his words. "He tells me that I should go to the posse people in Port Antonio and tell them I got a supply from off the boats and I want to do business with them. Then he gives me the drugs to show them. Now that I got a supply, I can get into the posse."

"And did it work?"

Neville nodded once. "Oh, it worked. They not only bring me into the posse, awhile later, after I supply more drugs, they take me to Kingston to meet the bosses."

The waitress brought his curried goat just then. It smelled delicious, but he didn't touch it.

"Those bosses, they bragged at me. I hear about all kinds of crime they do and what they gonna do."

"And you told Knowles, the investigator, I suppose."

"That's right. And you know what happened?"

"Tell me."

He turned and spit on the ground at the edge of the patio.

"Nothin' at all. That's what happened. Not to them, at least. It happened to me."

Willie's gaze narrowed as if he were trying to see all the way to Jamaica.

"What was it that happened to you?"

"Knowles, he rats me out to the Rain Posse. Tells them I'm a police spy, a snitch. They pay him a lot of coconuts for that."

"Coconuts?"

Neville rubbed his index finger and thumb together in the universal symbol for cash, for the payoff. With his other hand he swigged his Red Stripe and then slammed it down on the metal table.

"And that's his game from the beginning. Knowles, he knows I want to get even and he puts bait in front of me like a fish—the chance to pay them back for my brother. I go for it and he pulls me in," the kid said, cranking an imaginary reel. "I get friendly with the posse, find out what they do, how bad they are, and I tell him. Does he bust them then? No. He goes to them and he sells me out. He puts the Rain Posse on my tail."

Willie's lips curled. "So, he used you to infiltrate them, not to bust them, but to collect evidence, to collect dirt. And then he exposed you to them, so he could cut himself in on their profits."

"You got it."

Big drug money had corrupted lots of cops, in the US and just about everywhere else. Willie figured the Jamaican justice system couldn't pay its agents much. All that cocaine and heroin cash would be too much to resist. He sipped his tea to wash away the bad taste in his mouth.

"How did you get here? Why aren't you lying dead in an alley in Jamaica?"

The kid got a sly smile on his face.

"Because a girl who hangs with the Rain Posse in Kingston, she likes me. Her name's Therese. She finds out they comin' for me and she tips me off. A guy I know in Port Antonio, he's got a small plane and I pay him to bring me here."

"You paid him with drug money?"

Neville Spear shrugged. "I pay him with Rain Posse money. That's the way it should be."

Willie didn't argue.

"Now what? Why are you coming to Willie Cuesta?"

Neville Spear speared a piece of curried goat with his fork and dropped it in his mouth.

"Because the Rain Posse people, they afraid I came here to talk to the American drug police."

"The DEA. Drug Enforcement Administration."

"That's them. So, now they're telling Knowles that he needs to hunt me down and kill me, or they be runnin' him out into the ocean and droppin' him over the side for the sharks to eat. He's here lookin' to kill me right now."

"Did Therese tell you that too?"

Neville nodded.

"Why don't you go to the DEA, tell them what you just told me? They'll protect you."

The kid smirked.

"You think they gonna believe me and not Knowles? They already work with him, they already know him in Jamaica. Me, they think I belong to the Rain Posse. He's telling them that he's here huntin' a gangster. And they say, 'Okay, we be helping you.' Those guys, they stick together."

Willie took it all in. If his story was true, the kid sitting before him certainly had reason not to trust law-enforcement agents of any nationality. And the fact of the matter was he was probably right. It would be difficult to convince DEA agents that one of their old collaborators had gone rogue, given that you yourself were a member of the biggest, most violent smuggling organization on the island. Neville would be trying to convince them that he was the one member of the posse who was secretly on their side. But how were they to know that the leaders of the Rain Posse weren't setting up this Jamaican cop? How was Willie to know?

"Why should I believe what you're telling me?"

The kid popped another piece of goat into his mouth and chewed on the question.

"What you need is to go find the man I'm tellin' you about. He has a sister here. He stays with her. I can tell you where he is. You go follow him. You watch what he does. Find out who he talks to. You gonna see what I tell you. He's dirty."

Neville reached into his baggy pants and pulled out a thick wad of bills.

"I pay you. You tell me how much."

Willie shot an anxious look around. The kid was being reckless, but if you felt you were being hunted like an animal by dangerous people, maybe you had little choice. Willie had different day rates, depending on the difficulty of the assignment and the degree of possible danger. This case he would rate as highly risky. A Jamaican drug cop would be armed. And if Willie was trying to rob him of a generous livelihood and send him to prison, he would be dangerous.

But taking money from the kid raised tricky issues. It was drug money—dirty, just as Neville said. And if it was all a scheme to set up this agent, then Willie would be a paid participant in the plot. He thought of walking away, but by that point he couldn't. He wanted to know if Neville Spear was telling the truth. If he was really a victim who had only wanted to avenge his brother.

Willie cited an amount that would cover three days of dangerous duty. Without a qualm, Neville peeled off the cash. Willie reached across the table and shoved it in his pocket. He had already decided to drive directly to the office of his attorney, Alice Arden, tell her everything, and have her hold the money.

"How do I find this Raymond Knowles?"

Neville told him an address and Willie wrote it down. It was just north of Miami in a town called Villamar, which Willie knew was rife with Jamaicans.

"And he hangs out in a reggae club called Montego Bay right near there," Neville said. "You can't miss him. Skinny guy, real tall, not old but his hair all white."

Neville stood up as if to go, but he wasn't finished.

"His real name, it's Raymond Knowles, but nobody calls him that. He smokes menthol cigarettes, always has. Everybody calls him Menthol."

"Menthol?"

"That's him. You're lookin' for Menthol."

He turned, walked across the backyard and disappeared through the wooden gate. Willie waited moments, followed him and peeked through a space between the door and the jamb. He watched as Neville climbed into a car occupied by three other young black men in dreadlocks. They pulled away into traffic before Willie could copy the license tag.

Neville had made it sound as if he was a hunted animal all on his own, but it turned out he had backup. Who were those traveling companions of his? Were they simply local friends, relatives or were they members of the Rain Posse? Was the story he had told Willie true, or was it all a tale designed to set up a member of the Jamaican Constabulary Force, using Willie as an unwitting accomplice? Willie would have to try to figure that out before he went too much farther in his attempt to find Menthol.

⏀⏀ ⏀⏀

Willie paid for his tea and headed for Alice Arden's office. Alice was in court, but Willie left the money with her secretary, Selma, whose eyes widened with trepidation when he told her it was Jamaican drug-gang money. She shoved it in the safe and slammed the door as if she was trapping a demon in there.

Willie went home. He occupied the second floor of a house in Little Havana, which he also used as his office. He went to his desk in a corner of the living room, turned on his computer, opened his "Phones" file and found the number of Anita Briones.

Anita was an agent with the DEA. Willie had worked with her on several occasions when he was with the Intelligence Unit of the Miami PD. Willie's main responsibility back then was tracking foreign criminals trying to do business in South Florida. The kinds of commerce they were most often involved in were drug smuggling and money laundering—many times both. So, Willie had a considerable amount of contact with the DEA.

Anita was a girl of Puerto Rican extraction—small, thin, green-eyed and raven-haired. She was often used as an undercover agent because her good looks allowed her to get close to suspects. She was particularly effective in the nightclub scene, where her provocative salsa and *merengue* dancing would catch the attention of any guy with a pulse. Many a cocaine or heroin dealer had lured Anita back to his house or hotel room for a sample of his wares, only to find himself staring at Anita's badge and the mouth of her .38 Colt.

Anita answered the phone with her trademark throaty whisper.

"Is that you, Willie? What you up to, buddy boy?"

"I caught a case and I thought you'd be interested."

"Tell me more."

Willie filled her in on the phone call from Neville Spear, the meeting, his accusation against Raymond Knowles and the claim that he had been targeted for killing by the same.

"You ever hear of this Jamaican law-enforcement guy?"

"I never heard of no Raymond Knowles. But they don't put me on anything to do with Jamaica. They leave that to the guys and girls who operate only in English. Me, I do Colombia, Mexico, Puerto Rico, Cuba, the Dominican. Only the Spanish-speaking countries. Our people, Willie," she chuckled. "But that don't mean I'm not interested in your case. What you want me to do?"

"Can you ask around and see who in your office might know this Knowles? What they hear about him? Tell them what I told you and see what they think? I'm trying to figure if he's really dirty or if this Neville Spear and his buddies are trying to do him wrong."

"Can do, doctor."

"Depending what they tell you, I might want you to put on your slinkiest outfit and go with me to a Jamaican nightclub called Montego Bay. That's where he hangs out."

"Oooooo. Reggae dancing. I love reggae dancing, dude. Slow and sexy."

"We'll talk tomorrow."

꧁ ꧁

Willie climbed in his car again and headed north before rush hour started. The address Neville Spear had given him was about a half-hour north of Miami. Willie knew from past cases when he was a cop that the town of Villamar featured a good-sized, middle-class immigrant population, including a large contingent of Jamaicans. In the Miami metropolitan area, just about every Latino and Caribbean population had its favored enclaves, and Villamar was a home away from home for many from Jamaica.

He left the highway and entered the city limits. The town featured numerous tall condo complexes, mostly built in the Mediterranean style with ample balconies. Other neighborhoods were reserved for single-family homes, some of them in gated communities with names like Windsor Palms, Monarch Estates, Victorian Forest. Some Anglophile real-estate developer had really sunk his teeth into the town.

Willie used his GPS and found the address on Windsor Street, in a neighborhood that was not gated but featured relatively new, spacious, two-story stucco houses that were well cared for. If Knowles was, in fact, dirty, maybe he was sinking some of his ill-gotten gains into Florida real estate for him and his family members. A Jamaican cop who was clean didn't make the kind of bread to buy such a spread. Then again, maybe his sister had her own money. Who knew?

The house was painted sea blue, complemented by a Spanish-style red-tile roof. Two cars sat in the driveway, both pretty new, but nothing gaudy. Willie cruised by slowly, jotting down the license numbers.

He parked in front of a house three doors down and facing away from the Knowles family residence. He positioned both his rearview and side-view mirrors so that he would see anyone going in or coming out. Then he turned on sports radio and settled in for a wait.

He was in the middle of an interview with a Miami Dolphins middle linebacker when a black SUV pulled up in front of the blue house. Moments later the front door opened and out came Raymond Knowles. As Neville had commented, you couldn't miss him. He was a man of about forty, around six five, rail thin, with café au lait skin, long, prematurely white hair and shades. He dressed in a white shirt, cream-colored linen pants and white shoes—totally tropical. He had a cigarette dangling from his mouth—almost certainly a menthol.

His long strides took him to the SUV, where he leaned in the driver's-side window and spoke to the passengers. After several minutes of conversation, he turned and went back in the house, carrying a paper bag he hadn't had before. Who knew, maybe they were bringing him doughnuts, but Willie didn't think so.

The vehicle took off again, and as it sailed by Willie saw three men in the car. They were all black, but unlike Neville Spear's traveling buddies, these fellows didn't do dreadlocks. They wore shorter haircuts and, on quick study, looked a bit older. Both Neville and Knowles had their entourages. Maybe it was because they both needed buddies to help cover their backs. The crucial question was why.

Willie scribbled down that license tag too. He waited until they were almost a block away and then fell in behind them. He tracked the SUV across town and then watched it pull into a gated development called Cornwall Estates. A uniformed guard was at the gate and Willie decided discretion was called for. He kept driving past the place.

Before he headed home, he found the address of the Montego Bay Nightclub on Google and entered it into his GPS. He was led to a side street in the older part of town where he found a strip mall occupied by a florist, a travel agency with posters of the Caribbean taped in the window, a Jamaican restaurant named Nemo's and the nightclub. The front of the building was decorated with a mural of the Jamaican coast, highlighted by bright blue Montego Bay. It looked like it might have been painted by the same artist who had beautified Emil's Cafe in Miami. The club was still closed at that time of day, but a sign out front announced it was open from nine p.m. to five a.m. Wednesday to Saturday.

Willie headed home. When he arrived, he opened a cold beer. He also opened the computer programs that allowed him to identify the owners of vehicles and also run them for possible criminal backgrounds. Both of the vehicles parked in the driveway at the Villamar residence were registered to Regina Knowles Cassidy, presumably Menthol's sister. Willie checked her for a criminal record, but she came up clean. He also entered the tag number of the black SUV Menthol's friends had driven away in. He found it was registered to a seventy-year-old woman with the surname Arthur, who was also clean. Maybe the guys in that car were solid citizens. But just maybe they were up to no good and trying to hide behind Granny. Who knew?

Willie opened another beer and called it a day.

ഇ ഇ

It was midmorning the next day when Anita called back.

"I talked to our main liaison with Jamaica. He's a white guy named Norman Blair. He's never heard of this Raymond Knowles, doesn't know if he's dirty or not, but he's very interested in your case. I told him about that club, Montego Bay, where that dude hangs out, and he said he was going to check it out tonight. The chance to bust Rain Posse *hombres,* and their dirty Jamaican cop friends, he's enthusiastic about that, *amigo.*"

Willie winced. He wasn't too happy about the DEA insinuating itself into his case. Feds—whether it be the FBI, DEA or any other federal law-enforcement entity—weren't known as great collaborators. They were always the 888-pound gorilla in any investigation. A private operator like Willie would be very small change to those guys. But he didn't say that to Anita, who had only done what he had asked.

"You going with them tonight, Anita?"

"You bet, buddy boy. I told you, I really like that reggae music."

Willie disconnected and sat dissecting his case. He now had three "posses" to deal with—Neville's, Menthol's and the DEA. They were all armed and dangerous. Menthol did business with the DEA and, if he was dirty, maybe one or more of them were as well. You couldn't rule it out.

Willie didn't have any firm idea who were the good guys and who the bad in that triangle. Given that he was at the middle of it all, that was a very, very bad situation. It occurred to him that he might simply walk away, but he already knew too much to do that. He would have to watch his back for who knew how long. On top of that, he wasn't the kind of guy who was good at walking away.

Instead, he placed another phone call. This time it was to Mario Díaz, a homicide detective he had sometimes worked with on the Miami PD.

"Hey, Willie boy, what's goin' on?"

"You guys have an unsolved homicide from a few months ago. The dead man was named Malcolm Jones, up in Overtown. I have a client related to the victim. Maybe you guys can help me with some information and maybe I can help you too."

"What ya got?"

So, Willie repeated what Neville had told him about the murder of his brother.

"I want to get ahold of the case file," Willie said. "I need any details that might have turned up in the investigation. Maybe I can connect dots that weren't clear at the time."

"It isn't my case, but I can find out who handled it. Come down and I'll fix it up."

Willie made the short drive over to Miami PD. The file was waiting for him on Mario's desk when he walked in. For the next hour he pored through the original police report on the shooting, plus accounts of interviews done by the detectives. No eyewitnesses were found, only people who had heard it happen in the alleyway outside the dead man's apartment building and looked out windows too late to see the perpetrator. Willie wrote it all down, thanked Mario and then made his way to the scene of the killing a couple of miles away. There he knocked on doors and talked to neighbors for about an hour. Then he headed home to rest before making for the nightclub.

ᘒᕽ ᘒᕽ

It was ten that night when Willie pulled into the parking lot of Montego Bay. It was already crowded, and from inside the club he could hear the muffled sound of music. He parked, walked to the door and encountered two unusually large gentlemen, both dressed in black and both sporting deadlocks. They were the bouncers, but they could have been one side of the Miami Dolphins' defensive line. One of them asked Willie politely if he was carrying weapons and Willie answered honestly that he wasn't. He would have preferred to carry his handgun, but he knew that guns were prohibited in most clubs and Montego Bay was no exception. The lineman on the left asked if he could frisk him just to make sure, and Willie acquiesced. The frisk was quick, and he was waved in.

Montego Bay was a sprawling dark space that featured a bar just inside the door and beyond that a spacious dance floor. At the far end stood a stage where a DJ sat behind blinking digital equipment, flanked by tall speakers. The obligatory portrait of the dreadlocked patriarch, Bob Marley, was painted on that back wall, staring benignly out over at the dancers, like a demigod. The ceiling was low and painted with phosphorescent stars simulating the night sky over Jamaica. At the moment, the DJ was playing Jimmy Cliff's reggae standard "The Harder They Come, The Harder They Fall." The dance floor was crowded, a mass of bodies bobbing, swaying, writhing in sync, in time to the languorous anthem.

Dress was decidedly casual. Lots of guys wore baseball caps. The ladies largely wore pants, some even wore shorts for greater freedom of movement, but there were flashes of style. One particularly tall lady dancing near the bar wore a bright blue sequined halter top and a tiara that sparkled in the pulsing of strobes placed here and there.

Willie waded into the crowd. He saw the interior walls of the club were also painted with murals, breaking waves and palm trees. At one point he found a long aquarium built into a wall, with brightly colored fish drifting slowly along a sandy bottom. They were just about the only creatures in the place not moving to the music.

Side rooms jutted off from the dance floor, where people sat at tables, drinking, talking, laughing, waiting for the next tune. Willie searched the crowd for familiar faces—Menthol, Anita, Neville. It wasn't until he reached the back of the club and nudged open a louvered wooden door leading to a private room that he found the one he was looking for.

Seated at one table facing the door were Menthol and three friends of his, maybe the same individuals Willie had spotted in the SUV earlier that day. Menthol was still dressed in white and had a cigarette in his long thin fingers. Standing just inside the door facing him was a group of three people that included Anita. Willie assumed the other two were her fellow DEA agents, including Norman Blair, a stocky blond guy and the only white person in the room. Willie assumed they had been in dialogue, but they had apparently fallen into a silent standoff. As Willie stepped in, they all turned to look at him.

Anita spoke up. "Norman Blair, this is Willie Cuesta, the private investigator I told you about."

Blair barely nodded. Just then Willie felt someone else enter the doorway behind him. Blair's eyes shifted. At the table, Menthol and his men frowned and then they glared. Willie turned and found young Neville Spear standing stock-still just inside the door, returning Menthol's murderous gaze. They all fell into a frozen standoff, with the painted waves on the walls crashing noiselessly around them. Blair broke the silence.

"Who is this?"

It was Willie, the only one besides Menthol who knew all three sides, who filled him in. He introduced Neville, explained that the kid was his client and how he was trying to avenge the murder of his brother, Malcolm Jones.

"He was killed in Miami, allegedly by members of the Rain Posse."

Blair's blond eyebrows went up. "Allegedly?"

"Yes, that's what Neville was told by Jamaican law-enforcement agent Raymond Knowles here."

Menthol's gray eyes now glared at Willie.

"That's exactly what came down, Cuesta. They killed him because he knew they were part of a criminal enterprise operating on his street and he was going to report them to the local police."

Willie shrugged. "According to neighbors I talked to, everybody knew who was associated with the Rain Posse and who wasn't. Everyone had known that for a while, including the late Malcolm Jones. Those posse members didn't talk about their doings with any-one local and they didn't do any dealing in the neighborhood. If they were involved in business here, it was macro-economics—money laundering—not small stuff like local drug dealing. They didn't mess with locals and locals didn't mess with them. Everybody said that."

Menthol glowered and his voice rose. "Well, that wasn't true of Malcolm Jones. When I bumped into him here, he told me all about the Rain Posse, about them bringing in big-time drugs and weapons too."

His cigarette had burned down, so he stubbed it in an ashtray, reached into his shirt pocket and pulled out his pack. It was a brand of menthol cigarettes called Matterhorn that was sold in the Caribbean and that Willie had seen around down there. The package bore the image of that famous peak in the Swiss Alps, tinted an icy blue. Menthol plucked out one with his long fingers and was about to put the pack back. Willie reached out.

"Can I have one of those, if you don't mind?"

Menthol frowned but held out the pack. Willie crossed to the table and drew out a single cigarette. He made no move to light it, but simply held it in the palm of his hand.

"As I was saying, I went to the neighborhood. People said they saw a very tall, thin, light-skinned black man sometimes showing up at night to visit the Rain Posse guys. They didn't know who he was, but that was because they weren't from the same town in Jamaica he was from—Port Antonio. The one person in the neighborhood from that town was Malcolm and he recognized that night visitor right away."

Willie locked eyes with Menthol.

"From that moment on, Malcolm knew you were dirty, Mr. Knowles, and word got back to you that he had spotted you. You couldn't allow him to live and to tell anyone. You staked out his apartment, waited until he came home that night, pulled your gun, forced him into the alleyway and shot him in the head. When his half-brother, Neville Spear, began making calls to Miami, trying to find out who had killed Malcolm, you knew eventually you would be found out. That's when you hatched your plan to get rid of him. You fed him a story about a Rain Posse thug killing Malcolm over a woman. Then you led him into a trap where the Rain Posse would rub him out for being a police spy. He would be dead, and you would be sitting pretty with the Posse."

The tall man smiled through a cloud of his own smoke.

"You're spinning a tall tale, Cuesta. Nothing at all like that has ever happened. Where are your witnesses that I killed Malcolm Jones? Where is your evidence?"

Willie reached slowly into his pants pocket with his free hand and pulled out a small, clear plastic bag. In it was a single item: the butt of a filter cigarette. He held it up.

"Do you see this, Mr. Menthol? Apart from going to the neighborhood today, I also went to the Miami Police Department Homicide Unit. In the evidence locker corresponding to this case I found various items. Among them was this cigarette butt, which was found right next to Malcolm Jones' body."

Willie lifted the bag higher so that it better caught the light.

"You'll notice it's a Matterhorn, Mr. Menthol." He also lifted the cigarette he had just taken from Knowles. "That's your brand, which is well known in Jamaica, but quite rare here. I'm betting when we take a sample of the DNA from the filter of this cigarette end it will match yours exactly."

Menthol glowered at the plastic bag as the silence mounted. Everybody else was fixed on it as well. Then he did something decidedly foolish. As a law-enforcement agent, he had been allowed into the club carrying his concealed weapon in the waistband of his pants, beneath his long shirt. He reached for it right then.

But of course, the three DEA agents had also not relinquished their weapons at the door. Anita had apparently slipped her hand into her purse early in the conversation. By the time Willie caught a glimpse of Menthol's gun, Anita was already firing. Three quick shots caught the dirty cop right in the chest. The force of them knocked him and his chair over backwards. His gun clattered to the floor.

By then Willie had hit the deck as well, with Neville Spear right next to him. Willie covered his head and waited for more shots, but they didn't come. When he scrambled to his feet he found Menthol's men all standing with their hands up and the three DEA agents holding them at gunpoint. Menthol himself lay without moving, his lifeless gray eyes fixed on the painted stars above. Static stars in the eyes of a dead man. His cigarette had fallen to the table, still emitting a ribbon of smoke that rose, like his departing spirit, toward those stars.

Bouncers barged in the door but were met by the DEA agents holding up their shields. The dance floor behind them, in fact the entire club, was clear of people. Everybody had run for their lives.

Minutes later, the place was crawling with local cops, county sheriff's deputies and also ambulance personnel there to collect Menthol's body. The cops interviewed Anita, and after that she stood next to Willie, still shaken by what she'd been forced to do. Willie put an arm around her and held her close until she stopped trembling. Then he reached into his pocket with his free hand, removed the baggie with the cigarette butt in it and dropped it into a trash basket.

Anita scowled at him. "What are you doing, Willie boy? That's evidence in the homicide of that guy shot in the alleyway."

Willie shook his head. "No, it isn't. There was no cigarette butt next to the body. That's just one I found on the street outside my house. It wasn't even the right brand. Menthol never smoked it."

Anita's eyes went all big. "Willie, you sneaky son of a gun."

"Ya gotta do what ya gotta do, Anita. Right now, I'm heading home."

"This ain't no time for dancing, but one of these days you still owe me," she said.

"Give me a rain check."

"A rain check for when I'm finished dealing with Rain Posse?"

"You got it, girl."

Willie headed home then, out from under those painted stars.

THE GENTLEMAN FROM SHANGHAI

W illie Cuesta sat in a lawn chair under the mango tree in the backyard, keeping a keen eye on the branches above. It was mid June, the mangoes would begin falling any day, and then it would become dangerous to sit where he was. He had once been hit on the nape of the neck by a plummeting mango bomb—unripe and hard—and it was not something he wanted to undergo again. He told himself the next day he would move his chair onto the porch across the yard for safety's sake.

He was still staring up when his cell phone sounded and he reached to the tray table next to him.

"Willie Cuesta, private investigations."

"Is this Mr. Cuesta himself to whom I am speaking?" asked a man's voice.

It was a heavily accented voice but not of the variety Willie was accustomed to. Many of his clients were Latinos. He advertised both in the Yellow Pages and online as being bilingual—English/Spanish. He was also a former member of the Miami Police Department Intelligence Squad, which handled crimes of an international nature—usually involving Latin America—and he received referrals from old friends on the force. If a client had an accent, it was usually of a Latin flavor.

But the gentleman on the other end of the line now spoke with an Asian lilt.

"Yes, this is Cuesta. Who do I have the pleasure of speaking with?"

"My name is Mr. Chu."

"And where are you from, Mr. Chu, if you don't mind my asking?"

"I come from Shanghai, China, Mr. Cuesta."

Willie's eyebrows elevated.

"Are you calling all the way from Shanghai?"

The Chinese man chuckled.

"Oh, no. I no longer live in China. I am right here in your city of Miami, and I am calling to see if you are available to accept a very confidential assignment for me."

"Well, that's why they call it private investigations, because it's confidential."

"And you are free for an assignment that might take several days, or as long as a week?"

"I sure am."

Pickings had been slim of late, and a week's work sounded very good. About ten days before he had handled the case of a nineteen-year-old Brazilian girl who had come to Miami on vacation and suddenly fallen out of touch. The Brazilian Consulate contacted Willie and put him in touch with the parents. The father was worried, and the mother was frantic. Willie would have liked to stretch the case out, but he couldn't bring himself to make the poor woman worry any more than she had to. In one day, he had found the girl shacked up with the doorman from a South Beach club off Ocean Drive. Those guys who worked the velvet ropes—and decided who got in the club and who didn't—always did very well with women. Their romantic lives were like revolving doors.

The parents had wired Willie one day's pay and very sincere thanks, which didn't contribute much toward the rent.

"Yes, I'm available for a week's work, or even more," Willie said to his prospective client.

"Oh, that is very, very good," Mr. Chu said. "I would like to meet with you, Mr. Cuesta. Would it be possible for you to come to the Mandarin Oriental Hotel?"

Willie's eyebrows wiggled again. The Mandarin was about as ritzy as it got in Miami. Maybe, if you were Chinese—a very well-off Chinese—it was a touch of home. The case was sounding better and better to Willie because anyone with the loot to stay there would have more than enough to pay him. Willie agreed to meet Mr. Chu in an hour.

He disconnected and was just about to get up when he heard a faint rustling in the branches above. He glanced up, made a stab with his right hand, and caught a large, green mango just before it did damage to his left thigh. Willie fingered the fruit. It would take about a week to ripen—maybe like his new case.

☙ ☙

Willie parked a couple of blocks away from the Mandarin and crossed Brickell Avenue on foot. Then he walked across the short bridge that connects the mainland to Brickell Key, the exclusive island in Biscayne Bay that plays host to the Mandarin—and the mandarins who stay there. He could have parked at the hotel, but it would have cost him half a morning's pay.

He entered the hotel lobby, a space three stories high, with tall windows looking out on the bay. All that glass allowed a lot of sunlight to enter and to nurture an arching, graceful stand of golden bamboo that grew right in the middle of the lobby. Orchids were arranged on tables on either side and suffused the space with their powerful perfume. The walls were made of gorgeous wood that Willie couldn't identify and the floors of a brilliant, ocher-colored marble. The moment you walked into the Mandarin you were in another world.

Willie passed through the lobby and, following Mr. Chu's directions, emerged onto an outdoor deck that hosted the pool and some tables shaded by large white umbrellas. That was where Mr. Chu had said they would meet, and it wasn't hard to pick out his new prospective client. To begin, it was the off season, and the hotel was probably half empty. Secondly, Mr. Chu was the only Asian anywhere in sight.

The other man got up as he reached the table and Willie realized he was meeting an unusually large Chinese man. Mr. Chu had to be at least six foot two and easily weighed two hundred twenty pounds. He was wearing a long, buff-colored silk shirt and beige linen pants. Willie guessed that he was between forty and fifty. His hair was still jet black, long and straight. He wore large shades with thick black plastic rims.

"Thank you for coming, Mr. Cuesta," he said and motioned Willie into a chair.

Willie looked about and beamed.

"Nice place to spend the nights."

Mr. Chu nodded.

"And the days too, Mr. Cuesta. It is very comfortable."

"So what is this important matter that you might need my help with?"

Mr. Chu was smoking. He drew on his cigarette, exhaled a plume into the bayside breeze, shifted a bit uncomfortably in his seat, leaned forward over the edge of the table and dropped his voice.

"What I need help with, Mr. Cuesta, is locating a boat captain who might be willing to transport some people from Puerto Rico to Florida."

His words froze Willie. What he was talking about wasn't transporting perfectly legal persons from the one place to the other. If that were the case, he would have contacted an airline, not Willie. That was crystal clear. What he was proposing was people smuggling, human trafficking, illegal immigration, and Willie could lose his private investigator's license if he let himself become involved. He shook his head.

"No matter what you may have heard about private investigators, Mr. Chu, we are not allowed to operate outside the law."

Mr. Chu shook his large head.

"I will not ask you to do anything that is against the law. I will only ask you to help me contact someone who may be willing to serve my purposes. I will make sure that you are able to operate anonymously. You will have no role in the actual transfer, and I will never mention to anyone that I have consulted you, Mr. Cuesta."

That was all very easy to say, but who knew what might happen down the line. Smuggling people across the Caribbean could be very tricky business. The US Coast Guard didn't cotton to people in that business. Willie didn't know Mr. Chu and couldn't predict just how much he would sing if, in the end, he got caught.

"I'm not in the smuggling business, Mr. Chu, not even as a confidential consultant. You would be better off finding someone who is."

Mr. Chu smoked. Through the cloud he emitted, and from behind the big shades, he studied Willie.

"I'm turning to you Mr. Cuesta, because we both know how dangerous it can be if you place your loved ones in the hands of human smugglers whom you don't know and for whom you have no references."

Willie wasn't going to argue with that. Every day you opened the newspaper and read about people hiring smugglers down on the Mexican border and eventually being abandoned in the Arizona desert, left to die of thirst. Closer to home, how many Haitians had ended up dying when ramshackle, overcrowded smuggling boats went down in the middle of the Caribbean. The owners of those boats could be found back on shore counting their money—nice dry money. Or sometimes the human cargo was dropped on an abandoned spit of land off the Bahamas, told it was part of the US, and left there to starve.

As for the frequent trips from Cuba, it was usually fellow Cubans in the US who smuggled their countrymen from the island, and they had a better record. But even then smugglers could get careless, boats could fail, people could die.

So, Willie knew what Mr. Chu was worried about, but that was more reason not to get involved in the human smuggling business himself.

"I'd like to help you—" he began, but Mr. Chu cut him off.

"I'm convinced you will understand, Mr. Cuesta. These are three persons of my own blood. Persons who, for political reasons, are in danger from individuals in power in China. Persons whose only desire is to live here in this country in a democratic way. They have made it all the way to Puerto Rico and have only a small portion of the voyage left. I'm sure a person of your Cuban heritage can understand why it is I am so desperate to see that they arrive here."

Willie's gaze narrowed. It was as if Mr. Chu had been reading his mind and had decided to play the Cuba card. The Cubans who had been smuggled to Florida over the years had come fleeing Cuban communism. Willie was Cuban American and Mr. Chu either had done his homework and found that out, or he was playing the odds because so many Latinos in Miami were Cubanos. He figured Willie would sympathize with anyone running from a repressive government and in that he was right. Willie was sympathetic to people who wanted nothing more than a bit of freedom, but that didn't mean he was ready to play a role that might get him imprisoned and stripped of his investigator's license.

He reiterated that to Mr. Chu and the other man nodded.

"I promise you again, Mr. Cuesta, that you will not be asked to do anything that will place you in danger of arrest. In addition, I will agree to pay you for five days of work in advance, in cash, and if at any time you feel the terms of this agreement have been broken, you are free to walk away."

Given Willie's meager cash flow of late, five days in advance was extremely attractive, but even then he was wary. At that point Mr. Chu reached into the pocket of his shirt, brought out a cell phone, poked it a couple of times, swiped it twice and then handed it to Willie. On the screen was a photograph that depicted a pretty Asian woman about forty years old and two children, a boy and a girl, about eight and ten years old. They all stared warily at the camera, as if trepidation was a family trait. They seemed to be saying: "Willie Cuesta, please help us."

Mr. Chu was playing the family card now and that was more than Willie could resist. He couldn't say no to the rent money, the call of his Cuban blood and those faces too. That was too many soft spots. A minute later they had cut a deal. Willie could already feel his fingers wrapped around the cold steel bars of a detention cell, but at least he would have enough cash to make bail.

ꙮ ꙮ

He left Mr. Chu at the Mandarin with an agreement that he would be back in touch that afternoon. From his car he made a call to an old investigator friend who had worked at the federal Immigration and Customs Enforcement agency. His name was Víctor Ávila, another Cuban American, and Willie had worked with him on a couple of cases during his days on the Miami P.D. Víctor was retired now and was happy to hear from an old fellow warrior.

"How can I help ya, Willie?"

Willie hesitated just a wee bit.

"I have a kind of delicate question for you, Víctor."

"Delicate how?"

"Would you be able to identify for me a boat owner experienced in transporting people from a Caribbean island to the sunny shores of South Florida these days?"

The proposition was greeted with a profound silence. Willie knew exactly what Víctor was thinking. He believed that Willie was asking him who might smuggle some folks from Cuba. Willie was trying to sneak in his own relatives, or at the very least family members of a close friend. All Cuban Americans, no matter what their former professional responsibilities, would feel torn by such an inquiry. They had all, at some point, been confronted with the need to bring loved ones from the island. No one wanted to say no to their own flesh and blood, which was why perfectly respectable persons often paid thousands of dollars to smugglers to do the deed. This was also why Cuban-American immigration agents didn't bother certain smuggling operations that had been in business for years. In some circles the smugglers were considered patriots who braved the Cuban government patrol boats to bring refugees to freedom. As long as no one got hurt, or ripped off, the agents looked the other way.

That was the history that lay beneath Willie's question, the reality that Víctor was mulling over. By the time he spoke it was clear he had made up his mind.

"You and I never had this conversation. Am I correct, Willie?"

"No, we never spoke, Víctor."

Víctor's voice dropped.

"You're going to drive US Route 1 south, down into the Florida Keys. You're going to go more than three-quarters of the way down and at about Mile Marker Twenty—twenty miles from Key West— you'll cross a short bridge to Sugarloaf Key. Two miles down you'll see a gas station. There you'll turn east, left, and you'll see a small restaurant called the Keys Clam Shack. Go in there and ask for a guy named Gutiérrez, who runs the place. Tell him Tomás Sosa sent you."

"Who's that?"

"Tomás Sosa is me, at least that's how he knows me. Tell him I sent you. After that, you're on your own, *amigo*. I'm going to hang up now, even though we never had this conversation."

A moment later the line went dead.

Willie called Mr. Chu and told him they would leave the next morning for the Keys and that he should pack a bag. Mr. Chu agreed to meet him in the lobby of the Mandarin Oriental. He sounded very happy, as if he were going on vacation.

ꙅ꙳ ꙅ꙳

By ten-thirty the next morning Willie and his client were cruising down US 1, well south of Miami. For the trip Mr. Chu had donned a colorful tropical shirt imprinted with palm fronds. It was a large, baggy shirt and held a whole jungle of fronds.

Willie always loved the drive to the Keys. Most of the way it was one lane in either direction, a narrow ribbon of road connecting small, sandy island after small, sandy island. Those spits of land were stitched together by short bridges from which you gazed out at the gorgeous water of the subtropical Atlantic on one side, and the equally beautiful, somewhat calmer surface of Florida Bay on the other. Willie was flanked by shades of aquamarine and jade on either side, and that made his Caribbean blood sing.

Along the way they passed the roadside restaurants and motels, all aged by sun and hurricane winds; T-shirt emporiums and knick-knack vendors who found every possible use for a conch shell; the dive shops and dive bars. The landscape was not only bathed in sunlight but in that habitually laid-back, beachcomber vibe that was the year-round atmosphere of the Keys.

This time Willie was not as relaxed as he usually was on his voyages through the Keys. He checked his rearview mirror more than once looking for police, as if his car had a sign on the back announcing "Human Smuggling Operation."

Mr. Chu, on the other hand, looked composed. He took in the views and didn't talk very much. That was generally just fine with Willie, but he was curious about his client and asked a couple of questions of his own. The first was about Mr. Chu's English, which was heavily accented but otherwise excellent.

"I went to college in California," he said, without specifying what school.

"And what do you do now, if you don't mind my asking?"

"I'm a businessman."

To say he was a man of few words was an understatement. So, Willie felt him out on a subject that he hoped would elicit a more expansive answer.

"You must miss your loved ones very much. It is a very beautiful family. I'm sure you're anxious to be with them again."

This time Mr. Chu didn't answer right away. Willie could sense the emotion in him as he stared silently down the narrow, empty highway.

"Are you married, Mr. Cuesta?" he asked finally.

"I was once, but I'm not now."

Willie's ex-wife was a woman who had arrived in Miami on a raft from Cuba about ten years before. They had loved each other very much, but then the currents of life in her new country had swept her away from him again. They had drifted apart and divorced.

"Do you have children?" Mr. Chu asked.

Willie shook his head. "No, I don't."

Mr. Chu nodded stoically, but that was all. He again fell silent.

It was only when they were more than halfway to Sugarloaf Key that Mr. Chu suddenly spoke again.

"I talked last night with a person in Puerto Rico. He told me that I should inquire about one boat in particular that has picked up people there and brought them here to Florida. He said it was called the Las Olas and it operates from down here in the Florida Keys. He said the owner is very dependable."

Willie nodded, although he felt Víctor Ávila was probably a better source of information on the smuggling business than some anonymous person in Puerto Rico.

"We'll see," he said.

Willie followed the directions Víctor had given him, turned off US 1 at the appointed mile-marker, drove east on a rutted road and found the Keys Clam Shack exactly where he'd expected. It was a small, pink-stucco structure with a Spanish-tile patio holding about a dozen tin tables, the whole place topped with a thatched palm roof. The smell of frying fish permeated the still air. It was the ultimate Keys eatery.

One table was occupied. Willie and Mr. Chu took a table on the opposite side of the patio with a view of a narrow inlet. Nearby stood a flock of snow-white egrets, pecking the sand at the water line, hunting for lunch.

A honey-blond waitress in white short-shorts and a sky-blue tank top took their order. It was around noon and Mr. Chu was hungry, so Willie requested two orders of hogfish fillets, a local delicacy. Mr. Chu chugged beer while Willie stuck with water.

When they were done Willie summoned the waitress and asked for Mr. Gutiérrez, the owner. After a few minutes a slim man about sixty, with a wreath of curly white hair around his well-tanned bald pate, came out of the kitchen to the table. He was wearing a long white apron splattered with cooking oil, wiping his gnarled hands on a dishrag, and it was clear he had done the cooking.

Willie introduced himself and congratulated him on the hogfish.

"It was excellent," Willie said. "My friend Tomás Sosa said it would be and he was right."

The name Willie dropped made Gutiérrez cock his head and squint. He looked around, but the other customers had left, so he lowered himself into the chair next to Willie.

"Mr. Sosa sent you?" he asked. His voice was whispery, like the sound of surf on sand.

Willie nodded. "Yes, he told us you might be able to help with an errand we're on."

The other man's eyes narrowed. Then he turned away from Willie and fixed on Mr. Chu. A Cuban like Willie he understood. An Asian was another matter. Willie explained.

"We're looking for a person who might be able to make a quick trip to Puerto Rico and bring back some special cargo."

Gutiérrez grunted and nodded. Willie lowered his voice.

"Would you know anyone who has experience running that particular kind of errand?"

Gutiérrez began to mull that question, but Mr. Chu didn't give him much of a chance. He leaned his large body across the table.

"Have you ever heard of a boat called Las Olas. I understand the owner of that boat is extremely experienced."

Gutiérrez considered the question carefully.

"Yes, I'm familiar with that boat. It's owned by a man named Raul Correa and he keeps it at a marina about ten miles down the road on Shark Key. There's only one road on that key. You turn right there, and you'll find him. But I never told you that. In fact, we never talked." Gutiérrez got up and disappeared back into the kitchen.

Mr. Chu left cash on the table that came to about double the bill and they headed for the door. Willie would have preferred that Gutiérrez recommend someone for the Puerto Rico venture and he told Chu as much as soon as they were headed south again.

The big man nodded, not looking at him, but staring intently down the road.

"I understand, Mr. Cuesta. But this boat the Las Olas comes recommended very, very highly."

Willie shrugged and kept his mouth shut. He had a five-day advance and if that's what the client wanted, he wasn't going to argue. He was getting paid to take a tour of the Keys, which he would have gladly done for free. What was there to complain about?

They crossed Sugarloaf Channel, where a couple of boys were fishing off the bridge, then passed through the next islet, Saddlebunch. Finally, they crossed a narrower, aquamarine channel onto Shark Key. In the shallow shore water about a dozen flamingoes stood on their pencil-thin legs, as if they were on stilts. Their vibrant pink color was beautiful against the blue surf.

Less than a mile down they found a turnoff to the west in the direction of Florida Bay. Willie took it and two hundred yards later arrived at an inlet where several boats were parked in slips.

Willie spotted the Las Olas right away, a white, sport-fishing craft about thirty-five feet long. It featured rods stored in racks against a bulkhead, swivel chairs on the rear deck from which anglers could battle the large creatures they hooked, next to them a fish well to store their catch until they reached shore and a large cooler, probably for beer, with which they could toast their triumphs. The Las Olas appeared innocent enough at the moment, your standard charter fishing boat.

But Willie also saw how it could serve as a very efficient smuggling vessel. It was low to the water, but he saw a couple of portholes on its starboard side, which meant that it was equipped with enough room below decks to stow paying customers being secreted across the Caribbean. Such a boat came from the factory with a big inboard motor, about three hundred horsepower, but smugglers often juiced them up until they had twice the horsepower. Customized in that fashion, an innocent-looking charter fishing boat could fly across the water faster than any Coast Guard patrol vessel, which was the idea.

They were almost at the entrance to the slips when Mr. Chu spoke up.

"Stop here, please, Mr. Cuesta."

Willie did as requested. "What's wrong? Don't you want to talk to the owner?"

Mr. Chu shook his head.

"There is a motel back at the intersection. We'll go there and I will rent a room. I want you to make contact with this Captain Correa and tell him you have a client who wants to go fishing. Then you will bring him to me at the motel."

"Why don't you speak to him here?"

"Look at me, Mr. Cuesta. Around here I stick out, as you express it in English, like a sore finger. It is smarter for all of us if Mr. Correa and I conduct our business in private, not where we can be observed by persons on the other boats. Once we are together, you can leave us alone and I will tell him the true nature of my request. You will only say to him that I'm interested in fishing and there is nothing illegal in that. You will be protected, just as I promised."

Willie couldn't argue with that. He made a U-turn and headed back.

༄ ༄

They drove back the short distance to the Coral Reef Motel, which consisted of cabanas made out of coral rock topped with blue tile roofs. Mr. Chu rented one toward the rear of the complex where it was almost concealed by a grove of palms. Willie left him there and walked back to the inlet. He drifted down the splintered wooden dock to the Las Olas and called out a greeting. When that drew no response, he raised his voice a bit more and waited. He was starting to think no one was aboard when the varnished wooden door leading to the sleeping quarters creaked open and a man stuck his head out.

He was about fifty, maybe fifty-five, dark brown, unshaven, soft in the gut, wearing white shorts, no shirt and a dark blue captain's cap with a gold anchor embroidered on it. He had the look of a drinker and appeared to have been sleeping one off. His gaze was as friendly as a grappling hook.

"What do you want?" he asked in a rasping voice.

"I'm looking for Captain Correa."

"For what?"

"For a client of mine who wants to go fishing. Are you Correa?"

"That's right, but today it is already too late to go fishing."

"Then we'll go tomorrow. He wants to go very badly."

Correa scratched his hairy stomach.

"Tomorrow I am already busy. Tell him to try somebody else."

"But he has heard that you're the best at what you do, and he is willing to pay you very, very well."

Correa stared back for several moments, his breath audible, his big gut rising and falling. He climbed slowly up his captain's chair behind the controls, fell into it, retrieved a well-chewed black cigar from an ashtray and fired it up. His gaze had turned suspicious. Maybe he had never heard himself called the very best fishing guide. Maybe he knew it wasn't true. The guys who were good didn't risk their careers smuggling human beings. He knew it. Willie knew it. His bloodshot eyes narrowed even more.

"Where are these fish that your client wants to catch? And how much will he pay me for each fish he hooks?"

Whatever the vocabulary, the code, they were talking smuggling now, not trawling. That was clear.

"The fishing grounds he is interested in belong to Puerto Rico and he will be glad to pay you well for the three fish he would like to catch there."

"How well?"

"Let's just say he has come a long way and these fish are very important to him."

Correa considered that.

"Where is this client of yours? Why doesn't he come here to meet with me?"

"He didn't want to be seen here speaking to you in public, but he's right up the street in the motel. I'm sure he'll be glad to order a bottle of rum so you can talk over the fishing expedition."

That last line won him over.

꧁ ꧁

The captain went below, put on a sleeveless T-shirt and reemerged. Apparently, he didn't discuss real business bare-chested. They walked down the road to the motel and made their way through the overgrown garden to Mr. Chu's cabana. Willie knocked, and moments later the wooden door swung open. He and Correa stepped into the air-conditioned room and the door quickly closed behind them.

Since Willie had last seen him, just minutes before, Mr. Chu had acquired company. Two young Chinese men, probably in their twenties, were also in the motel room. Willie had seen a black SUV parked outside and had assumed it belonged to a guest in another unit. But now he figured it belonged to the two young fellows. Maybe Willie had been right. Maybe he had been followed all the way down the Keys highway from Miami, not by police but by these two individuals. Now the question was why.

Mr. Chu sat on the edge of the king-sized bed. The two youngsters flanked the door behind Willie and Correa blocking any escape. Correa looked at them, from one to the other, and then scowled at Willie.

"You didn't tell me they were Chinese."

He obviously had an issue with the ethnic identity of his prospective clients.

For a moment Willie forgot the whole ruse of the fishing expedition.

"What's the difference? They are still people trying to reach freedom, and they are willing to pay."

Mr. Chu had taken off his shades and had his dark, almost-black eyes fixed on Correa.

"You don't understand, Mr. Cuesta. Your friend here thinks Chinese people are very different from other human beings."

Willie was confused. "What do you mean by that?"

"I mean he believes that Chinese people really are like fish and that they can swim for long distances through the ocean without the danger of drowning."

Willie still didn't understand that, although apparently Captain Correa did. He suddenly bolted toward the door, but the two young men blocked his way. A struggle ensued but ended quickly when one of them caught Correa right in the diaphragm with a short, piston-like punch. The captain gasped, emitted a gust of alcohol-laden breath, keeled over, hit the floor hard, moaned, held his gut but didn't move.

Willie jumped between the kids and Correa. One of them squared up as if he was ready to do the same to Willie, but Mr. Chu held up a hand, said something in Chinese and the kid relaxed.

"Mr. Cuesta, I want you see to something."

A black briefcase lay next to him on the bed, and he took a folder from it. He opened it, removed several newspaper clippings and laid them on the coverlet. Willie craned over to study them. They were cut from a paper in the city of Naples, Florida, about two hundred miles away over on the Gulf Coast. They all concerned the same story, which had occurred about a year before. Would-be immigrants from China were being smuggled into the US at night, apparently from somewhere in the Caribbean, when a Coast Guard helicopter spotted the boat. The persons aboard had either chosen to jump into the sea or had been ordered into the ocean by the smuggling crew almost a mile from the beach. The boat, which had its name covered by a tarp, then hightailed it back into the high seas.

Coast Guard cutters had been summoned but were unable to reach the site in time to rescue anyone. Over the next day nine bodies were recovered, including women and children. A photograph showed corpses of different sizes wrapped in white shrouds lined up on the beach. Willie read the headlines and the top sections of the stories. With only the dead as possible witnesses, the Coast Guard had eventually given up trying to identify the smugglers and closed the case.

Mr. Chu took out a photo of the woman and two children, similar to the one he had shown Willie the day before on his phone, and laid it next to the newspaper photos.

"Three of those bodies were my wife and children."

Willie studied the photo. The trepidation in their gazes had not been misplaced. Willie remembered Mr. Chu asking him if he had his own wife and children. Maybe he had thought of confessing his plan, but figured Willie was someone who would never understand. Willie couldn't imagine the pain Mr. Chu had experienced. He was dumbfounded and didn't say a word. The other man tapped one of the news clippings.

"What these stories don't tell you is that one man managed to get to shore and escape."

Willie fixed on him. "And he didn't go to the authorities to turn in the smugglers?"

Mr. Chu shook his head.

"He was illegally in this country and was afraid to contact any police. Instead, he made contact with relatives in Miami. They rescued him from where he was hiding and hid him in their home. But he contacted those of us who had lost loved ones. He told us the captain, at gunpoint, had forced all the terrified Chinese to jump overboard. Then he had left them there to drown."

He looked down at Correa as if he were gazing at some brand of slimy sea creature. Willie kept his gaze on Mr. Chu.

"So you've traveled here to exact your revenge."

Mr. Chu nodded. "Mine and that of the others whose hearts he has broken."

"Why don't you let me tell federal immigration police I know. They will make him pay the price."

Mr. Chu shook his head. "There is only one proper price for what this man did."

"You know I can't let you do this."

"Yes, I know," he said and then he nodded at his two henchmen.

One of the boys came at him, but Willie was able to grab him by the shirt and sling him across the room, where he fell onto a dresser and sent a vase full of artificial flowers crashing to the floor. By that time the second youngster had jumped on Willie's back and Willie backpedaled and slammed him against a doorjamb. That knocked the wind out of the attacker, but he managed to utter a breathy phrase that sounded very much like a curse in Mandarin. Willie let him drop to the floor just as the first fiend launched himself again. Willie was just about to punch out his lights when he sensed Mr. Chu just behind him. He whirled around just in time to see the big man pull a handgun from beneath his baggy shirt and swing it at his head. It caught Willie flush on the left temple. He keeled over, landing right next to Correa. Two he could handle; three was another thing.

By the time Willie could gather his senses, his hands were tied behind his back, his ankles were loosely bound and a cloth had been shoved in his mouth. He was marched out to the black SUV and shoved in the backseat. Correa was tied up and gagged as well, wrapped in a blanket, carried outside by the two young guys and dumped into the luggage space behind Willie. Mr. Chu and his two helpmates hopped aboard, and they drove to Correa's boat.

It was midafternoon in the dead of summer and the air pulsed with heat. Nobody else was around in that ragged, miniature marina, and the Chinese had no trouble transferring Willie and Correa onto the boat without being observed. Moments later, the lines had been loosed; one of Mr. Chu's young mates manned the controls and backed the boat into the inlet. They cruised out into the bay, but then looped around through the channel just south of Shark Key and made a beeline into the open sea. Gulls followed them for a short while but then peeled off as if they didn't want to see what was about to happen.

Willie was propped just behind the captain's chair. Correa had been dumped in the empty fish well. He was the catch of the day. When they were a few hundred yards from land Mr. Chu reached down, lifted Willie into one of the swivel chairs usually occupied by clients and removed the gag from his mouth. Willie stretched his stiff jaw muscles.

"We're not going fishing, are we, Mr. Chu?"

The other man shook his head. "No, Mr. Cuesta. We are going to add to the population of the sea, not subtract from it."

About twenty minutes later, the young driver suddenly cut the engines and the craft's momentum began to slow. The boat was quick, and Willie calculated they were about ten miles out from the coast. No other craft were in sight. The two mates then lifted Correa out of the fish well and stood him straight up, still bound, but they removed the gag.

Correa craned around trying to spot a spit of land or another boat but found nothing. His eyes, flooded with fear, finally fixed on Willie, as if he had just spotted a life preserver floating in a turbulent sea.

"You can't let them do this to me," he cried, his voice cracking. "I didn't do what he says I did. I am innocent."

Willie looked up at him, squinting against the glare.

"He says you killed his wife and four children. That you left them to drown."

Correa's face stormed over, and he strained against the ties binding his hands.

"Four?" he screamed. "There were two. There were only—"

He caught himself in mid scream, but it was too late. A silence as profound as the bottom of the sea suddenly surrounded them. They were still staring into each other's eyes, and Willie could see Correa's hopes sinking out of his gaze and deep down into his quavering flesh.

Mr. Chu stood before him, holding the photograph that he had shown Willie earlier.

"Do you remember these three faces, Correa? The last time you saw them they were pleading with you for help. Now you are going to join them and all the others you left to die."

Correa screamed and fell to the deck, trying to escape his fate, but it did no good. The two helpers picked him up, shoved him to the edge of the boat, very quickly cut the ties around his hands and feet, and tipped him over the side. He screamed as he fell, was submerged for a moment, but bobbed back up, his captain's hat floating nearby. By that time the driver had jumped back in the chair and gunned the motor just enough to move the boat ten yards away from him. Correa tried desperately to swim to them, but the boat was drifting away from him. He met Willie's eyes one last time, pleaded to him, but there was nothing Willie could do.

Even if there had been, Willie wondered right then what he would have done. Back in the motel he had tried to stop them, but that was his long years as a cop coming to the fore. Now his Cuban blood was speaking to him. Relatives of his, and other Cubans, had braved those waters on rafts just to reach a US beach and freedom. His own wife had made that terrible voyage, terrified by the thought of ending up at the bottom of the sea. Or worse, knowing what it was to be torn apart by sharks. But here was a Cuban, Correa, who was capable of forcing other human beings into the sea. It boggled Willie's mind. He couldn't do anything to rescue Correa, but that saved him from having to decide if he would have. For the first time in his life he had encountered a human being who he might not have saved even if he could.

Mr. Chu ordered the boat to head back to shore and the sound of Correa's cries disappeared beneath the roar of the motors. Willie turned away before they lost sight of him.

As they approached land again, Willie was moved below decks, placed comfortably on a berth in the sleeping quarters, the gag reinserted in his mouth.

"Unfortunately, we are forced to leave you here, Mr. Cuesta," Mr. Chu told him. "Once our escape is assured, I promise you I will call the authorities and you will be rescued. I want to thank you for your help. You are a good man, and I am sure you have done much to help your clients over the years. But men can be instruments of justice in different ways, and this time you were an instrument used by someone else. I hope you can forgive that in time." Then they disembarked.

☙☙ ☙☙

Local police received an anonymous tip several hours later, after nightfall. Willie was dozing when he heard clambering on the deck above him. He was soon freed and gave them the entire story, although he insisted he had no notion that Correa was a smuggler.

The Coast Guard searched for Correa for twenty-four hours, but he was gone. Police went to the Mandarin Oriental in Miami and found that no Mr. Chu had ever been registered there, nor had anyone matching his description. Willie had only met him in the patio cafe and in the lobby and it was clear Mr. Chu had simply been using it as a meeting place. In fact, Willie assumed his real name was not Chu. Who the man truly was, Willie would never know.

☙☙ ☙☙

Two weeks passed and one day a FedEx envelope was delivered to Willie's door. No return address or name of sender was written on the waybill. Inside Willie found a small package wrapped in newspaper written in Chinese characters. He unwrapped it and held a wad of bills, equal to the advance he had received the first day. No note was included, but the exotic wrapping told him all he had to know.

IN THE WAR ZONE OF THE HEART

W illie Cuesta sat in a singles joint in South Beach called the Unicorn. He was positioned at the bar nursing his second margarita, ostensibly studying the ladies in attendance. But only ostensibly. Willie was single, but he wasn't there to socialize. He was working, tracking an errant husband who sat at a nearby table with a young woman who was definitely not his wife. Willie knew because in his pocket he carried a wedding photo of the man and his true bride.

Willie lifted his cell phone, as if he were checking his messages, and surreptitiously took a couple of snaps of the clueless couple. Sitting just behind them were two women about Willie's age, and moments later one of them got up, found an opening at the bar right next to him and ordered another drink.

"Since you were gazing my way I thought I'd give you a closer look," the lady said. She flared her brown eyes brazenly and then chuckled at her own cheekiness.

"Well, isn't that wonderful," Willie said, watching the couple in question over her shoulder.

Tracking wayward spouses had never been Willie's preferred work, but it paid the cable bill and then some. And his current client was a perfectly nice woman who deserved better than the lothario at the table. At that moment the husband began nuzzling his busty tablemate. Willie raised his phone.

"Now that you're up close, give me that gorgeous smile again," he said to the lady.

She complied, and he snapped a couple of shots, making sure to catch the illicit nuzzling over her shoulder. Then he bought the lady's drink as a way of recompensing her for her incidental service.

As they toasted, his phone pinged with an incoming text message. It came from Alice Arden, the immigration attorney he had helped on many cases in the past and who threw him work when she could.

"What's up, Willie boy?"

"Furtive love," he texted back.

"Lucky fella. Can u come to office 2pm tmrw? Got a case 4 u."

"With bells on."

Whatever Alice had in mind had to be more interesting than his current assignment. Luckily, the couple at the table got up right then and made for the door. Willie paid his tab hastily and stood up.

"Going home to the wife?" his neighbor asked.

"I'm married to my work," Willie said.

She gazed into his eyes mischievously. "How about if I change my name to 'work'? Then what?"

They smiled at each other.

"I'll see you here again, Ms. Work."

Then he headed out.

At two p.m. the next day Willie was standing across a desk from Alice Arden. Her Brickell Avenue office featured a wall of windows overlooking beautiful Biscayne Bay and the Atlantic Ocean in the distance. The view was spectacular, but Alice was even more distracting than the seascape. A lithe blonde just a few years older than he, with a lively intelligence and wicked sense of humor, Willie never tired of gazing at her. And she never failed to tell him that she didn't date the help.

In this instance, Willie skipped his usual personal appeal. That was because Alice's latest client was seated there with them. She was a wide-shouldered, big-busted Latina woman who appeared to be about seventy-five years old, but still strong, stolid. Her hair was thick and white like a cloud over her head, her swarthy skin deeply lined, her eyes dark and sunken with a grave gaze. She wore a short-sleeved black dress that reached modestly below her knees. On her left forearm Willie saw a deep, jagged scar that ran up past her elbow. Whatever had done that, it had been painful and bloody. But given the stern, unblinking look in her eyes, you had to wonder if she had even let out a small yelp when it happened.

Alice made the introductions in Spanish.

"Willie, this is Señora Isabel Guevara, originally from Nicaragua. And this, Isabel, is Willie Cuesta, whom I told you about."

"Originally from Little Havana right here in Miami," Willie added.

They nodded to each other courteously and Willie cozied up in the next chair.

"So how is it that I can help you, señora?"

The woman glanced at Alice, and it was the attorney who answered.

"So, here's the situation, Willie boy. Señora Guevara has twin sons. They were in their late teens when the civil war broke out in Nicaragua between the Sandinista government and rebels who called themselves the Contras. You were just a boy then, but you may have heard about it over the years from Nicaraguans who fled here to Miami to escape the war."

Willie nodded. While working as a law-enforcement officer with the Miami Police Department he had met lots of Nicaraguans. Some of them were victims of crimes, some of them perpetrators. Along the way you couldn't help but soak up the dramatic stories about what had driven them from their homeland. He told Alice he had heard about the war, and she continued.

"Well, the Guevara family owned a farm in the northern mountains, where most of that war would be fought. In that region, some of the young men chose to support the government. Others sided with the opposition. Sometimes members of the same family chose opposing sides and ended up going to war against each other. That is what happened in the Guevara clan."

"The two twin sons?"

"Exactly, *amigo*. The one, named Sergio, sided with the Sandinistas and joined the Sandinista Army. The other, named Oscar, threw his lot in with the Contras. They ended up in units that staged firefights against each other all through those mountains. Since the twins were both expert woodsmen and familiar with that territory, they both served as scouts, which was extremely dangerous duty."

Señora Guevara broke in just then, her tone grave.

"Always out in front of other forces, always running the risk of falling into ambushes. That was their job. One for one side, one for the other. I knew that's what they were doing, and I waited the whole war, every day expecting to hear that one or both of them were dead."

Willie now understood the unusually deep lines in her face. They came from years of worry, of daily fear for her sons.

"But luckily that didn't happen," Alice interjected. "The civil war finally ended, and both sons had survived. Minor wounds, nothing major. By that time Isabel had moved here to Miami with her two daughters to escape the war. Her husband had died years before and she was afraid to stay on the farm with no men."

The older woman shook her head.

"It wasn't that so much," she said, "but the battles were sometimes close. I couldn't know when one side might arrive to camp on my land and draw an attack from the other. I did not want my daughters, or myself for that matter, getting caught in the middle of gunfire. So, we left our land and came here, the same as many other Nicaraguans."

"And you didn't go back after the war ended?" Willie asked.

She shrugged. "Yes, but not to live. By that time, both my daughters had married here and had children. I wanted to be with them. And I had become too old to do the work the farm required. I hired a manager to run it for me."

"And your sons, what did they do once the war was over?"

She gazed out the window over the aquamarine bay, vaguely toward the south, as if she could see all the way to her homeland. The memories she was left with obviously didn't make her happy.

"My son Sergio, he stayed in the army. He made that his career and rose to the rank of captain." She shrugged again. "For some mothers that might make them proud, but I never wanted either of my sons to be soldiers. As I said, a mother only worries."

"And your other son, Oscar?"

Her gaze came back to Willie. "He went back to the farm at first, but feelings were still raw in that region. Many people had died and some of their relatives wanted revenge. It wasn't safe for him to stay there, so eventually he came to Miami to live with us. He brought with him a girl from home. He found work, they married and settled here. They have two children."

To Willie it all sounded like a fairly typical Miami immigrant saga. Violent strife in the homeland followed by refuge in South

Florida. You named almost any of the Latin American countries and families from there had lived that same story over the past fifty years. All around Miami were communities of Salvadorans, Hondurans, Guatemalans, Chileans, Argentines, et cetera—and, of course, Cubans like Willie himself. All had arrived on the run and stayed. But that didn't explain why he, Willie Cuesta, was being called in for consultation at the moment.

"So, what exactly is the issue now, señora?"

The question made the older woman press her eyes closed, take a deep breath, and then stay staring at him in profound sadness. It was Alice who finally answered.

"What has happened, Willie, is that Isabel's son Sergio, the one who spent his career in the Nicaraguan Army, is heading this way. He hasn't told his mother that, or his brother, but another relative called and gave them a warning."

Willie frowned. "A warning?"

"Yes, a warning. You see, Sergio has made it clear that he has nothing but hatred for his brother Oscar. He has never forgiven him for joining the opposition rebels. He says Oscar brought shame on the family and blames him for the deaths of friends who fought with him in the army. Isabel is afraid he is coming here to kill his brother."

That made Willie whistle. "Wow!"

"And there is another reason he wants to seek revenge against Oscar," Alice said.

The older lady had listened patiently, but now she broke in.

"Sergio has said to people the reason he hates his brother is because of the war," she said, "but the real reason is that the woman Oscar brought here from Nicaragua was once the girlfriend of Sergio. Her name is Natalia and she grew up on the neighboring plantation. She is very beautiful, and Sergio was in love with her all his life. But after the war ended, he had to go where the army sent him in another part of the country. Oscar, as I said, went home to the farm, but decided it was unsafe to stay there; he convinced Natalia to leave with him. It is she that he married. Sergio, meanwhile, has never married. He has never stopped loving Natalia. I'm convinced that is the real reason he wants Oscar dead."

The three of them sat in silence for several moments while Willie took it all in. The guy they were talking about, Sergio, was no shrinking violet. He was an army veteran, experienced in guerrilla war. If he was, in fact, intent on killing his brother, he might be an extremely dangerous operator.

Willie leaned toward Isabel Guevara.

"Have you or Oscar spoken to the police about this?"

She nodded somberly.

"Yesterday I asked a policeman who patrols in our neighborhood. He told me if Sergio shows up to call nine-one-one, but that they can't afford to have police guarding only my house. Of course, I'm afraid that by the time I call nine-one-one, it will already be too late."

The response didn't surprise Willie. Cops couldn't work as personal bodyguards.

"So, you turned to Ms. Arden here."

"Yes. I didn't know where else to go, and we have run out of time."

"When is Sergio supposedly coming and how is he coming?"

"I was told by the family member that he left Nicaragua five days ago and flew to Mexico. From there he was to be smuggled across the border by coyotes," she said, using the slang for people smugglers.

Willie knew if you were prepared to pay enough, you could be smuggled across the Arizona or Texas border in short order. He probably wouldn't be able to fly due to lack of valid documentation, but a bus could get him to Miami in two days. In other words, he might be in Miami already or close to arriving. He said as much to Doña Isabel.

"Oh, I know that he's here already. The same relative heard from him and called me."

And once Sergio was in the city, buying a weapon—any kind of weapon he wanted—would be a piece of cake. It wouldn't take long. Willie knew that but wasn't about to say it to Doña Isabel. He had arrived at that office minutes before and already felt under the gun.

"Does he know where you live and where Oscar lives?"

She nodded grimly. "We all live in the same house and, yes, Sergio knows the address. He has written me there."

"Well, all of you need to get out of there as quickly as possible. Do you have someplace you can go to hide?"

Doña Isabel thought and then nodded pensively.

"Yes, I have a friend, a Nicaraguan woman, who has a house up near Fort Lauderdale. Sergio doesn't know of her and would have no idea where we were. I, Natalia, and the two children could go there. But the problem will be with Oscar."

Willie squinted. "Why is that?"

"Because Oscar has told me that he refuses to run. He said to me that if Sergio comes to kill him, he will wait for him right in our house. He has guns there. Not just a handgun but a big gun that shoots many bullets."

Willie winced. "An automatic weapon?"

"That's right, like the ones he used in the war. He says if Sergio shows up there, he will kill him, or die defending himself."

The grief in her voice and her face hit Willie in his gut. He had an older brother, named Tommy, whom he loved. The idea of one trying to harm the other, let alone kill the other, was unthinkable. But this woman was faced with what was apparently the very real possibility of having the blood of one, or maybe both, her sons spilled in her house before long. Willie thought of his own mother and how she might have been affected by such a possibility. That thought scared the hell out of him.

The older woman shook her head.

"Ever since they were born I have been afraid this would happen. All their lives they have been at each other's throats. When one said white, the other said black. When one was happy, the other was bitter. When Sergio joined the army, I should have known Oscar would enlist with the opposition. That was an excuse to try to kill each other. In Nicaragua that failed, so now the lifelong feud comes here."

She reached into a big black handbag on her lap and brought out several photos. The top one was decades old and depicted her and her young family posed before a large, rustic house made of logs, a hillside thick with forest in the background. She stood next to a dark, husky man who Willie figured had been her husband. They were flanked on either side by the two boys, who looked no older than five. Their faces were identical, and they wore the same striped T-shirts and shorts. But while one was smiling broadly, the other looked as if he were afraid. Of what, Willie couldn't know.

The next photo showed just the two boys, but about ten or twelve years later, in their teens, at a school function. Again, the faces were identical, and both wore the white shirt and dark pants that was apparently the school uniform. They were thin, clean-cut. And again, all that distinguished then was their expressions. One smiled, while the other one glowered at the camera as if he were seeing the vicious guerrilla war in their not-too-distant future.

Willie tapped the two images. "Which one is which in this photo?" he asked.

Doña Isabel focused intently and then tapped the boy on the right.

"This is Sergio. I can tell because of the small scar below his eye."

Willie noticed the scar now, just barely visible.

"How did that happen?"

"They got into a terrible fight once; he fell and hit his face on a sharp stone. He was bathed in blood, but it healed. That's the only difference, but in person they never looked the same. When one was happy, the other was miserable. After this, there are no more photos of them together."

She handed him a third snapshot. "This is Oscar, taken just this year, at the house here in Miami."

It showed him standing before a barbeque grill in a backyard. His expression was neither smiling nor angry. But he looked much like he and his brother had looked in the previous photo, still slim, well-groomed, but obviously older.

"I have no recent photo of Sergio," Doña Isabel said. "He has never sent me one."

Willie asked if he could keep the last photo, and the lady agreed.

"Now we should go to your house to get you, your daughter-in-law and grandchildren out of there," Willie said. "And I will speak with your son."

He turned to Alice. "Although first we have to talk business."

"I've already told Isabel your day rate and she has agreed to hire you for at least three days."

She passed Willie a check that he folded and tucked in his pocket. It wasn't all that much, given that he would have to deal with veteran guerrilla fighters. But it would pay the rent—if he survived until the first of the month.

☙ ☙

The house in question was in the town of Sweetwater, just west of Miami in the direction of the Everglades. It came as no big surprise to Willie that that was where the family lived because the town was the biggest settlement of Nicaraguan exiles anywhere in South Florida. So much so that it was known as Little Managua—after the capital of the homeland.

He and Doña Isabel took Willie's car, headed out the highway west past the airport, and eventually turned south into Sweetwater. You knew you were within the city limits when the restaurants and prepared-food emporiums went from advertising American or Cuban fare and tried to seduce you with Nicaraguan cuisine. *Nacatamales* were bigger versions of the Mexican *tamal*. *Vigorón* involved cabbage, pork rind and yuca and was tastier than it sounded. And then there was the *fritanga,* a large platter covered in grilled beef, fried cheese and plantains, rice and beans, and anything else tasty lying around. When he had been a patrol cop in Little Havana, Willie and his partners had nipped over to Sweetwater from time to time for late-night *fritanga*—in the days before he had started policing his intake of fried foods.

But there was no time to eat right then. Following Doña Isabel's directions, Willie drove into a residential section of town, mostly one-story stucco structures. Eventually, she had him turn into a cul-de-sac and drive to the end of the street. There he pulled into the driveway of a house painted bright yellow, a bit larger than the others on the block, built on a double lot and surrounded by fruit trees. It was a quiet street, devoid of traffic, certainly not a setting where you might normally expect serious trouble. Then again, with only one way in and one way out, and the house isolated in its own private grove at the end of the street, it might be a perfectly good place for Sergio to close in on his brother.

Willie saw the crimson curtains covering the front window move. Somebody was keeping a close watch as to who might be arriving. As they climbed the front steps the door opened and standing there was Oscar Guevara. He looked the same as he had in the photo, although the gaze in his eyes was much more wary. He closed the door behind them and locked it.

"This is Mr. Cuesta," Doña Isabel said to her son. "He is the man the attorney recommended. He is a former policeman here in Miami and he is going to help us."

Oscar looked Willie up and down and didn't look particularly impressed. But he decided to be discreet.

"I'm sure Mr. Cuesta is very capable," he said, "but I don't think there is anything he can do. I am the person Sergio is coming to kill. I am the one who must defend himself and this house."

Willie glanced around the large living room. It was comfortably furnished, all as might be expected, except for one thing: Leaning against the sill beneath the front window was an AR-15 automatic weapon. It was loaded with an ammunition clip and two more clips sat on the sill. As a former guerrilla fighter, Oscar Guevara would be familiar with automatic weapons, probably more familiar than he was with handguns. And since his brother was also a veteran of the war and had almost certainly been armed with a similar weapon, it was best to make sure you weren't outgunned. Hence, the AR-15 was what he had chosen to protect himself and his home.

Oscar noticed Willie studying the weapon, looked at it and then back.

"Yes, that's my gun and yes, I own it legally."

Willie didn't want to enter a discussion with Oscar about the wisdom of the course he was taking. At least not at the moment. First things first.

"I have advised your mother that she, your wife and children should find another place to stay if you believe your brother is headed here with violence on his mind. I told them you should leave as well, but at least let's get the women and children out of here."

Oscar thought that over and then called over his shoulder to the interior of the house.

"Natalia, come here, please."

Moments later his wife walked in. She was probably in her mid-thirties, tall, with long, wavy black hair, dark green eyes and an exquisite body that now was clad in a very low-cut floral-patterned housedress. Willie understood instantly why both the brothers had wanted her and why the loss of her had led Sergio to thoughts of fratricide.

Doña Isabel introduced Willie.

"Mr. Cuesta believes that you, I and the children should leave here, that we won't be safe if we stay."

Natalia had already appeared scared, and now she only looked more so. She turned to look at Oscar.

"I think he's right," her husband said. "It will be better if you all leave."

Natalia frowned. "And you? You're not coming."

Oscar shook his head. "No. It is me Sergio is after. If I go with you, that only keeps you in danger. And he and I need to settle this once and for all."

It was clear that Natalia was picturing in her mind just what that might entail. Tears appeared in her emerald eyes, but it was Doña Isabel who spoke up.

"I'm the one who should stay. I'm the one who can talk to Sergio and get him to stop this madness."

Oscar shook his head once.

"No. You know that isn't true, Mother. You know this moment has been coming all our lives. If you stay and I go he will only believe that I am hiding behind your skirts. That will give him even more reason to hate me, and the threat will still be there. You know that is true. I can't allow you to stay here and risk being hurt. Your responsibility now is to Natalia and the children. There is only one way for this to be settled, and that is between him and me. We need this nightmare to be over."

The stress of the situation had obviously affected the older woman. She looked to be at the end of her rope and didn't argue.

Oscar turned back to Natalia.

"Pack bags, get the kids and my mother in the car and go as quickly as possible."

And that was what happened. Although Doña Isabel balked, Natalia and the grandchildren talked her into the car. Oscar and Willie stood on the front porch and watched them drive off into the dusk.

"Now you should leave," Oscar said. "There is no one left here for you to protect."

"Your mother hired me to help protect the whole family, and that includes you."

Oscar shook his head. "I don't need you to protect me. I spent years in the mountains during the war with people trying to kill me every single day. And look, I survived, didn't I? So, you can go home, Señor."

Willie held his ground.

"Your mother paid me to protect this home and that's what I'm going to do."

Oscar stared him down, considering his options. He could call the police and tell them he wanted Willie removed from his property. But then Willie would simply explain what was about to come down and then Oscar would have not just Willie on his hands but law enforcement. Oscar obviously wanted as few bodies as possible between him and his brother. For the moment, he didn't argue. He turned, entered the house and Willie followed.

For the next half-hour Oscar prepared for any attack that might come. He wedged a chair under the knob of the back door. Then he locked the windows, closed all the curtains and turned off all the lights inside the house, except one dim lamp in the living room.

He went into a closet, brought out two more clips for the AR-15 and placed them on the windowsill. Then he disappeared into a bedroom and when he came back out he had changed into black jeans and a shirt in a jungle camouflage pattern, with a pistol strapped to his waist on one side and a bayonet on the other. He stood still a moment so that Willie could study him. Then he offered an explanation of sorts.

"If he wants to go back to guerrilla war, we will go back to guerrilla war."

Willie was speechless. He suddenly found himself in the middle of a potentially murderous two-man showdown—on an otherwise quiet block in a residential neighborhood. He wore a flowered shirt and a black blazer, not camouflage. All he had was a .38 in his back holster, no match for an AR-15. And more than anything, he lacked the homicidal rage that drove Sergio Guevara. Willie should have walked right then, but he had taken Doña Isabel's money, and he had a thing about doing what he was paid to do.

Oscar crossed the room, picked up his AR-15, opened the front door and walked out onto the darkened porch. Willie followed.

The fruit trees blocked the view of the street. So, Oscar descended the stairs and strode out into that small orchard. Again, Willie fell in behind him, although he wasn't happy about it. He now had his gun in his hand and peered warily behind every tree and plant.

Oscar reached the front wrought-iron gate and closed the padlock hanging from it. He gazed up the cul-de-sac, which was dead quiet now.

"Do you think he'll come tonight?" Willie asked.

"I know he will. He won't wait."

Willie gazed down the abandoned street and back at Oscar.

"How can you be so certain?"

Oscar shrugged. "Because that is my brother. He is not possessed of patience. He could try to wear me out with anticipation, unnerve me with worry, but he won't do that. That was never his style, and I believe it still isn't. He's a hothead, and he will come as soon as possible."

He walked to the far side of the yard, positioned himself behind a large-leafed banana plant and peered at a patch of trees not far away. He picked up his analysis of the situation where he had left off.

"Me, I have the patience to sit and wait. That is the secret not only to surviving guerrilla war in the mountains but being successful at it. Being able to lie still for hours at a time, to lie in ambush concealed by the vegetation for most of a day or night, waiting for your enemy to come to you, to walk into the sights of your weapon. That is how most people die in guerrilla war—not knowing what hit them."

"But your brother won't be unaware. He will know he's walking into trouble and will try somehow to outflank you, surprise you. Don't you think?"

Oscar thought that over, his eyes alive and shining as they examined the darkness.

"We'll see."

"I still think you should call the police. Don't you see how crazy this has become? In fact, if you don't call them, I will."

Oscar glared at Willie. "If you do that, all you will accomplish is delaying the inevitable. If he sees police here, he will simply leave and come back when they have gone. Maybe he will come back when my wife and children are here, and I cannot allow that. You should just leave now. This is not your battle, no matter what agreement you made with my mother."

"I can get plainclothes detectives to come, no patrol cars. He won't know."

Oscar gave Willie a withering look. "Yes, he will know. He didn't survive all those ambushes in the mountains of Nicaragua to get trapped so easily here. And it is not the fight of those detective friends of yours either. It is mine."

He turned and stalked along the inside of the chain-link fence, inspecting the entire perimeter of the large lot. Willie kept up with him. When they reached the front of the house again Oscar climbed the steps, they went in, and he locked the door.

Oscar propped the AR-15 against the sill of the front window again, sat right next to it and opened the curtain just enough to be able to see out. He settled in for the expected siege. All Willie could do was wait with him. Hopefully, Sergio wouldn't show up. Maybe he was nowhere near Miami. Maybe it was all a ruse, meant only to frighten his brother, to rile him. Willie hoped that was the case, but he didn't really believe it.

After a while he needed to use the bathroom and found one in a back bedroom of the sprawling house. As he came out, he noticed that a window in that bedroom was open just a crack at the bottom. Oscar had closed and locked all the windows all around the house but must have missed that one. Willie closed it, locked it and headed back to his post in the living room.

They waited in complete silence, and each minute that passed made Willie question what he was doing there. What would he do if Sergio showed up? Would he try to get between them? That prospect seemed suicidal. Would he try to help Oscar vanquish the attacking Sergio? Wasn't that why Doña Isabel had hired him? But how happy would she possibly be if one of her sons ended up dead?

Willie struggled to see a way out. A moment later he heard a creaking sound from the back of the house and turned. Nothing loud, just the sort of noise all old houses made. Oscar must have thought the same thing. He glanced in that direction and then turned back to his surveillance of the street.

Willie got up and walked quietly toward the rear bedroom where he had found the open window. He was careful not to make a sound. Just short of the bedroom, still in the darkened hallway, he tucked himself into the doorway of the bathroom and pulled his handgun from his back holster. He waited there for about two minutes and then he heard the floor creak again. It came from the bedroom and moments later a man emerged from there. Even in the darkness Willie saw a gun in his hand. He couldn't see the man's face, but he didn't have to. He knew it was the same face he had just left in the living room.

From where he stood Willie could see Oscar, at the front window, his back turned. He knew he couldn't allow Sergio to reach the next room. If he did, one or both would be lying there with bullet holes in them, maybe both dead. He waited until the silhouette was just past him and then swung the butt of his gun so that it landed hard on the back of the skull. Sergio fell like a sack of rocks. Willie quickly turned the handgun around and fired four fast, resounding shots into the floor, careful not to hit the fallen twin.

He heard Oscar's heavy footsteps cross the living room in a hurry. The light came on suddenly in the hallway and Oscar was standing there, a cloud of gun smoke hanging before him, his AR-15 pointed right at Willie. Then his gaze fell to the body on the floor. Sergio was dressed in camouflage pants and a black T-shirt—the reverse image of his brother. Apart from that, Oscar might have been looking at his own self lying there before him.

He still held the AR-15, and for a moment Willie feared Oscar would fire down into the body to make sure Sergio was finished. But he didn't do that. Instead, he stayed staring in disbelief.

"You killed him," he muttered finally.

Oscar seemed astounded, as if he couldn't comprehend that after so many years of strife his brother was dead, but he hadn't done the killing himself. Or was it more than that going on inside him? Willie thought so, because as the moments passed that gaze was marked more by grief. Was it that the rivalry with his brother, which had begun when they were boys, had always remained something of a game, even during their war years, but now it had finally ended unexpectedly in real death. Was it the now lost hope that at the last moment they would somehow find a way not to spill blood, that they would go back to being sons of the same mother, neither of them wanting to cause her the pain of having a son die before her. Self-preservation was a powerful instinct, but exercising that instinct at the cost of causing your mother a tragedy out of Greek drama—was it worth it? Would he be better off dead himself?

Willie had no way to tell what went through Oscar's mind, he could only surmise. But he sensed that the man before him was reliving decades of rivalry, fear, hatred—and maybe love too.

Oscar finally leaned the AR-15 against the wall of the hallway and kneeled next to his brother. Willie stepped around him and grabbed the weapon. Oscar sprang back up to take it back, but Willie drove the stock of the rifle into his chest and Oscar went down, right next to Sergio, struggling for breath. Willie was about to tell him that his brother wasn't dead, but a moment later Sergio moaned and started to stir.

Oscar frowned, inspected more closely his brother's head and body, and understood quickly that he had been duped. He made a move to get up again, but Willie had the AR-15 trained on him.

"Don't move."

Sergio sat up then, leaned against the wall, shook his head and realized he was right next to Oscar. He flinched, searched for his handgun, but didn't find it. That was when he realized Willie was standing over both of them with all the guns. At that moment they seemed to stop hating each other and focused all their ire on Willie. That was fine with Willie. In order to hate, you had to be alive, and that had been the real job he'd been hired to do by Doña Isabel—keep them both alive.

"If either of you moves before I tell you, I will open up on you both with this AR-15, on your legs specifically. There will be no more war games for you, and your mother will be left with two cripples for sons."

Willie wasn't kidding, and the two-headed creature on the floor seemed to understand that. But that didn't answer the question of what he could possibly do with them now. He thought of calling an immigration agent he knew and having Sergio apprehended. He was in the country illegally and could be detained and deported. Of course, if he still had murder on his mind, he might just come back. So, what good would that do?

Or he could simply call the cops and have him arrested for breaking and entering with a deadly weapon and send him to prison for years. Was that what Doña Isabel would want him to do?

He didn't have to think about that for very long. Behind him he heard the floor creak and then Doña Isabel was standing next to him.

"I couldn't stop thinking of what might happen here. I couldn't stay away."

She stared down at her sons. With her standing above them, it was as if they were children again. She found the small scar beneath Sergio's eye and focused on him.

"Are you finished with this madness now? Do you understand that if you kill your brother you might as well be killing me? If you shoot him, I will die. Is that what you want?"

Before Willie could react, she reached over, pulled the handgun from where it was tucked in his belt and threw it to Sergio. He caught it and stayed fixed on her, obviously frightened.

"Go ahead. Get it over with. Don't bother to shoot your brother. Shoot me and put me out of my misery."

For several moments, no one moved or made a sound. Sergio could easily raise the gun and shoot Oscar; they both knew it. Oscar was scared at the prospect, but so was Sergio. In fact, maybe he was more scared because of what his mother had just said.

And Sergio could have shot Willie as well. After all, it was Willie who had deceived him and also dented his skull.

Willie felt his pulse throb several more times and then Sergio put the gun on the floor and slid it back toward him. Willie leaned over and picked it up as Doña Isabel spoke to him.

"I want you to take all the weapons and get out of here, Mr. Cuesta. Leave me here with my sons. I will be all right."

Willie hesitated, and Doña Isabel insisted.

"Go ahead. I believe the madness is over. I don't expect them to love each other, but I believe they will spare me the life I have left."

Willie backed away slowly. From the looks in the eyes of the brothers, he thought she just might be right. He crossed the living room, exited onto the porch and then paused. He waited there for several minutes, listening for any sign of commotion, but it didn't come. So, he took his small arsenal and headed home.

⤳ ⤳

He slept in the next day and called Alice Arden late in the morning to fill her in.

"Well, Willie boy, I don't know exactly what you did in Doña Isabel's house. She did mention bullet holes in her wooden floor. I'd rather you didn't give me the details on that. But she also says her sons are no longer intent on killing each other."

"At least for the moment."

"She thinks it's more than that. She has them staying in different places. Sergio is going back to Nicaragua and has promised not to come back anytime soon. She will go visit him there, and she's holding out the hope that in their old age they might even reconcile. Something is something. She told me to thank you."

"My pleasure," Willie said, although the night before hadn't been pleasurable at all.

Alice added a last word:

"And by the way, Willie?"

"Yes?'

"Doña Isabel said not to worry. You don't have to pay for the floor."

THE REVENGE OF THE PUMA

illie Cuesta was running the last lap of his morning jog when his cell phone sounded. The track at the local high school in Little Havana was a quarter mile and he was entering the back stretch, sweat suffusing his University of Miami T-shirt. It was August, just after eleven a.m., by no means the best time to run. But Willie was head of security at his brother Tommy's Latin nightclub and hadn't made it to bed until three in the morning. In Miami, only madmen and nightclub employees ran in the midday sun.

He slowed to a walk and pulled the phone from the back pocket of his running shorts.

"Cuesta Investigations."

"Willie. It's Esther from the Herald."

Esther Perry was a veteran police reporter at the *Miami Herald*. Willie had met her years before when he was a member of the Miami PD, and they had developed a rapport. Willie was able to talk to her about his cases off the record, without having to worry that his name would show up where it shouldn't. He hadn't spoken to Esther since he'd left the force several years before and was surprised to hear her voice now.

"How are you, honey? What can I do for you?"

"It's more like what I can do for you, Willie," she said. "I might have a client for you. A very famous one. Have you ever heard of Rafael Reyes?"

Willie shrugged. "You mean the writer?"

"Exactly. That Rafael Reyes. The Latin American novelist."

Willie wasn't exactly a member of the literati, but he had completed high school and eked out a degree at the local community college. Between those experiences and his relationship with his ex-wife—who loved literature—he had become at least acquainted with the most famous of the modern Latin writers. He had read selected books—mostly selected by his wife—by Gabriel García Márquez, Isabel Allende and the blind writer from Argentina, Borges—among others. He had also read a book or two by Rafael Reyes.

Willie remembered one in particular by Reyes—*The Revenge of the Puma.* It was about an Inca priest from the colonial era, murdered by Spanish conquistadors, who comes back to life in modern times to settle accounts with powerful people. The ghost compared himself to a puma, the long-clawed mountain cat that had also been hunted almost out of existence but which sometimes managed to ambush and kill its pursuers. Willie—who rarely got scared by books or movies—remembered that one vividly.

"What kind of trouble can Mr. Reyes be in?" Willie asked. "He must be pretty old by now."

"Yes, he's in his eighties. He lives most of the year in Peru, where he's from, and part of the year here in Miami to escape the winters down there. He has a small house in Coconut Grove."

"I didn't know that."

"Very few people know that. He has always guarded his privacy. And that's just the problem he has now. Someone is invading his privacy and doing it in a menacing way."

"How so?"

"A man Reyes doesn't know has appeared at his house several times, always at night. Reyes says he saw the man at the windows initially, but that the last time, which was a couple of days ago, he found this person actually in his writing room. The man had come in through a window."

"Did this guy try to harm him in any way or take anything?"

"No, he didn't attack Reyes, at least not yet. And as for taking anything, he didn't have a chance. Reyes surprised him and the guy skipped back out the window."

"I hope Mr. Reyes locked that window."

"He did, but he says he's almost positive it was locked already. So, this individual found some way to jimmy it, to get in. And he's afraid he'll do it again."

"Is the guy just some crazy fan?"

"He doesn't know, and he doesn't want to find out. He called the police, and they took a complaint, along with a description of the man. They can patrol the area a bit more but can't stake out the house. They don't have the manpower for that. He needs someone like you to act as his bodyguard and help grab this guy. He had his US publishers call me from New York today and they will cover your day rate. I'll send you their contacts as soon as I hang up, along with his number and address. I'm writing a story on the fact Reyes is here, but I'm not including the address. I'll wait until this guy is nabbed to report on the intruder."

Willie drank it all in and decided he couldn't pass up the opportunity to work for a literary lion. Truth was, he couldn't afford to pass up any assignment. He needed the money. But a last question did occur to him.

"What did he say this guy looked like? Is he bigger than me?" Willie was six feet, 175.

"No worry there. He said the intruder is short, very skinny, with long black hair and the bronzed, hawk-nosed face of a Peruvian Indian. He should be easy to spot. There can't be that many Incas in Coconut Grove."

"I guess I'll find out."

๑๖ ๑๖

Willie jogged home, took a shower and sat down at his computer. He found the e-mail from Esther and sent off a message to an editor at the publishing house in New York. He cited his day rate and requested two days' pay upfront. He added his bank information and within fifteen minutes received an e-mail from an editor named Regina assuring him that money would be wired that afternoon.

"Please take good care of Raffo," she wrote. "He's a great man."

Next Willie called the number he had for "Raffo." It rang several times and then a woman answered. It turned out she was the housekeeper and had been told to expect his call.

"Don Raffo is working right now. And after that he will take a nap and work some more. He asks that you come tonight at nine p.m. I will be gone by then so please ring the bell several times to make sure he hears you." Willie agreed to do all that and disconnected.

In his living room, which doubled as his office, a small bookcase stood against the far wall. He went to it now and found his old, dog-eared copy of *The Revenge of the Puma.* He hadn't looked at it in almost twenty years. He sat back down in his chair and opened it, figuring to fill part of the afternoon before he reported for duty.

It was early evening before he closed the book. Parts of the story were comical, the adventures of a five-hundred-year-old Incan man who suddenly finds himself in the modern world, with all of its baffling technology. But as Willie had remembered, it was also a horror story about the vengeance the old priest wreaks on the most corrupt, abusive and prejudiced people he can find. Along the way were some beautiful descriptions of the majestic Andes Mountains and other aspects of the Peruvian countryside, the only landmarks the old man recalls from his first stint on earth.

Willie got up, heated up some leftover Cuban takeout and poured himself an ice-cold IPA. By the time he finished it was time to get dressed and go. He slipped into a black *guayabera* shirt and white linen pants and headed for his car.

Twenty minutes later he was pulling up to the address Esther Perry had given him in Coconut Grove. People who lived in the Grove tended to favor lush vegetation and Reyes appeared to share that predilection. An old-fashioned, country-style mailbox stood outside a black wrought-iron gate and bore the number of the house. Apart from that, all he saw was tall, extremely thick plant life, which blocked any view of the actual dwelling. The first thought that occurred to Willie was that the junglish landscaping would make it very easy for a prowler to access the property. Not good.

He went to the gate, lifted the latch, passed through and followed a flagstone pathway to the front door. On either side of him the yard was planted with a variety of palms, ferns, crotons and flowering bushes, as well as fruit trees—mango, orange. The air was thick from the smell of jasmine as well. Near the front door he reached an arched trellis that was entwined with vines, creating a tropical entryway to the house. The white stucco walls were covered with moss and vines. A dim light barely illuminated a brass bell from which hung a leather cord. Willie rang the bell and, remembering what the housekeeper had said, he rang it again.

After about twenty seconds he heard a gravelly voice from the other side of the thick, wooden, studded door.

"Who is it?" the voice asked in Spanish.

"It's Willie Cuesta, the investigator, Mr. Reyes. Your publisher sent me."

Willie heard two locks tripped, including a deadbolt, and then the heavy door creaked open.

"Come in."

Willie did as ordered. Reyes closed and locked the door behind him. Hanging above the foyer was a kind of ship's lantern that looked several centuries old. It cast a soft light on Don Rafael Reyes, who stood beneath it. Willie found him an impressive-looking individual indeed.

He was of medium height but broad-shouldered and barrel-chested. His thick hair and wide moustache were both a pure white. His face was long, with bronzed cheeks that were hollowed and creased with age. The nose was arched and prominent, indicating a large dose of Incan blood. But what attracted most of Willie's attention were the eyes. They were large and gray-blue, the color of flint. Set in his dark face, they at first made him appear startled, but when he fixed on Willie they were piercing.

The air conditioning was on full blast: The house was chilly, and the old man wore a gray sweater that matched those eyes.

"Come into my study. I've just finished work."

They passed through the living room, which was simply and rustically furnished, featuring a large, very beautiful crimson rug woven with what appeared to be ancient Incan symbols. On the walls hung several oil paintings of mountains, probably the Andes. Hanging alongside them were various ceramic ritual masks, some of them very solemn faces, others ferocious, that appeared to be ancient Indian gods. If they were as old as they looked, they were worth a pretty penny. Don Raffo had imported a large dose of his native culture to surround him in his Miami hideaway. The place looked a bit like a private museum.

The study they walked into now was smaller. Three walls were lined floor to ceiling with mahogany bookcases crammed with books. Another Peruvian carpet lay on the hardwood floor and a large, intricately carved mahogany desk sat near a window in the far wall. On either side of that window hung photographs and diplomas. The old man ducked into a bathroom there and Willie took the opportunity to study that wall.

Don Raffo had received numerous honorary degrees from universities all over the planet. He had also won all sorts of literary awards from around the world. In the photographs he was posed holding those awards next to people Willie didn't recognize. Willie fixed on one where the much younger Reyes stood next to an extremely aristocratic-looking man in white tie and tails. Just then the author emerged from the bathroom.

"That is me standing next to the king of Spain the year I won the Cervantes Prize," he said. "The Spanish wine at the awards dinner was excellent."

He took a seat behind the desk, motioned Willie into the chair across from him, picked up a pipe, lit it and exhaled.

"So, you are a real-life private detective. I have only read about them in mystery novels."

"Yes, that's what I do for a living, although not all of my cases are as exciting as the ones you read about in books."

"Well, maybe this one will be. This person who is harassing me might be a dangerous character."

Willie crossed a leg. "Tell me about him."

The old man shrugged. "I can't tell you all that much about him. He has appeared here several times but hasn't spoken to me."

"Where have you seen him?"

The old man turned and indicated the window behind him.

"The first time was right here in this window. It was dusk, about ten days ago, and I'd had considerable trouble working that day. When you get older, the imagination is less efficient, the images less clear."

"I understand."

"I was just finishing my efforts that day when I got up and happened to notice a movement. I turned and there he was on the other side of this window just staring at me."

"What did he look like?"

"He is definitely of Peruvian Indian ancestry, in his thirties, I'd say, with long black hair, and he is always in peasant clothes, those a farmhand might wear."

Willie frowned. Farms existed in the county south of Miami and Latin Americans made up most of the field hands, but they were mostly Mexicans and Guatemalans. He had never heard of Peruvians working on those properties, but it was possible.

"What did you do when you saw him?"

Don Raffo shook his head.

"I didn't have an opportunity to do anything. The moment I saw him he turned and disappeared into the foliage."

"But you saw him again? He came back?"

"Oh yes. It was probably two days later at the very same time. This time I heard something behind me in the underbrush. I turned and he was there again just staring at me. This time I called to him, 'What are you doing there? Who are you?'"

"And?"

"And he didn't answer. He stared at me for several more moments and then, again, he disappeared into the vegetation. This time I went out into the yard after him, but he was gone."

Willie peered out the window and then back at his prospective client.

"I'm told that on one of these visits of his you actually found him in the house."

The old man's gray eyes flared now, and he grew agitated.

"That's right, two days ago. It was about eight at night, I was feeling tired and I went to make myself coffee. When I entered this room again, he was standing right in front of me, dead still. Somehow, he must have opened the window."

"That's all he was doing, just standing there?"

"Yes, but his stillness was very worrisome, let me tell you. And there's another thing. I had only seen him before at the window and from the chest up. This time I saw the full length of him and noticed that in his woven belt he carried a short machete, the kind that field workers might use." Reyes held up his gnarled hands and indicated that the machete was about a foot long. "This one was special, however. Its wooden handle was carved with the head of a llama."

"Did he take it out of his belt? Did he menace you with it in any way?"

The old man squinted in thought, obviously trying to picture the scene. Then he shook his head.

"No, he didn't. But it's like I told you, he stood very still as if he was deciding what he was going to do to me. At my age it would be very difficult to defend myself against someone so much younger and armed with such a blade."

"Then what happened?"

"He didn't run right away. We stood and stared at each other for several moments and then finally he turned, calmly, mind you, escaped back out the window and disappeared. He acted as if he owned this house, and I didn't. I have no doubt he will be back. In fact, he has told me so in the notes he has left me."

Willie scowled. "Notes? Nobody told me anything about notes."

Reyes reached into his desk drawer and dropped two pieces of lined paper in front of Willie. The notes were both short, written in block letters, in black pen and in Spanish. Reyes slid one of them toward Willie.

"This was the first."

The note read: "You have not written my story, old man." It was signed "F. S." That was all.

Reyes slid the second one toward him. It was longer:

"You have still not written my story. You know who I am. You know what you must do. I will be back. F. S."

Willie was still scowling.

"Where did you find these?"

"My housekeeper found them. Both times they were shoved through an old mail slot in the front door and were lying on the floor. They had not been there when I went to bed on either night, but she found them when she arrived in the morning, which means they must have been delivered late, during the night."

Willie glanced again at the notes.

"Do you have any notion what this person means in these notes? What he is talking about?"

The old man shrugged. "Yes, I have an idea. First you have to understand a basic fact. While readers around the world tell a writer such as I how wonderful I am, in my own country there are those who insist I have gotten their story all wrong or have ignored them altogether. It's like the scriptures say, 'A prophet has no honor in his own village.'"

"But why this particular person?"

Don Raffo puffed his pipe and shrugged.

"Several years ago, a man wrote to me to tell me about a very tragic case. His name was Fidel Sánchez and his fiancée, a beautiful young Indian woman who worked as a teacher, had been murdered in Lima. Her name was Ariela. A powerful government official was suspected of having killed her after she rejected his advances. Because that man was so powerful, the police would not move against him and none of the newspapers would investigate this man's claims either. The bereaved man turned to me."

"Did you believe his story, that this official had committed the crime?"

The old man squinted into the past.

"The girl, when last seen alive earlier that evening, had been at a government reception for educators and Peruvian congressional leaders. That was about eight p.m. Early the next morning, her body was found on the side of a highway outside the city. She wore the same dress she had worn the night before and had been raped, beaten and strangled. Rural residents living near there said they had seen an expensive car, like that provided to government personages, pulled to the side of the road there around midnight. They had no idea why it was there. That was all that was known."

Willie tried to picture what Reyes described to him.

"So, what did you do after her fiancé came to you?"

Reyes shrugged. "You have to understand, Mr. Cuesta, that I am not a professional investigator of crimes as you are, and my options were limited. In Latin America our law enforcement systems have often been compromised and, even if you determine who committed a crime, justice is elusive. At the time, I went to certain journalistic and government contacts I had and inquired discreetly about the congressman in question. His name was Raul Villa. I confirmed that he was an individual who owned large amounts of land and had a reputation for corruption and for brutality with his underlings. But I, like the young woman's fiancé, found no appetite on the part of any authorities to pursue the case."

He held out his empty hands and his expression was one of frustration.

"I did not have the hard facts, the evidence sufficient to make an allegation against this official on my own. I could do nothing for this young man trying to avenge the murder of the woman he loved. I tried to explain that to him. I was helpless. I needed someone like you, a professional, unbiased investigator, but there was no one like you to turn to."

He paused to puff his pipe and fixed on Willie.

"If a crime like this one had occurred here in Miami it would have worked differently, wouldn't it? What would you have done to investigate it? Tell me. I want to know."

Willie shrugged. "Well, I would have begun by interviewing everyone at that reception and determining what kind of contact the suspect had with the girl during that evening. That would include congressional officials, other educators, friends of hers, even the waiters."

"And you believe the members of congress would cooperate? In my country they would claim some kind of immunity, or at least try to."

"No, here there is no congressional immunity. Politicians some-times get away with murder in this country, but not literally."

Willie smiled, sipped his drink and went on.

"I would have looked, in particular, for any person who had seen them leave together, including the valet-parking attendants. I would obtain a warrant to inspect both the car and residence of the suspect or anywhere else he might have taken the girl. I would have DNA samples taken from both the victim and the gentleman in question and determine what kind of contact there may have been between them. I would interrogate neighbors of the congressman to deter-mine if they heard anything unusual that night, in particular the sounds of an argument or any other violence. I would locate surveil-lance cameras that might have captured the two of them together."

Don Raffo was grimacing. "We don't have anywhere near as many such cameras in Peru as you have here, and I don't know how sophisticated DNA science is in my country. But go on."

"I would obtain the cellular telephone records of both persons. At the scene where the body was found I would take casts of the tire treads on the side of the road where neighbors saw that car and com-pare them to the treads on the car of the suspect. I would press those neighbors to try to remember details about the car, maybe even a fragment of the tag number. People sometimes have absorbed more information than they realize."

"Would you hypnotize them? I have heard of that being done to tap the subconscious."

"No, I wouldn't hypnotize them, but I would request that they try very hard to remember exactly what they saw. I would also take samples of the dirt in that place and see if it showed up on the shoes, pants cuffs or anywhere else on the suspected perpetrator."

The old man drank it all in avidly. "Very meticulous," he mumbled.

Willie nodded. "Yes, and that is just the basics. Then I would begin questioning the people close to the suspect. Was he married?"

"Yes, he was—and is."

"Then I would question his wife. If he was cheating on her, maybe she would be willing to cooperate and reveal a detail about that night that I could use to undo him. You say he had a reputation for brutality; well, maybe he mistreated her and she had been waiting for her chance to take her revenge."

Don Raffo looked pained. "Both Villa and his wife are members of the privileged class. I doubt she would turn against him publicly."

"Then we would go to his servants and other employees. You said he had a history of mistreating them. And, finally, I would interrogate the suspect himself, or convince friends of mine who are still policemen to interrogate him. We would make him recount every second of the day the girl died from the moment he woke up until the second he went to sleep—if he slept at all after committing the murder. We would try to trip him up. We would press him for his attitudes toward women, towards Indian girls in particular, his past indiscretions—and who else he might have already exterminated in his life."

Don Raffo drank it all in.

"If only that had happened in this case," he said. "Instead, Villa still roams Lima, a free man. The fiancé is still bereaved, enraged, mute and apparently out of his mind with frustration of justice denied."

"But what on earth is he doing here?"

Reyes shrugged. "I know he made certain accusations against Villa publicly in Peru and I'm sure his life was threatened after he did so. Maybe he came here running for his life. Or maybe he is in Miami specifically looking for me. As I said earlier, others have shown up at my door with their hopeless causes, their sagas. I am the author, after all, of *The Revenge of the Puma,* a story about vengeance taken in the name of the entire Inca nation."

Willie glanced out the window again and back at the old man.

"Do you own a gun?"

Don Raffo shook his head.

"No. I have never before found the need to own one and wouldn't know how to use one. That's why I sought out your services. I need someone who has experience with this type of individual."

Willie shrugged. He wasn't sure he had experience with "this type of individual"—a Peruvian Indian who intimidated solely by showing up where he didn't belong and staring ominously.

"I can try to find this man and turn him over for arrest," Willie said.

"The police already tried to find him, to no avail. He is probably in this country illegally and leaving no trail."

Willie shrugged. "Well, if you want, I can come here in the evenings and wait for him until he comes back. That's the only way I can see to go about it. Your publisher has already agreed to pay me a daily rate."

"Can you start this very evening?"

"I think I already have."

ᕬ ᕬ

Willie stayed at Don Raffo's house until three a.m. that morning. The following two nights he arrived at nine p.m. and stayed until three. He always parked his car around the corner and made sure he wasn't being watched as he entered the house. He didn't want the stalker to know that anyone else was there besides the old man. Most of the time the two of them simply sat on opposite sides of the old man's desk, drinking pisco sours—a drink made from Peruvian brandy—and talking. What else was there to do? Occasionally Willie got up to stretch his legs. When he did, he would go out into the overgrown yard and make sure the intruder was not hiding there in the thick vegetation. He wasn't. Then he would go back in, sit, talk and wait.

The old writer regaled him with all kinds of stories from his long life. His childhood in the Amazonian region of Peru where he cohabited with anacondas, piranhas and jaguars. Walking several miles to school every day through jungle to get an elementary education. How he showed promise and ended up eventually at a university in the capital, Lima, where he was surrounded not by Incas such as he but mostly white people of Spanish descent. From there he received scholarships to study in Europe. He heard French, Italian, German for the first time and published his first paid work, an essay entitled "An Inca in Paris." He also met famous European writers and some of his fellow Latin American expatriate writers who would also later find fame. While living in Barcelona he wrote and published *The Revenge of the Puma,* the work that made his name.

By the time he returned to Peru, the country was embroiled in a guerrilla war. Many members of the guerrilla army were Incas, but so were many of its victims. Reyes found himself caught in the middle, his life threatened at times by government agents and at other times by the insurgents. It was then that he developed his modus vivendi of letting as few people as possible know where he lived.

"In addition to protecting me, I found the clandestine life was very good for my literary productivity," he said, puffing on his pipe. "I wrote many books and stories."

Don Raffo was a great raconteur, but each night, after he had recounted another chapter in his life, he would insist that Willie tell him about particularly interesting cases he had worked. Willie was nowhere near the storyteller Reyes was, but he managed to piece together some of his exploits, both as a police detective and lately as a private investigator. He told him of the case where he tracked down the killer of a legendary Cuban showgirl, a case with Mafia connections. The time when he was briefly kidnapped by some Colombian kidnappers, but still helped free a hostage and break up that ring. He recounted his run-in with illegal Argentine arms traffickers and a shootout at a tango club on the Miami River. Of course, those were the highlights. He didn't bother to bore Don Raffo with all his nights as a young patrolman when he had ridden around for hours in Little Havana answering only the most mundane types of calls. And now, as a private investigator, many days were spent simply waiting for the phone to ring.

The old man enjoyed the stories, often asking all sorts of questions, delving into the details of detective work. That was how they spent the first four uneventful nights—a bit drunk from the pisco, and word drunk as well.

ᕼ᪉ ᕼ᪉

It was on the fourth night that the intruder finally made his move. It was around eleven p.m. Willie had already been there two hours and was on his third pisco sour. The conversation had slowed down considerably. Willie, in particular, was running out of war stories and just couldn't keep up with the old fabulist. They sat in silence for stretches.

Don Raffo got up and shuffled from the study to the bathroom. Willie sat drumming his fingers on the armrest of his chair, staring through the window into the overgrown garden. Suddenly, he heard a shout, then a loud crash followed by a thump that shook the floorboards. He jumped up, ran from the study, streaked through the living room and found Don Raffo lying on the floor of his bedroom at the back of the house. Willie had not been in there before and found it decorated much like the rest of the house—bookcases, colorful Peruvian rugs, more masks, with an antique four-poster bed for a centerpiece.

One of the bookcases had been tipped over—causing the crash Willie had heard—and books were strewn everywhere. A ceramic mask had shattered. The one window in the room gaped open. Lying on his stomach amid the books and shards was Don Raffo. Willie lifted him and helped him onto the bed.

"Are you all right?"

The old man caught his breath, squeezed his rib cage and felt his head.

"Yes, I think I'm all right."

He pointed at the open window.

"It was him. I found him in here and he knocked me down. He went out that way."

Willie ran from the room, out the front door and onto the street. About a half block away he saw a man walking quickly under the beam of a streetlight and sprinted after him. He was about twenty feet away when the guy, hearing Willie's pounding footsteps approaching, suddenly stopped and turned around. Willie pulled up and stopped dead. He was staring at a boy of about twenty with blond hair. He was a big kid, football size, obviously not a Peruvian Indian. And he wasn't happy to have Willie looking like he wanted to tackle him. Willie raised his empty hands.

"Sorry. I thought you were someone else."

He turned, hurried back to the house and found Don Raffo still sitting on the bed.

"Did you catch him?"

"No, he was gone."

The old man pointed at the pillow.

"Look at what that vandal did."

Sticking from the pillow was the short machete that Don Raffo had described with a wooden handle in the shape of a llama. The wide blade had sunk into the pillow, loosed some feathers and pinned a note, written in the same block letters and black ink as the other notes. Willie plucked his handkerchief from his back pocket, pulled out the knife in a way that fingerprints would not be erased, and read the note.

"You have betrayed me and your people. You deserve to die, and no protector will help you."

Willie put it back down on the bed.

"I'm going to call the police," he said.

"No," barked Don Raffo. "They won't do anything. I'm going back to Peru first thing tomorrow. In Peru I have numerous places I can hide from this phantom. He won't find me."

He hauled himself up, rolled a suitcase out of his closet, began to empty drawers and tumble clothes into it right then. Afraid that the intruder might return, Willie stayed with him all night, even after the old man finally fell sleep. Only after the housekeeper arrived in the morning did he leave, handing her a note for Don Raffo, wishing him well and expressing his regrets that he hadn't been able to capture the criminal. Fact was, he hadn't even caught sight of the stalker.

That afternoon he received a call from the old man's publisher telling him that a check for five days' work was in the mail. It arrived days later, and Willie heard nothing else from or about the author for over a year. Then one day a package arrived in the mail bearing foreign postage. Willie torn it open and found a thin book, in Spanish, by Rafael Reyes, entitled Avenging Ariela.

Ariela had, of course, been the name of the young woman allegedly killed by the congressman. Willie had developed a taste for pisco sours and now he made himself one, sat on his porch and opened the book. On the acknowledgments page in the front of the book was a list of names of persons who had helped the author. Willie was among them.

He found that it was written in the same style as *The Revenge of the Puma*. But in this case it was the dead girl who came back from the dead and with the help of her fiancé—and another ally—they investigated a powerful congressman, suspected of her murder. The ally was an American private investigator named William Cole. He had the same initials as Willie. As Willie skipped around the book looking for that name, he found that Don Raffo had borrowed the case histories and investigative techniques Willie had recounted to him to flesh out the character and the action.

Tucked in the back of the book was a handwritten note from Don Raffo.

"Willie, my dear friend and protector, I want to thank you very much for all the assistance you gave me in the research of this book. It is an enormous success here in Peru, my most praised tome since *Puma*. I'm including some of the reviews and articles. You'll be glad to hear that the congressman on whom the story is based is in disgrace, has finally been forced to retire from public life and may even end up behind bars. Thank you again. Respectfully, R. Reyes."

Willie glanced at the reviews and articles. It was at the very bottom of one that he found a sentence:

"The fiancé in real life, Fidel Sánchez, died ten years ago, long before Reyes started work on the book."

Willie read the sentence and read it again. It had been nearly two years since he had spent those nights with the old taleteller. Had the face in the window and intrusions into the house been an old man's delusions? Or had Willie been played like a musical instrument by a master of magical realism researching his next master work?

A wry smile twisted Willie's lips. He sipped his pisco sour and dove back into the book.

THE CUBAN PRISONER

P rivate investigator Willie Cuesta leaned against a palm tree in a park just blocks from his Little Havana home, watching seven-year-olds play soccer. The kids dashed madly up and down the field in their striped jerseys, occasionally running into collisions that left several of them strewn on the grass. They sprang up right away and took off hell bent in the opposite direction, the careening ball never firmly in anyone's control and never quite making it into a net. On the sidelines, parents cheered them, gossiped a bit and then cheered some more when their kid touched the ball. Willie understood why soccer had become such a popular sport in the US: If you wanted to tire out your seven-year-old so that he or she went to sleep early and soundly, allowing you to sit comfortably with your carafe of wine, you nudged your child into soccer. In Willie's young days, he had played a lot of baseball, a more static, contemplative game, and had never wanted to sleep. His mother would have been better served if she'd been born thirty years later.

A pileup occurred near one goal, a whistle sounded and the referee called for a penalty kick. A young player with a mop of jet black hair reared back, booted the ball at a forty-five-degree angle, far from the net, into the crowd and hung his head. Shouts of reassurance rang out and the mad scramble resumed.

"Mr. Cuesta?"

Willie turned to a woman who had walked up. She was about forty, raven-haired, attractive, wearing a lime-green blouse, black Capri pants and comfortable mom sneakers for standing on the sidelines.

"You're Ursula Estevez?" Willie asked.

"*Sí, Señor.*" They shook hands.

155

Willie had received a call from Ms. Estevez about two hours before, midmorning Saturday. She said she might need his services. He had asked her what her problem was, but she preferred to meet in person. Her son was playing in a soccer game that started at noon not far from Willie's house, and he had agreed to meet her.

"Which of the boys is yours?" he asked.

She pointed at the organized disorder on the field.

"Number nine, in green."

Willie saw a smallish kid with her black hair and pale skin scurrying around the fringes of the action.

"But he's not why I called you. It's my mother, his grandmother." She pointed to the end of the line of spectators, where an elderly woman sat about ten feet from the sideline in a canvas chair. She wore a flowered dress, a sun visor and shades. Her hair was brown, although almost certainly with the help of her hairdresser. Willie guessed that she was in her mid to late seventies. She was fixed on the field of play with a smile on her face, apparently content watching her grandson and probably not all that concerned with the score.

"She appears to be doing pretty well," Willie said. "She looks happy."

Ursula Estevez nodded. "Yes, right now she is especially happy. But I'm worried that someone is out to take advantage of her, possibly hurt her, and that her life could turn very dark. I'm worried that would finish her."

The statement was stark and was matched by her tone.

"You better tell me what's going on," Willie said.

A park bench stood nearby and they sat on it, still able to see the field and the lady in question. Ms. Estevez folded her hands on her lap.

"My parents escaped Cuba in the early 1960s, soon after Castro took power. Like a lot of other Cuban exiles, they settled here in Miami. They started an insurance business together, largely serving other Cubans, and in time it did very well. Once they were solidly on their feet, my sister and I were born. Everything continued to go well and they retired a few years ago with a comfortable nest egg. Their only plan was to spend as much time as possible enjoying their grandkids."

She gestured toward the obviously contented lady in the canvas chair.

"But something must have spoiled that plan," Willie said.

Ursula's lips curdled and she nodded.

"My father died two years ago of a heart attack. From one moment to the next he was taken from us. Because of their history, escaping Cuba together, my parents had been unusually close, and my mother was lost. I mean terribly, terribly lost. She cried for months and then she was almost completely quiet for many months more. She was so sad we were afraid she might do something to hurt herself. She refused to move in with either me or my sister because she didn't want to leave the house that reminded her of him. We had to be there as much as possible to make sure she was all right and didn't do anything crazy."

She stopped to take a breath and Willie nodded in commiseration.

"My father died several years ago and my mother is a widow. I understand. Go on."

She stared off across the park. "Finally, we and an older lady friend convinced her to get out of the house. She started to go for walks and lunches with this friend. And eventually this lady even convinced her to go to the community center for the elderly here in Little Havana. People meet there to play dominoes and canasta, or just to talk. I can't tell you how relieved my sister and I were when this happened. We had been worried sick for months about her and now we finally saw her coming back to life."

"Well, that all sounds good."

Ursula rolled her eyes. "Yes, it was too good. One day she was at the community center playing dominoes when a man sat down at her table as part of the foursome. His name is Norman Cruz. He is a man in his sixties, about ten years younger than my mother. He is handsome, tall, well built, just as my father was. He told my mother that he had come from Cuba only recently. When my mother asked him why it had taken him so long to leave the island, he told her it was because he had been held for more than twenty years as a political prisoner in Castro's jails and had only recently been released."

She fixed on Willie.

"You can easily imagine what that meant to my mother. She despises the Castros and here was a man who had lost twenty years of his life because of his courageous opposition to them. She was dizzy with admiration for him."

Willie nodded. He had grown up in the Cuban exile community as well and knew that former political prisoners were greeted in Miami like heroes returned from the war. There was no greater position of honor in the exile world. But Ursula wasn't finished with her tale.

"From one moment to the next, my mother was in love with this man. She had missed my father so much and now God had sent someone to take his place. They started spending almost all their time together and now, just six weeks after they met, my mother has announced that they are going to be married next month. We have no idea who this man is, Mr. Cuesta. My mother is a woman of some wealth and at a very vulnerable stage of her life. We need to make sure she is not simply being taken advantage of."

"So, you need me to do background checks on this Norman Cruz."

She looked pained. "We have a family lawyer and he has tried to do that. But the Cuban government won't give any information on who was or wasn't a political prisoner."

That didn't surprise Willie. Governments, in general, didn't admit to having political prisoners at all. Everybody in jail was catalogued as a common criminal.

"And the lawyer has also tried to get information here locally," Ursula said. "There is an organization of former political prisoners here, but they admit they don't know everyone ever held in those prisons. Dozens of detention centers exist all over the island. They found an old listing in human rights records of an N. Cruz, but nothing else about him. This man Cruz says he was held in a small facility in the city of San Sebastián on the eastern end of the island. The lawyer found that there is a detention center there, but he could find no one else who was detained in that facility and who might know Cruz."

"How about members of Cruz's family? Most exiles have family here. They would have information about him."

Ursula shook her head. "He says he was an only child, that his parents died when he was young, and that he lost touch with other relatives while he was in prison. He has no one here."

Willie soaked that all in. He was starting to comprehend Ursula's plight.

"You need someone who can size this guy up—get enough out of him to determine whether he's on the up and up."

"I don't know what else to do."

Willie stared at the elderly woman propped in the chair, then at the young soccer players galloping up and down the field and back at Ursula—three generations of Cubans. He gave Ursula his day rate, advised her that he needed a two-day minimum up-front, and moments later she had made out a check. Willie tucked it away.

"Okay. I want you to contact Mr. Cruz and tell him a representative of the family wants to talk to him, to welcome him to the clan and firm up some details on the wedding. Whatever. Have him call me."

One of the kids on the field finally scored a goal and a great cheer went up. The lady in the canvas chair clapped. Willie wondered if she would still be clapping when he finished his investigation.

⁖ ⁖

He went home and warmed some leftover chicken and rice for lunch. Then he turned on his laptop, brought up Google and looked for information on Cuban prisons. He found a list that went province by province and even included some photos of the facilities. About one hundred prisons were listed, including the San Sebastián unit in Santiago province. The photo showed a box-like cement structure about three stories high, which might have been a very unattractive public housing project, except all the windows were blocked with bars and it was surrounded by a tall wall with barbed wire on top and guard towers rising high at each corner.

Willie left that site and found others that named political prisoners. The long lists he scanned named people imprisoned over the years, but the compilers warned that the logs were not complete. They wrote that some persons who were in fact political prisoners had been convicted of trumped-up common crimes, or were simply never listed as prisoners of any kind by the government. Willie scanned the lists nevertheless, but did not find the name Norman Cruz.

Many of the sites were run by human rights groups and included reports of troubles at the facilities—mistreatment of prisoners, hunger strikes, prison riots, et cetera. A couple involved the San Sebastián facility. He scribbled down notes, closed the sites and moved on to other business.

In addition to his private investigations firm, Willie served as chief of security for the Latin dance club Caliente, run by his brother Tommy. It was the most popular Latin club in the city, wall-to-wall people, especially on the weekend nights, rum and tequila flowing like rivers, and it required plenty of staff. Willie spent the next hour making out schedules for the security details, posting that information and confirming payroll figures for already completed shifts.

He was just finishing all that when his cell phone sounded. He answered and found a man with a deep but soft voice on the other end.

"Is this Mr. Cuesta?"

"Yes, it is."

"This is Norman Cruz calling. Ursula Estevez asked me to contact you. I understand you want to meet me?"

He spoke slowly, cautiously.

"Yes, that's right. I was hoping we could get together sometime today. Would that be possible for you?"

The other man took several moments to think that over.

"Yes," he said finally. "Maybe we could meet for dinner. Normally I would eat with Lydia, that is Ursula's mother, but today she has another matter to attend. Maybe we could meet at a restaurant near where I live. It's called Café Santiago."

"Yes, I know where that is. Right on Calle Ocho."

Calle Ocho—Eighth Street—was the main drag in Little Havana.

"That's right," Cruz said. "Can you meet me there at five o'clock?"

Willie frowned. That was early for dinner and especially for Cubans, who liked to eat late. The other man seemed to read his mind.

"I know that's very early, but that was when they fed us in prison and I have found it a habit hard to break."

Willie didn't argue. He described what he would be wearing—black silk shirt and cream pants—so that Cruz would recognize him. Then they signed off and Willie went back to his accounts.

He arrived at the restaurant about five minutes early. Café Santiago was small—maybe twelve tables—and certainly nothing fancy. Those tables were Formica. The chairs were made of well-aged wood. The décor consisted of faded black-and-white photos of the beautiful Cuban colonial city of Santiago and of its local beaches. The lights were hanging fluorescents and the food was cooked right behind the Formica serving bar.

What was luxurious about the place were the aromas emanating from the stoves and ovens. Right then they must have been roasting and/or frying the pork dishes for the expected dinner crowd. The air was suffused with the delicious scents of the meat, seasoned with traditional Cuban spices. Willie—given his Cuban-American nose—also picked up the aroma of boiled yucca smothered in butter and onions, as well as the narcotic nose treat that was fried sweet plantains. He had walked in not hungry at all. Within five minutes his mouth was watering.

Norman Cruz arrived at exactly five p.m. Willie knew who it was right away because he matched the description provided by Ursula. He was tall—about six feet—somewhere in his sixties, square-shouldered and ruggedly handsome. His complexion was sallow—fitting for a man who had spent years in a prison. His cheekbones and chin were pronounced, his cheeks hollowed. His eyes were narrowed in a squint and were gray, approximately the color of concrete. He wore a white shirt with black stripes and gray dress pants. The clothes looked new, just as Willie had often seen with recently arrived exiles from Cuba. After years of living under a communist government, most often meagerly, when they arrived in the US they got makeovers.

Cruz fixed on Willie, identified the black shirt and shuffled over.

"Mr. Cuesta?" It was the same deep but quiet voice he'd heard over the phone.

Willie stood, they shook hands and Cruz sat to the left of Willie, not across the table from him. He smiled slightly and pointed toward the entrance.

"I never sit with my back to the door. Any door."

"Is that something that comes from your years in prison?"

Cruz shook his head. "No, actually it began during my time in the anti-Castro underground, although I kept it as a rule in prison as well. There were many men who could be dangerous there too. Especially the guards."

A waitress brought menus and Cruz considered his.

"Order anything you want," Willie said. "It's on me."

The other man's eyes flared. He liked that idea. He closed his menu and when the waitress came over he ordered an appetizer of fried pork chunks, a black-bean soup, a churrasco steak, with rice, beans, fried plantains and a beer. Despite the seductive aromas all around, Willie decided it was still a bit too early to eat and ordered only the beer.

Once the waitress was gone, Cruz looked at him sheepishly.

"I eat a lot of meat. They say it isn't good for you, but I went so many years almost never getting meat in prison that I can't resist."

He dipped into the basket on the table and buttered a piece of Cuban bread.

"This also we didn't get much of," he said, biting into it lustily.

"You were in the prison at San Sebastián?"

Cruz nodded, still chewing. "Yes, that's right."

"Did you know a political prisoner there by the name of Alberto Ramos?"

It was a name Willie had found in the online accounts of human rights disputes at the prison.

Cruz swallowed his bread and swigged his beer. "Oh yes. We all knew Alberto. He was famous for once managing to escape. He did it by hoarding salt, then rubbing it all over his body very hard, which caused a terrible, bleeding rash. That got him admitted to the infirmary. Late that first night he snuck to a phone, called the local civilian hospital, passed himself off as the prison doctor and ordered an ambulance to have himself transferred to that hospital. With no doctor on duty that late, other prisoners on orderly duty carried him out. Once at the hospital, he ran away."

Cruz chuckled at the memory. "What was brilliant about his scheme was that prisoners planning an escape attempt often hoarded pepper. Once outside they could scatter the pepper in their tracks so that the bloodhounds' noses would get fouled and they couldn't be tracked. Alberto did the unexpected; he found a way to use salt. So smart of him."

Cruz swigged and shrugged.

"Of course, he was caught. Cuba is an island and he didn't have access to a boat. On an island they have you trapped from the moment you make it out the gate. Do you know what they tell the troops searching for an escaped prisoner in Cuba?"

Willie said he didn't.

"They tell them look for somebody who is unusually pale. Most Cubans get as much sun as they want. The island has plenty, but inside we got almost none. You escaped, but you looked like an albino and almost as easy to spot. Pale or not, Alberto at least enjoyed a couple of nights with his girlfriend before they grabbed him, although later they locked him in solitary for a long, long time."

Cruz sipped his beer and so did Willie. What Cruz had related about Alberto Ramos was what Willie had read in the online accounts.

Cruz's first course came then—the chunks of fried pork. They weren't very big and Willie would have probably just popped each one in his mouth whole. But Cruz meticulously cut each chunk into three pieces and ate them bit by bit, chewing each morsel thoroughly. It took him a while to finish his appetizer and at one point he noticed Willie's amusement.

"In prison you learn to eat very slowly, precisely. You have so little to do locked between those walls, you suffer so much boredom, that any activity you stretch out for as long as possible. Even if the meals were awful, as they were in San Sebastián. Sometimes we even found insects in the food. Jokesters called it Asian cuisine because in Asia people sometimes eat insects. But even then we took our time eating."

At another point he reached across the table for the salt, which was near Willie. He froze, still holding the shaker.

"Now, that is something I would never have done in prison, reach across a dinner table for anything."

"Why's that?'

"Because another prisoner would instantly think you were trying to grab his food and you would find your hand pinned to the table," he said, jabbing his fork down in the direction of the Formica.

He finished his pork and soon his black bean soup arrived. He savored that, spoonful by spoonful, much as he had his appetizer.

"I'm told you spent twenty years of your life there," Willie said.

Cruz shrugged. "That's what it turned out to be. We didn't have calendars and you lose count. But yes, just over twenty years."

"It must be quite a shock to suddenly find yourself free."

Cruz spooned the last of the soup into his mouth and dabbed his lips with his napkin.

"You don't realize all that prison has done to you until you are no longer in there. I slept in a large cellblock for years and there were always men snoring, grunting, arguing. That's not to mention the ones with nightmares, screaming nightmares, because they had been mistreated. That went on every night, but I grew accustomed to it and learned to sleep through it all. Now that I'm out, do you know what wakes me up?"

"No. What?"

"The quiet. Every night I wake up because my mind is searching for the sounds that it's accustomed to hearing. I lie still and listen, trying to hear something. Anything. The quiet concerns me, scares me."

He punctuated that thought with a flick of the eyebrows, sipped his beer and went on.

"Like I told you, I can't sit with my back to the door. Also, when I was behind bars in Cuba I always kept a shiv tucked into my sock, along my ankle. I had made it from a piece of bedframe. I brought it with me when I left the island and I still have it here where I'm living. I can't bring myself to throw it away."

He pointed toward the street.

"Another matter is walking through the city. When I first arrived here I would walk a block or two and then turn around and walk back. It had been so long since I had been able to walk long distances, that my mind would tell me to turn around. Now I walk farther, but I am still very wary, as if I've escaped from prison and someone may come after me or even shoot me. Walking with Lydia is curing me of that little by little."

By this time his steak had arrived and he gazed at it as if he were looking at a beautiful woman. He started to dig in, then stopped and laughed.

"There is another problem I had briefly with the walking." He pointed down at his shoes. "In prison I always kept any little bit of money I had or anything else small that I valued stuffed in my socks. That way even when I was sleeping no one could rob me. When I first got out, sometimes, without thinking, I would still do that with money. Then I went for a decent walk and I got a blister. Finally, I could go as far as I wanted, but I limped."

He laughed and dug into his steak. Willie gave him time to enjoy it. Cruz asked Willie absolutely nothing about himself, although Willie sensed he was being sized up by the man across the table just as much as he was sizing up Lydia's suitor. The gray eyes had an animal wariness to them, just as you might expect from a man who had been in a prison for years.

Willie ordered two more beers and sipped his.

"Do you have contact here in Miami with any of the men you were in prison with?"

Cruz shook his head. "No. The men I was locked up with are either dead now, or they are still stuck in that prison."

"How was it that they let you go?"

Cruz winced slightly, as if Willie had asked something that made him uncomfortable. Willie wondered for a moment if maybe Cruz had turned into an informer in prison, maybe bought his way out by snitching on fellow inmates. That tended to happen in prisons everywhere. Cruz certainly wouldn't want anyone to know that, although Willie wasn't about to judge him. You had to wonder what you yourself might do after twenty years in prison. There was no way of telling. Then again, maybe that wasn't the reason behind the discomfort. Cruz explained it moments later.

"They were trying to save money by reducing the prison population. So, they chose prisoners who had caused the fewest problems. I never joined any of the protests, the hunger strikes. Some of my fellow political prisoners didn't like that. But once I was in I just wanted to get out as quickly as I could. It still took a long, long time." He shrugged.

Willie wondered whether Cruz did know of other former San Sebastián inmates in Miami or elsewhere but didn't want Willie to talk to them because they would have nothing good to say about him. That could be the source of his uneasiness.

Cruz finished his meal and Willie paid the waitress. They drifted out the door.

"Do you think we could meet again tomorrow, Mr. Cruz? There are some matters regarding the wedding I'd like to discuss with you, but right now I need to be somewhere."

Willie hadn't discussed the wedding at all, but that didn't seem to surprise Cruz. They both knew what was going on: The would-be groom was being vetted. He didn't argue.

"That will be fine with me," Cruz said. "Why don't we meet tomorrow around noon down where they play dominoes."

Willie knew exactly where he meant, a roofed patio right on Eighth Street where elderly Cubans met to play the Cuban national pastime.

They shook hands. Willie started to turn away but Cruz held his hand and added a final word. "Make sure to watch your back, *hombre.*"

Cruz continued to grip his hand. Was this a man who had lived twenty years in a dangerous environment giving another man friendly advice? Or was Cruz issuing a not very veiled threat. Willie's mind flashed to that shiv Norman Cruz had carried with him from San Sebastián. The other man finally let go, turned and meandered away.

۵୬ ۵୬

Willie went home, poured himself another beer, sat on his back porch and stared at his backyard where the mango tree was just starting to bud. He thought about everything Norman Cruz had told him and wondered what he should do next. Halfway through that beer his next move budded as well: He would call his mother.

Willie's widowed mother, Silvia, was the owner of her own *botánica,* several blocks east on Eighth Street. It was a narrow storefront where many people—mostly Cubans—showed up with their chronic complaints. Physical, emotional, romantic, economic. You name it. Indigestion, impotence, insolvency, Silvia had a suggested remedy. She would listen at length to the problem—which was a crucial element in the service she offered—and then identify an herb that was indicated for treatment of that malady. Or she would offer the patient the image of a saint who was known to specialize in miraculously curing that condition. The likenesses she featured on her shelves were not just of Catholic saints but of spirits enshrined by the Santería religion, which Cuban slaves had brought from Africa. She covered all her bases.

The herbs were piled in bins on one side of the store and the plaster casts of religious figures lined shelves on the other. The middle aisle separated the natural from the supernatural, like two sides of the same brain. Her customers consulted with medical doctors for serious illnesses, of course, but they brought their everyday ailments and issues to the *botánica,* just as they had done back in Cuba. She didn't charge much; it was a volume business. Willie figured that over the decades almost every family in Little Havana had had dealings with his mama. Consequently, she knew everybody in the neighborhood.

She picked up the phone now, recognizing Willie's number.

"Finally, you call your mother," she said in Spanish. "You would rather talk to criminals and other strangers than to me."

This was her standard greeting to him. No matter how often he called it would never be enough. He apologized as he always did, told her he loved her and then got down to business.

"Mama, who do you know who came here from San Sebastián in Cuba? I need to find someone who knows that city well."

Silence ensued on the other end as his mother reviewed her internal Rolodex, the vast collection of names and personal stories she had accumulated over the decades. It took her the better part of a minute before she found the right name.

"You should speak with Hilda Sánchez. She came from San Sebastián decades ago, knows everybody else from there and she likes to talk."

"Where do I find her?"

She described a large, pink, aging Art Deco apartment building just off Twenty-Seventh Avenue, still in Little Havana. Willie was familiar with it.

"You go there and ask for Hilda. Everyone knows her. I'll call and tell her you're coming."

Willie thanked his mother, repeated his love for her and disconnected. He printed out the information he had on San Sebastián and headed for Hilda's house.

She was waiting on the steps for him when he arrived—a short, dark, silver-haired lady, about seventy. She led him to a neat second-floor apartment. Willie knew that Cuban exiles were eternally connected to the cities they came from and loved to reminisce. Exile did that to a person. For the next hour he fed Hilda questions about people, places and events in San Sebastián over the years and listened as she luxuriated in her memories. She brought out old black-and-white snapshots of her own to illustrate her recollections and Willie studied them. At one point, in response to a question from Willie, she even picked up her cell phone and a long-distance calling card, dialed a number in San Sebastián and put Willie on with an old friend of hers, named Amelia Martínez, who had never left.

Willie stayed on the line with Mrs. Martínez for the next fifteen minutes. By then he had what he needed, thanked her, gave Mrs. Sánchez enough money to buy a new calling card, thanked her too and headed home. He then made a quick call to his old friend Frankie Lagos, a Miami P.D. detective he had worked with before he'd turned private investigator. They agreed to a rendezvous the next day.

At that point, Willie poured himself yet another beer and sat on his back porch poring over what Hilda and her friend had told him. All the time he kept considering the man who called himself Norman Cruz. He was still at it when he went to sleep.

ꙅ ꙅ

Willie arrived a few minutes early for his meeting with Cruz. The place was popularly called Domino Park, but it was actually a patio about thirty feet square, surrounded by a black wrought-iron fence and covered with a red tile roof. Under that roof sat tables made of thick plastic and especially constructed for the playing of dominoes. The tables included troughs where each of the four players could line up his or her tiles, out of the sight of opposing players. From those troughs the players would choose a tile and slap it down, extending the line of tiles played in one direction or the other. The new number had to match the number last played. A curling snake of dominoes was created and the first team to expend all its tiles was the winner.

Near noon, the twenty tables were always full. The participants were almost all elderly and almost exclusively men. They played, kibitzed, chewed on cigars and played some more. Those waiting to participate observed the action and offered commentary, adding to the constant hum of conversation in guttural, cigar-smoker Spanish.

At the very back of the patio stood a couple of tables with chessboards imprinted on the surface for anyone who might prefer that game. One of the two tables was empty and Willie sat there, his printed material on the table before him.

A few minutes after noon, Norman Cruz arrived. He sat down across the chess table from Willie, facing the front gate. He was dressed as he had been the night before. Willie couldn't tell if he was carrying his shiv or not.

Cruz peered around the patio.

"I played a lot of dominoes in prison. We had so little to do that I became quite accomplished at the game."

Willie gazed around and then back at Cruz.

"It just so happens that my mother has an acquaintance from San Sebastián."

On the surface, Cruz expressed only mild interest, but behind his gray eyes he was wary. He glanced down at the paperwork lying on the table and at the empty chessboard, as if he were considering a move, then back at Willie.

"Is that so? Well, I doubt very much that I know her. I grew up in a small town in that province but far from the city of San Sebastián. I rarely got there when I was a child and later, the time I spent in the city I was locked up."

Willie stayed fixed on him. "She told me she went to the school right next to the city hall. The building was painted a light green color and white statues stood along the street in front, heroes of the independence war against Spain."

Cruz smiled and shrugged. "I don't really recall."

"Her family ran the movie theater right on the central square. It was called the Athena and had murals of the Greek gods on the walls inside. Everybody went there to see movies made in Mexico and Spain and American movies too."

Cruz was shaking his head. "My family were farmers. We didn't get to the movies."

Willie cocked his head.

"The government took over the theater and later her mother worked as an aide in the government health clinic. It was right next to the old Catholic church."

Cruz convulsed his face in efforts to remember. "I recall that there was a church but that is all."

Willie smiled. "Of course, there was at least one Catholic church in every city in Cuba back then."

Cruz could only shrug. Willie glanced at the chessboard and then back at his opponent in the game of wits.

"Here's something I'm sure you'll remember. This lady told me the prison is on a hill not far from the beach."

Cruz nodded enthusiastically. "Yes, it is."

"And she said the girls used to go to the beach in their bikinis and they would wave and wiggle at the men they could see through the barred windows. The men would whistle back."

Cruz nodded and laughed. "Oh yes. They used to do that all the time."

"That must have driven you men crazy."

Cruz rolled his eyes. "Absolutely. They were very beautiful girls too. They would call to us and strike provocative poses. The idea was to drive us wild. They were terrible."

"I can imagine."

Cruz shook his head at the memories of frustration.

Willie leaned forward, elbows on the table and he squinted at his adversary.

"It's funny that you remember it that way. What the lady actually told me was that the men they waved to at the prison weren't the prisoners, they were the guards in the watchtowers. The prisoners were behind walls. They couldn't see the beach or be seen from there. The only people at the prison who could see the sand were the guards in the surveillance towers. The girls waved to them to taunt them because they'd all had relatives locked up one time or another and hated the guards. They called them cretins, savages and worse. They questioned their manhood."

Cruz had turned to stone, including his gray eyes. He didn't move. Willie whispered at him.

"The name Norman Cruz appears in the list of political prisoners held over the years in San Sebastián. Yesterday I spoke to a woman there, a Mrs. Martínez, whose older brother is now dead, but who was once imprisoned there. She remembered her brother telling her of a prisoner named Norman Cruz who was killed many years ago. He died after trying to escape and being badly beaten by guards. Just as you said, he had no family. His parents were dead and he had no siblings. He was buried with no headstone in a potter's field. There was no one to keep his memory alive. He was forgotten."

The other man's mouth was twitching at the corners. Behind his eyes desperate thoughts dodged one way and another, but still he didn't move. Willie went on.

"You know so much about life in prison not because you were a political prisoner, but because you were a prison guard. You were not one of the heroes, you were one of the villains. Maybe you were one of the guards who beat Norman Cruz to death. When you arrived here you knew you could claim his identity and his standing as a hero. And you've used that to deceive Lydia Estevez in order to lay your hands on her money. You're a fraud, a criminal and possibly a murderer."

Now Cruz placed his palms on the table and started to get up.

"Don't move!" Willie ordered and his right hand fell to his belt. His handgun was holstered there beneath the flap of his shirt.

"You won't shoot me," Cruz muttered.

Willie gazed around the patio and then back. "I don't need to shoot you. All I need to do is shout out, 'This man was a guard in a Cuban political prison.' Some of the men here might have been in such prisons. All of them have relatives or friends who were in them. Maybe some of those loved ones died there. What do you think they'll do if I yell that? Do you think you'll make it to the gate alive?"

Cruz—or whoever the man really was—looked around like a trapped animal. He was sweating now, frightened to his bones. He didn't move.

Willie waved to Frankie Lagos, who was waiting just inside the gate with another officer. They came, quietly read the impostor his rights and charged him with using a false identity to enter the country. Fraud charges might follow. Now the former prison guard really would be a prisoner. He gave Willie one last withering, bitter glance and they led him away.

☙ ☙

Ursula and her family were generous with Willie. It had only taken him a day to ferret out the phony, but they paid for a week. Given the money they had saved, they still came out way ahead.

A few days later, Frankie Lagos contacted him to say the guy had been identified through an old former inmate at the prison. His real name was García and he had, in fact, been a guard at the San Sebastián facility.

"A particularly nasty one at that," Frankie said. "He's locked up and the feds are looking at human rights charges against him."

A few weeks passed and one day Willie ran into Ursula at the park.

"How's your mother?" he asked.

"She's fine. She's gotten over the brief romance without much grief. She said she had already started to dislike things about him."

"Is that so?"

"She said he ate too slow and he would always make her sit with her back to the door. That bugged her."

THE UNDERGROUND MAN

T he plane banked, and private investigator Willie Cuesta gazed down at the gorgeous aquamarine waters off the coast of Miami Beach. He was on his way home after tracking down a runaway husband up in Atlantic City. The sea there had been dark blue and icy cold. Now his eyes fixed on the warm flow of the Gulf Stream below. Whenever he'd been away, he loved coming back to the Caribbean colors of his home waters. He had mentioned that once to his mother.

"Your father and I were both born and raised on the coast of Cuba, always within view of that sea," she said. "You were born here, but you are a child of the Caribbean. Your blood is those colors."

It wasn't, really, but Willie understood the sentiment.

The wheels touched down two minutes later, in twilight, and Willie turned on his phone. In voice mail he found messages from his mother and from his brother Tommy, who owned the popular Latin dance club called Caliente—Hot—where Willie was in charge of security. They were telling him to check in, which he would.

The last message was from Alice Arden, the immigration attorney who often hired Willie to investigate her cases. "*Señor,* I hope your bounty hunting up north went well. Please be in touch as soon as you hit town. I have a client who is in urgent need of your help. I think the case could interest you."

Willie was in his car, leaving the parking garage, when she picked up.

"Cuesta here, Counselor."

"Welcome back, Willie boy. Where are you?" She told him.

"Well, since you're on the road already, why don't you come to my place, drink a beer with me on my balcony and get the lowdown on this new customer?"

Twenty minutes later, Willie pulled up to Alice's low-rise condo building right on the Miami River. She lived on the third floor, facing the water. He was soon sitting on her veranda, sipping an IPA and gazing down at a small, rusty cargo ship heading slowly downriver in the direction of the Caribbean.

Alice was blond, blue-eyed, beautiful and only a few years older than Willie. Right now, she wore a blue tank top and very short, cut-off white jeans. As always, she looked fetching. But she also adhered strictly to a policy of not mixing business with pleasure. Over time, Willie had subtly tried to steer their dealings into more personal channels, to no avail. So, he stuck to business.

"So, tell me about this new client of yours. What's his story? Or is it a she?"

"No, it's a he. Let me see, where do I begin?" She crossed her long, elegant, bare legs and then fixed on Willie. "My client was trained as a mining engineer. He then became a master builder of tunnels, which were used to break political prisoners out of Latin American prisons. He engineered some of the biggest and boldest jailbreaks in the history of the hemisphere. Does he sound interesting enough for you?"

Willie whistled. "That's quite a résumé. Tell me more."

Alice sipped her suds. "The gentleman in question comes from Uruguay. You know where that is, right?"

"Yes, it's just south of Brazil."

"Exactly. Just like many other Latin countries, in the 1960s and 70s movements sprang up in Uruguay to fight poverty. They went into poor neighborhoods, set up soup kitchens, education programs and also did political organizing. In most cases, there was no violence of any variety. But military leaders decided the groups were Communist fronts, started to round up members, put them in prison and, in some cases, to torture them and kill them. This led other activists to take up arms, a guerrilla war erupted, blood was spilled on both sides and even more people were imprisoned."

Alice was pretty much encyclopedic about the contemporary history of Latin America. She had represented immigration clients from almost every country in the hemisphere and had heard many tales of terror. She sipped more beer, brushed the suds from her lovely lips and continued.

"Like I said, those same conflicts arose in countries all over Latin America back then, with the same bloody results. What distinguished the Uruguayan insurgents was a particular skill they developed, a skill that created headlines around Latin America and the world."

"Tunnel digging? Like *The Great Escape?*"

"Exactly, but they operated in Latin America, not in Europe, like the World War Two prisoners of war in that movie. Their two biggest jailbreaks came within a short period of time. Twice in the space of a few months they dug secret passageways—first into a men's facility and later into a prison where many of their female members were being held. Altogether, more than a hundred of their members went free. The government was grossly embarrassed. The international press had a field day. But right after that, the military cracked down on the groups and they had to go way underground. Many of them were killed. Some others managed to make it out of the country. My client, who was a master tunnel digger, is one of those."

"And he arrived here?"

"No, not right away. He worked for several other clandestine groups in other countries, helping to free prisoners, until he finally decided that life was just too dangerous. That's when he came here. That was almost twenty years ago. Since then, he has worked in construction, specializing in laying water pipes, cable lines and other underground systems. He has used his engineering skills here and done well for himself. In other words, he's been digging tunnels, but without the legal issues."

Willie shrugged. "So, what's the problem? That sounds like honest work."

"It is. The trouble is that recently he was recognized by some people who are involved in work that is not at all honest. They specialize in robbing jewelry stores, and they are blackmailing him into participating in their next job by using his tunneling skills."

Willie frowned. "Why doesn't he go to the police?"

"Because he's been living in this country under a false name, which is enough to get him deported. On top of that, he has all those years collaborating with clandestine groups down south, which even now won't make the State Department happy. They'll deport him in a Miami minute. He has a wife and kids here and he doesn't want to be thrown out of the country."

Willie didn't argue with Alice on questions of immigration law. The fellow was in a fix. But Willie had his doubts about taking the case.

"Is he the sort of guy we should be helping? An individual who initiated prison breaks."

Alice shrugged. "Most of the people he broke out of jail were not armed militants. The armed ones ended up dead. The prisoners were only locked up because the government didn't like their ideas. If somebody locks me up because of what I think someday, I hope someone like him is around to find a way to get me out. And he's kept his nose clean here for two decades. So, I have no trouble trying to help him."

Willie couldn't argue with that either. And he needed the work.

"What's this guy's name."

"Here he goes by Roberto Corvo. That's all you need to know."

"And what is it you want me to do?"

"We need somehow to dissuade these bad guys from forcing Roberto to participate in the heist. They have threatened to turn him over to immigration authorities if he doesn't take part. You need to keep them from doing that as well. And since this caper is planned for about thirty-six hours from now, you have to move quickly."

Willie stifled a chuckle. "And just how am I supposed to accomplish all that?"

Alice Arden beamed at him. "I have no idea, but Willie Cuesta is the most persuasive, inventive, brilliant private investigator I know. You'll think of something."

Willie rolled his eyes. "Flattery will get you everywhere, *amiga*."

He sipped his beer and watched the river flow by.

☙ ☙

Alice called her client and he and Willie arranged to meet at nine p.m. that same evening. They didn't have time to lose. Corvo chose an all-night Cuban coffee stand called Conchita's Café, right on SW Eighth Street, the main drag of Little Havana. Willie knew it well. It was a place he had frequented during his days as a third-shift patrol cop on the Miami PD. When it was three a.m. and you still had four hours of policing to do in that neighborhood, it was the place to go. He still stopped there for a pick-me-up from time to time.

"It's also right near the jewelry store they want to rob," Corvo said over the phone. "I'll be able to show you the place."

Conchita's featured archways decorated with traditional Spanish tile facing the street. Willie arrived first, parked and took a stool at the outdoor counter, just as he always did. The small open-kitchen area was stuffed with espresso machines, juicers, blenders to make Cuban smoothies, a narrow griddle and glass cases that held Cuban pastries.

The waitress behind the counter, a hefty, boisterous, middle-aged lady named Blanca, had been there for years. She put a *café con leche* in front of him without even asking, as she always did, and spoke to him in Spanish.

"How are we, Willie? Working?"

"Maybe, Blanca. We'll see what happens."

Corvo showed up a few minutes later and climbed onto the next stool. Willie saw right away how the new client might have become a master tunnel rat. Swarthy and hollow-cheeked, with wavy black hair, he was no more than five feet three inches tall, narrow-shouldered and wiry. On top of that, when Willie reached out to shake hands he found that Corvo had paws that were large for a man his size and, if his grip was any indication, they were very strong. He had the strength to wield a pick and shovel and if he had encountered underground obstructions while tunneling—rocks, roots, whatever—he had the large claws to deal with them.

Blanca knew him too and put a Cuban coffee in front of him. Corvo glanced both ways down the street, wary about who might be around, then turned to Willie.

"Ms. Arden says you may be able to help me," he said in a near whisper.

Willie shrugged. "I can try, but first I need to know exactly how you got into this trouble."

Corvo's face stormed over at Willie's words.

"I didn't do anything to create this mess. I have a female acquaintance here, a former lover also from Uruguay, who knows my history. For years, she said nothing to nobody, but one night, with a few drinks in her, she said some things she shouldn't have said about my past. Don't ask me how that story spread, and how it reached the wrong people, but about a week ago I get a knock on my door. It was a man I'd never met before and he was the one who proposed this robbery."

Willie sipped his coffee. "Who is this individual?"

"He goes by the name of Oscar Robles. At least that's what he told me. He's a Cuban, one of those who came over here years ago when Fidel Castro decided to empty his prisons and send his criminals here to Miami."

Corvo was talking about the early 1980s, when tens of thousands of ordinary Cubans fled the Communist island in a massive boatlift engineered by Cuban exiles in Miami. Castro took advantage of that exodus to open his prisons and escort common criminals to the docks, so they could emigrate as well. It was his revenge against Miami. For the next few years, those criminal elements caused havoc for law enforcement in South Florida, involving themselves in the drug trade, prostitution, extortion and other crimes. Many had ended up in prison stateside. Others turned up dead, having killed each other off in turf wars. They were a nasty bunch.

Willie drank it in, along with his coffee.

"So, this Robles character survived all that old mayhem and is still committing crimes."

"That's right. He and a partner of his named Solís, another old Cuban criminal, specialize in committing burglaries on jewelry stores and private homes. The target this time is a store right here in Little Havana."

"And they want you to help them tunnel in?"

Corvo nodded somberly. "Exactly."

Willie frowned. "Where in Miami can anybody possibly dig a tunnel? The water table here is so high, so near the surface of the earth, that nobody even has a basement. You'll be tunneling through water."

Corvo held up one thick index finger. "Yes, that is true for ninety-nine percent of the buildings and private homes in this county. We deal with that in my job, laying pipe and electrical conduits. But there are a few areas that are slightly more above sea level and these gangsters managed to locate a jewelry store operating in one of those areas. In fact, the store owner took advantage of the solid ground underneath his place of business to create a cellar where he stores all his valuable pieces when he is closed."

"How did these gangsters get ahold of that information?"

"Robles has a contact in the county construction department, and he has blueprints of that building."

Willie whistled. "That's quite a contact."

"Yes, it is. The guy will get a cut of the job," Corvo said.

"So, they are willing to divide the take four ways, including you."

The little man smirked. "I don't believe for a second that these Cubans would ever cut me in. I think the moment they have their hands on the jewels, I get bashed in the head with a shovel and left for the police to find."

Willie winced. He himself was Cuban, and Corvo was talking about his people. But Willie knew the old tunnel jockey was probably right. Those old Cuban gangsters could get greedy and grisly.

"So where is this robbery supposed to happen?"

Corvo pointed west down Eighth Street—known locally as Calle Ocho.

"It's about ten blocks that way. I'll show you."

They drained their coffees and Corvo climbed in with Willie. Calle Ocho is the commercial lifeline of Little Havana. Except for Conchita's, a bar or two and a few "love motels," most of the businesses on that stretch were closed by that hour. The traffic was light.

They passed individual businesses and also strip malls. The jewelry store in question was located in one of those small malls. Corvo had Willie pull over about a hundred feet short of the place and across the street. They parked and turned off the lights.

"There it is, on the first floor."

The collection of stores was two stories high, a half-block long, and crammed with about twenty small businesses. Little Havana was an immigrant neighborhood and the variety of storefronts reflected that. One slot was occupied by an immigration attorney; another sold cellular phones and long-distance calling cards with special rates to Latin America. The locales included a Cuban bakery, a Nicaraguan lunch counter, a Korean nail salon and a tattoo parlor that advertised "Ink in All Languages."

Near the far end of the first floor was the jewelry store in question: Joyeros El Rey—or The King's Jewelers. It was narrow, with a grate pulled across the windows and a glass door. A ragged banner sagged from the eave and trumpeted in Spanish: "We Buy Gold and Old Jewelry." Despite the name, it certainly didn't look very royal. Willie said as much to Corvo.

"Yes, but it turns out that guy does very good business. His family owned a jewelry store in Havana before the revolution there, and many of the old Cuban families come to him to sell jewels when they get in financial trouble."

Willie gazed at the place with a new appreciation. Corvo pointed in that direction.

"Now look at the place right next to it."

It was a locale about twice as wide as the jewelry store, with no grate to protect it. Imprinted in gold lettering across the large window was "Iglesia de Dios Pentecostal."

"A Pentecostal church," Willie said.

"Exactly," said Corvo, "and that is an important part of the criminal plan."

Willie's eyebrows twitched. "Really. How's that?"

"The jewelry store is closed on Sundays and Mondays. The church has services Sunday most of the day, but then sits empty Monday and Tuesday. The plan is to break into the church after services Sunday night and tunnel from there down into the cellar of the jeweler. They will have all night Sunday and all day Monday, until Tuesday morning when the jeweler opens again, to finish the job."

Willie studied the place as if he himself were casing it out for a criminal act. He noticed that the windows of the church had no curtains. Anyone could see right in.

"Once they are in there, how will the bad guys keep from being seen by other people using the strip mall?"

Corvo pointed. "Pull up in front for a moment. I'll show you."

Willie did as asked, with his lights still off, and stopped right in front of the church. It was a room about thirty feet square, filled with folding chairs. At the front stood a slightly elevated stage with a podium on it. A drum set stood off to one side, along with several music stands. On the back wall hung a plain wooden cross about a yard tall.

"Look just to the left of the cross," Corvo said. "Do you see the outline of a door there?"

Willie said he did.

"That leads to a narrow storage area in the back of the building. A back door there gives onto the alleyway behind. The plan to is break in through that outside door and do all the work there in that confined space. They won't be seen from either the front or the rear. And on the other side of that alleyway is a vacant lot, so nothing will be heard there either."

Willie pulled out and headed back to the coffee bar.

"How do they know about that storage area?"

"Because they've already broken in once. They have even attended the services there, Robles and Solís. They've pretended to be believers just to get the lay of the land."

Willie shook his head. What the criminal class of Miami wouldn't do to pull a job. He could just see the crooks feigning piety while they sized up the property.

They arrived back at the coffee bar and parked. Corvo fixed on Willie, his face bathed in worry.

"What do you think you can do to help me, Mr. Cuesta? We only have hours."

Willie squinted into the darkness. "We have to somehow foil the job without them suspecting that it was you who spilled the beans. If they think that, they'll rat you out to the feds."

Corvo nodded bleakly.

"I'll have to think this out," Willie said. "Do you know where this Robles lives, or the other guy?"

Corvo shook his head. "No, they have always come to my house, or we have met in a public place. But I do know Robles plans to come to the church tomorrow during the services, just to make sure there is no change in the weekly schedule of the devotions. They need to know that no one else will be there Sunday night and Monday. One of them will come to pick me up and take me there tomorrow night."

"What do they look like, this duo?"

Corvo described the two men in detail. Willie scribbled it all in his notebook.

"Do they carry weapons when they work? Did they tell you anything about that?"

Corvo shook his head. "Robles told me they never carry guns."

Willie studied that statement. He knew this was almost certainly true. He had dealt with lots of break-and-entry pros during his days as a cop. Professional burglars always avoided firearms because if they got caught armed they would be facing much, much more prison time. If they got caught carrying guns, they could kiss ten or twenty years goodbye, depending on their priors. These Cubans sounded like pros. He turned back to the tunnel rat.

"Okay. Go home but meet me here tomorrow just before the ten a.m. church service. We need to do some surveillance of our own. Hopefully I can figure out how to handle this."

Corvo inquired about payment and Willie cited him a day rate down near the bottom of his scale. The small man thanked him profusely.

"You're saving my life, Mr. Cuesta." Then he climbed out and disappeared into the darkness.

Willie sat without moving for several minutes. He only wished he was as confident as Roberto Corvo.

☙ ☙

Willie went home, poured himself a beer and pored over his problem. How to foil the burglary without leaving Corvo at the mercy of his Cuban criminal colleagues. He went to bed that night without anything close to an answer.

The next morning, he shaved, showered and dressed in a sports jacket with dress slacks. A short while later, he was parked across from the church with Corvo at his side. They gazed through Willie's tinted windows as worshipers filed in for the morning service. They were single people, couples, families, mostly Hispanic. They were all dressed in their finest Sunday duds.

It was just before the ten a.m. starting time that a car pulled into the parking lot and a man in late middle age emerged. Corvo poked Willie.

"That's him. That's Robles."

He was of medium height, thin, slope-shouldered, bald on top but with a three-day beard and horn-rimmed glasses. Like Corvo, he was narrow, constructed to operate in tight spaces. He wore a dark blue knit shirt and black pants. Maybe, being a burglar, he only owned dark clothes. Or maybe not, but that was his current outfit.

They watched as he entered the church and took a folding chair in the last row.

"I'm going in," Willie said. "You get behind the wheel. If he comes out before I can get back here, you follow him and find out where he lives. Then come back for me."

The small man nodded confidently. He was once again involved in clandestine action after a long time of following the straight and narrow.

Willie crossed the street, passed through the glass door of the church and stood at the back. From there he had a clear view of Mr. Robles, or whatever his real name was, who was seated in the back row.

The pastor was just stepping up behind the pulpit. He was a husky, white-haired Latin man with mahogany skin, wearing a baby-blue suit the color of the heavens. A three-man band was positioned behind him to one side—drums, organ, guitar. The musicians swung into a rousing religious number in Spanish, invoking the glories of the Promised Land.

The pastor put his Bible down on the pulpit and began to sing and clap. His congregation joined in enthusiastically. Moments later, the pastor went to the back of the stage, opened the door there, reached into the storage area, brought out a tambourine and fell into the rhythm of the music. If you weren't wide awake when you walked in, you soon would be.

Willie watched Robles out of the corner of his eye. The jewel thief was not singing or clapping, but only staring at the still-open door and the view it afforded of his future work space behind the stage. His hooded eyes were fixed on it. The only Promised Land he was interested in, apparently, was where he might fly with his profits from the burglary. He stayed staring until one of the musicians closed the door again.

The worshipers continued to sing and were soon waving their hands above their heads in jubilation. An older woman standing next to Robles beamed at him ecstatically, her extended arms lifted toward the skies. Robles responded with a crimped smile and lifted his arms as high as his shoulders, waving his hands minimally. But there was no sign on his solemn countenance that the spirit had entered him. He was casing the place, pure and simple.

When the song ended, the pastor swung into his sermon, a soaring summons to faith. He strutted the stage and waved the Bible above his head, shaking one Biblical verse after another out of it to support his arguments. He had the rousing style of a revival preacher and his listeners chimed in regularly with calls of "Yes, Jesus! Yes, Lord!" Robles was unmoved. He studied the space around him, maybe searching for an alarm he had overlooked.

The band swung into another hymn and this time some of those who were particularly taken by the spirit danced before the stage—strutting, trembling, contorting their bodies as if possessed. They shouted, "Hallelujah," and a couple spoke in unintelligible tongues. Willie found himself transfixed. It was an exercise in abandoning inhibitions and it was wild. When he glanced at Robles, he found the old criminal frowning. He obviously didn't approve of the spectacle before him. Burglars had to be precise, painstaking, methodical, contained. Religious transport wasn't to his taste. A minute later the ushers passed the wicker collection baskets and Robles let it go by without contributing, not even a nickel.

After Communion and another song, the pastor announced the schedule for that week's services. Sunday worship would end around eight p.m. and the next prayer meeting would not be until Wednesday. He then swung into some final sermonizing. But it was clear that Robles had heard all he needed. He quietly slipped from his row and out the door. Willie tracked him as he climbed back into his car and drove away. Behind by a few lengths was Corvo, doing a credible job of tailing him.

Willie stayed where he was, waiting for Corvo to come back while the congregation sang. It was while he stood there, half listening to the singing, half ruminating on his case, that an answer to Corvo's problem occurred to him. It was as if he had been touched by the spirit—the private-eye spirit. He stared at the back wall of the church, as if he could see right through it into that storage space where it would all happen.

It was a risky solution, and just the thought of it made him recoil at first. If Robles and his partner did, in fact, carry guns, then it could all go to hell fast. The success of his plan would depend on the burglars being professionals—a calculated risk, but he could think of no other way. And he told himself that even if they did travel armed, he would have the drop on them, not the other way around. He didn't know Roberto Corvo much at all, but he liked him and sympathized with him. And he found Robles and his blackmailing of the little man reprehensible. With only hours before the burglars swung into action, Willie decided to take his chances.

Moments later he saw Corvo pull up in the car across the street. Willie slipped discreetly out of the church and climbed in.

"Were you able to follow him?"

Corvo nodded. "Yes. They are living in a rooming house in East Little Havana. I saw them both there."

Willie nodded. "Good work. Meanwhile, I think I've found a solution to your problem."

Corvo eyes widened expectantly. "What is it?"

"Right now, you are the one who is afraid of them, aren't you?" Willie asked. "Afraid that they will ruin your life."

Corvo nodded warily.

"Well, by the time tonight is over, they will be afraid of you, my friend. To the point that they will never bother you again."

Corvo appeared incredulous. "How does that happen?"

"I'll explain," Willie said. "Just drive."

☙ ☙

It was just before eight o'clock that night and Willie sat on a dark side street staking out the church. He wore his old dark-blue uniform pants from the Miami PD and a windbreaker of the same color with no markings. Next to him on the seat sat his old uniform hat, but without the badge. If the plan went awry, he didn't want to be charged with impersonating an officer.

The last service of the day had just concluded. Under the fluorescent lights that illuminated the sanctuary, Willie could see the pastor, in his sky-blue suit, shaking hands with the last worshipers to leave. Willie waited, biding his time.

After leaving the church that morning, he and Corvo had driven back to Willie's place. It was there that Willie explained his plan. As expected, Corvo had freaked at first. Willie had to admit that the scheme sounded scary. But he explained the mechanics of it, especially the fact that he and Corvo would know what was coming, while the two Cuban burglars wouldn't.

"You have a choice," Willie told him. "You can try to escape them, which will mean uprooting your family and living on the run. You can do what they want you to do—commit grand theft—and risk having them turn you in, or you can do what I'm proposing. And you have only hours to decide."

Corvo, a man who had participated in dangerous, clandestine operations in his youth, eventually accepted that he would have to take the risk in order to escape his plight.

Now, Willie waited. He watched the pastor turn out the lights, lock the front glass doors and drive away. The entire mini-mall was now dead quiet.

Willie hid the hat under the windbreaker and stuck a flashlight in his pocket. Tucked in his back holster was his handgun, but he hoped like hell he wouldn't have to fire it. He got out, walked around the block and approached the church through the rear alleyway. He had taken the same route that afternoon, when no one was watching, and he had found that the empty lot directly behind the church featured thick bushes separating it from the alleyway. It was pitch dark and dead quiet there. Willie tucked himself into those bushes, where no one could see him, and waited some more.

It was a full hour later that he saw headlights on the side road that skirted the mini-mall. He heard a car approach slowly, the lights were doused and the engine killed. A minute later three silhouettes appeared at the head of the alleyway. He picked out Corvo, the smallest, and Robles, slim but slightly taller. The third man would be Solís. Willie couldn't see his face, but he was stockier than the other two. Willie figured Robles employed him just in case he required muscle to dig and to move whatever might need to be moved. Robles and Solís carried what appeared to be duffel bags, probably holding picks and shovels.

The three moved quickly and arrived at the back door of the church. Robles went to work on the lock while the other two kept watch. Willie, hidden no more than twenty feet from them, didn't move a muscle.

The church's security was no match for the career criminal. Robles picked the lock in a matter of a minute. The three men passed through the door into the storage space and closed it behind them. Willie saw only the faintest line of light appear beneath the door. Minutes later, he heard, just barely, the sound of a pick hitting concrete.

He had told Corvo he would commence the plan exactly at that moment and he did. What happened next all happened extremely quickly. Willie put on his hat, took out the flashlight, turned it on, crossed the alleyway and entered the storage area. It held a large old wooden cross, some music stands, folding chairs and, on a shelf, spare hymnals.

The three of them were all crouched at the end that abutted the jewelry store. A small electric lantern illuminated them. Willie pointed his flashlight at them nonetheless.

"Security here. What are you doing?" he said.

Robles and Solís were both shocked into immobility. But Corvo responded just as he and Willie had planned. He reached under his dark windbreaker, pulled out a handgun with a silencer on it, pointed it at Willie's chest and pulled off three quick rounds. Willie grunted, staggered, dropped his flashlight and fell hard to the ground. With his cheek pressed against the cement floor he could see through squinted eyes from under the bill of his cap.

Robles and Solís stayed frozen for another two counts, their faces gripped in horror. Then Robles turned on Corvo and exploded in a seething whisper.

"What are you, crazy? I told you no guns."

Corvo responded with ice in his voice. "I've been in prison. I'm not going back."

The big man, Solís, started to move toward Willie, but Corvo barked at him, pointing the gun. "Don't go near him."

But Solís paid him no heed. He wasn't going to check on Willie, he was heading for the hills. He ran through the back door, with Robles right behind him. Willie heard them sprinting back down the alleyway. Corvo went to the open door and watched. Moments later Willie heard the car start and the screech of tires as they tore away.

"They're gone," Corvo said. He closed the door to keep the light from spilling out.

Willie stood up. His shirt exhibited no bullet holes, no blood. He reached for the gun equipped with the silencer—loaded with blanks—and Corvo handed it to him. Moments later they had shoved the tools into the duffel bags, extinguished the lantern and locked the door behind them. The only sign that anyone had been there was a slight chip in the concrete and Willie covered that with the spare cross.

Ten minutes later they were back at Willie's place. Willie sipped a beer. Corvo was still shaking too much to hold a glass.

"You understand that those two guys will never bother you again," Willie said. "Together you committed a burglary that resulted in a murder. That's what they think. As far as they know, they are facing the death penalty. Not only will they never approach you again, I will be very surprised if they don't get out of Miami altogether, and quick. I'll bet they head to New York or Los Angeles, some other place where Cubans are found in numbers. They are now much, much more afraid of you than you will ever have to be of them. And we did it all without spilling a drop of blood, or even waking anyone up."

Corvo nodded like a hummingbird, still all nerves.

"The one thing we must agree on is not to tell Alice Arden what happened tonight," Willie said. "She would kill me if she found out." Corvo agreed.

The next day, Corvo settled with Willie for his services, throwing in a bit extra as a bonus. Willie folded the check into his wallet. Then just to make sure, he went to the rooming house Corvo had identified, where Robles and Solís had been staying. He found the owner, an older lady in a housedress with a disgruntled expression.

"Oh, those two," she said. "They left their room in the middle of the night without a word. They owed me a week's back rent—and they stole the clock radio too. The rats!"

THE LOVERS OF TRABER

T he town of Traber is located southeast of Tampa in the midst of tomato fields that stretch as far as the eye can see. Private investigator Willie Cuesta, who called Miami home, had driven all morning to reach it. He cut across the Everglades in the early hours of the day, greeting the egrets, herons, alligators and other habitués of the great swamp. Just short of Naples he swung north and headed into farm country, which in Florida tended to be fertile, flat—and even flatter. Four hours after leaving home, he cruised down the two-lane blacktop that brought one into Traber.

On either side of the treeless road he saw acre after acre of tomato plants, arranged in super-straight rows that ran like rail lines to the horizon. It was spring, harvest time, the leafy plants had grown waist high on their stakes and were hung with bright green tomatoes. Here and there amid all that green, Willie saw a splash of color. Those were teams of tomato pickers who wore wide straw hats and also various layers of clothing to insulate themselves against the dehydrating sun. They preferred bright colors, especially red, maybe so they could find each other easily in the fields thick with plants. From a distance they looked like flocks of birds, maybe cardinals or macaws, feasting on the crop.

Willie continued down the road until eventually the tomato fields ended and he encountered houses. It was the second house that interested him, a large, three-story, white clapboard place with green shutters, a structure that resembled an old plantation manse. Willie followed the semicircular driveway and found his friend Francisca González Camp waiting for him on the front steps.

"Willie, ¿cómo estás?" she said and wrapped her arms around him.

They had grown up together on the streets of Little Havana. While Willie had stayed, Francisca had gone off to the University of Florida to study education and had never come back to the Cuban barrio to live.

In her junior year she brought home a boyfriend to meet the family, a farmer's son named Fred Camp who was majoring in agrobusiness. The next time Willie saw Francisca she held out her hand, which was weighed down by a large engagement bauble.

"Look, Willie, the redneck gave me a ring."

She called Fred that in fun, even though his neck really was rosy in color.

Willie had attended the wedding but had seen his old friend only sparingly over the next two decades, on Francisca's occasional visits to her family. So, he had been surprised to answer the phone the day before and hear her voice.

"I have a nasty problem on my hands, and I need your help, Willie."

She preferred not to discuss it over the phone and assured Willie that she and Fred would pay him for the time it took to make the trip. Willie said he wouldn't take a dime from her but would be there as early as possible the next day.

Now she escorted him into her living room, which featured Colonial-era furniture, Audubon prints on the walls and large rear windows overlooking the family farm. Moments later, Fred entered and greeted Willie solemnly, even grimly. He was a lean, square-shouldered man, with a face burnt and furrowed by the sun and a head of reddish-blond hair.

Willie knew he had a dry sense of humor and there was usually a glimmer of it in his green eyes. But that glint wasn't in evidence now.

Fred offered Willie an easy chair and he and Francisca sat on the sofa. She poured unsweetened iced tea and then did the talking.

"I called you because we have a serious problem with our daughter, Susanna. She's twenty-one and she's taken up with a young man who works for us. They got engaged three months ago and the plan was for them to marry in the fall."

Willie sipped his tea. "Who's the lucky fellow?"

"His name is Fernando Ortiz. He's originally from Mexico, came to the United States as a migrant farmworker about seven years ago, started here with us, worked very hard, learned English, and is now keeping the books for the company."

Willie shrugged. "Sounds like he's making a success of himself."

Francisca nodded once. "On top of that, he's taking courses in business administration at the local college. He plans to get a degree as soon as possible. He's also attractive and polite. There's only one problem."

"What's that?"

"Apparently he's already married."

Fred, who'd sat quietly until then, suddenly stirred and spoke up.

"Apparently nothing. The woman has all kinds of proof. He's a married man. He wants to marry Susanna just so he can qualify for citizenship. He's a fraud."

Willie looked from Fred back to Francisca.

"What woman is that?"

"A week ago, a woman showed up here," Francisca said. "Her name is María Valdez and she said she had just arrived from Mexico, looking for her husband, Fernando Ortiz. She had a little girl with her who she says is Fernando's daughter. She's six years old and her name is Teresa."

Fred looked at Willie fiercely. "He abandoned a wife and child in Mexico and wanted to marry our daughter. He's lucky I haven't put a slug in him."

Francisca grabbed Fred's arm to calm him down. Willie sipped his tea.

"What happened after they showed up?"

Francisca turned back to him. "We summoned Fernando and confronted him with her."

"And?"

"And he denied it all. He said he'd never seen this María Valdez before, had never been married, and had no children."

Willie shrugged. "So, it was her word against his. You don't even know her, while he's been a trusted employee for some time."

Fred jumped to his feet. "Not exactly. She presented proof."

He crossed to a roll-top desk against the far wall, grabbed two pieces of paper and presented them to Willie, who read them over.

"She has the originals. I made copies."

Both documents bore the seal of the city of Veracruz in Mexico. The first was a marriage certificate that stated that Fernando Ortiz Grijalbo had wed María Valdez Juárez on May 15, 2007. The second document, a birth certificate dated six months later, announced the arrival of a baby girl to the same couple. Her name was Teresa.

To Willie, who had seen his share of documents from Latin countries during his days on the Miami police force, they looked legitimate enough.

"What did Fernando say when the woman produced these?"

Fred was still standing. "He admitted he was from Veracruz but insisted she was lying and that the documents were fakes. Just then our daughter, Susanna, showed up, heard what was going on and took his side."

Suddenly, behind Willie, another voice was heard. A female voice.

"And I still do. Fernando is not that woman's husband and he's not the father of that child."

Willie turned and saw Susanna. He hadn't seen her in at least six or seven years. And in that time she had turned into an extremely lovely young woman. She had long, lustrous auburn hair, her father's green eyes and her mother's skin, which was as white as dogwood flowers. Willie had no trouble understanding why a young Mexican man, or any man for that matter, might want to marry her.

Fred frowned at her. "We asked you not to interfere with this meeting."

"So you could fill this man full of lies about Fernando. Well, I'm going to marry him anyway, no matter what you say."

"Not if he's married already, young lady. It won't be legal."

Susanna stormed out again. Francisca's gaze followed her, full of a mother's grief. It broke Willie's heart to see her anguish. Fred's face, on the other hand, had hardened into something resembling stone. He looked down at Willie.

"What we want you to do is prove to our daughter that this man is deceiving her."

Francisca stood up and faced her husband. "That's not what we want at all," she said. "We want to find out the truth, whatever it is."

Willie stood up as well, which put him between them. There was strain in the relationship that Willie didn't recall seeing before, but he didn't know them that well. Fred walked out without saying another word. Again, Francisca's face fell.

"Where do I find Fernando?" Willie asked.

She pointed farther down the road. "He lives about a half-mile that way, in a small white house we own. Fred wanted to throw him out, but I convinced him if he did Fernando would leave town, Susanna would follow and we would lose her altogether."

"And the woman who arrived? María Valdez?"

"She's staying at a trailer park where many of the local tomato pickers live. Past Fernando's house about a mile you'll see a dirt road to the right. She told us she's staying with friends there."

Willie headed for the door and Francisca followed.

"Please, help me figure this out, Willie, before it tears my family apart."

Willie squeezed her arm and said he would do what he could.

ﾟ) ﾟ)

He climbed back into his car and continued down the road until the large houses ended and he saw the white cottage Francisca had mentioned. An aging white pickup was parked in the driveway.

Willie walked up to the front door, found it open. Through the screen he peeked in and saw a young man who he assumed was Fernando Ortiz propped in a chair facing a television set. But it wasn't on and he was staring into nothing. He didn't notice anyone at his door at first, affording Willie the chance to give him the once-over.

As Francisca had said, he was a good-looking guy—mid to late twenties, slim, café au lait skin, curly black hair. He was in a white T-shirt and jeans and looked clean cut, well groomed. At the moment he appeared very serious, solemn, but that was understandable given the way his plans had come undone in recent days.

Willie knocked lightly on the door. That brought Ortiz out of his chair quickly and he hurried to the door. He stopped abruptly the moment he spotted Willie. It was clear he had expected someone else—probably someone named Susanna. His expression turned suspicious.

"Yes, what do you want?" he asked in accented English.

"Are you Fernando Ortiz?"

"That's right."

"My name is Willie Cuesta and I'm a friend of Mr. and Mrs. Camp."

That made Ortiz's mouth turn down and his dark brown eyes narrowed into a squint. Willie held up his hands and spoke in Spanish.

"Listen, I have nothing against you, amigo. I'm just trying to discover the truth. I want to talk to you."

Ortiz hesitated, but then opened the screen door and let Willie in. The small, one-story house was plainly and neatly furnished. Ledgers lay on a wooden desk in the corner. Ortiz offered Willie the one stuffed chair while he sat in the hard-backed wooden chair just feet away.

"If you want the truth, it's this," he said. "I have never seen this woman María Valdez in my life before this week."

He stopped and stared into Willie's face, allowing Willie to search for any lies behind the eyes. There was nothing but anger there now, no obvious lies.

"And you have never been married?"

"Never."

"And you have no child that you know of?"

"None."

"Why would this woman say these things? Why would she make all these accusations?"

"I have no idea." His tone remained tough, but Willie thought he saw a slight shifting in the gaze.

"Are you sure she has no reason to say these things?"

Ortiz got up and stalked the room. "Yes, I'm sure. I've never done anything to her."

"I understand she's from Veracruz, same as you."

"She says she is, but I never met her there. It's a big city. Many people live there. I don't know them all and that includes her."

His pacing seemed to reflect not only his anger but a desire to escape a situation that made no sense. Not to Willie, nor to himself. But he couldn't escape it, no matter how much he stalked.

Willie stood up. "You're a young man. Maybe you made a mistake once. If you do the right thing now, if you tell the truth, it can still come out right. Susanna loves you."

Ortiz whirled and scowled at Willie.

"I'm telling the truth," he shouted.

He stalked to the screen door, opened it and held it that way. Willie went through it.

He walked to his car and headed for the trailer park. He found it where Francisca said he would, a mile down that road bordered by tomato fields. If Fernando Ortiz's cottage was a comedown from the Camps' house, the trailer park was another large step down Traber's social ladder. In fact, it had to be at the bottom.

A narrow, unpaved road left the main thoroughfare, cut through some stunted trees and low brush, opening into a clearing that accommodated about two dozen trailers. Weeds grew between them and rainwater, from an out-of-season downpour, sat in puddles and sustained the mosquito population. Clothing sagged on lines between the trailers, much of it kids' clothes. Some of the Latino kids they belonged to played here and there on the grounds. The trailers were in various degrees of dilapidation—dented, rusted— and old cars parked outside some of them matched the trailers. A few of the inhabitants apparently hadn't gone to work that day. Work shoes and plastic buckets used for picking tomatoes sat next to the stairs of a few units.

Willie drove into the clearing, careful not to splash the kids. He stopped next to the first group and spoke in Spanish.

"Do you know a woman named María Valdez? She came to live here a few days ago with her daughter, Teresa."

The kids all turned in unison and pointed at a pretty, ponytailed girl of about seven, dressed in denim overalls, who stood among them.

"That's her," the biggest of them said.

The girl grew embarrassed at the attention.

"Can you take me to your mother?" Willie asked in Spanish.

The girl hesitated and Willie shook his head.

"Don't worry, I'm not the *migra*," he said, using the common slang for immigration agents.

The girl turned and trotted off toward a rear trailer. Willie got out of his car and followed. A young woman sat on the front steps of the trailer staring warily as Willie approached. The little girl led him to her.

The woman wore blue shorts and a yellow halter top. She was dark-skinned, black-haired, curvaceous, wore bright red lipstick and was probably in her early twenties, although her stern expression made her appear older. Her eyes were slightly slanted and that gave her an exotic, indigenous look. Willie noticed that the little girl resembled her and didn't really look much like Fernando. If push came to shove, the Camps could use DNA testing to settle the question at hand, but that would take time and would probably tick off Susanna even more.

"Excuse me, are you María Valdez?" Willie asked in Spanish.

She nodded but said nothing.

Willie introduced himself. "I'm a friend of Mr. and Mrs. Camp and am here to ask about your relationship with Fernando Ortiz. Can you tell me where you first met him?"

María Valdez wasn't very anxious to speak to Willie. She looked as if she was about to jump up, duck into the trailer and lock the door behind her. But she held her ground.

"I met him in Veracruz. Our families are both from there."

"I see. When was it you met him? What year?"

That threw her for a moment. "I don't know."

"Think. Was it seven years ago? Eight? How old were you?"

Computation was not her forte. It made her eyes fidget.

"I was fifteen or sixteen."

"I see. And where was it you saw each other the first time?"

She frowned and fell silent. Willie softened his tone.

"Don't tell me you don't remember," he said. "Women always remember when they first saw the man they love. It was in Veracruz, but was it near the port, in the cafés downtown where they play the marimbas?"

María Valdez's eyes grew very wide. She was surprised he knew so much about Veracruz. While he was with the Miami P.D. Willie had once traveled there on an extradition case and he recalled just enough to impress her. But she still wasn't talking.

"Or did you meet him on Vallarta Beach?" Willie asked. "That's where most of the young *veracruzanos* I know meet each other."

She nodded tentatively, but still said nothing. Willie rested a foot on the stair of the trailer.

"Why don't you name a friend of his for me, someone you both knew back in Veracruz. Maybe that will be easier."

Her eyes brightened.

"Martín," she said. "Martín Mendoza."

He had finally asked a question she could answer. Willie did not believe for a moment that she had known Fernando Ortiz back in Veracruz. To begin, there was no Vallarta Beach there. The strip of sand where young people gathered was called Copacabana Beach. But she and Fernando might have a connection to this man Mendoza, and that could explain why she was lying.

"Where is this Mendoza now?" he asked. "Is he in Mexico still?"

She started to shake her head but stopped herself.

"I don't know where he is," she said, but Willie knew that wasn't true.

She stood up, giving him to understand that the interview was over. He thanked her, patted the little girl on the head and walked back to his car.

He wanted to ask some questions of the neighbors, but that would have to wait. Most of the adults were still at work in the fields.

Instead, he cruised out of the trailer park. Two hundred yards up the road he pulled up under a tree with Spanish moss hanging from its limbs and made a call to the Camps' house. Fred answered, which was fine.

"Fred, it's Willie. I have a question for you."

"Uh-huh." He was still irritated.

"Have you ever heard of a young Mexican man around here named Martín Mendoza?"

Fred grunted. "Yeah, I've heard of him. He used to work for me."

Willie's black eyebrows went up.

"Really? How long ago?"

"I fired him two years ago. He worked for me for about three years. He was an assistant foreman."

"Why did you get rid of him?"

"Because he wasn't doing his work. Plain and simple. I'd find him hanging around in the air-conditioned offices here in the house when he ought to have been overseeing the tomato crews out in the fields."

"Do you know where Mendoza is now?"

"He's still around here, I'm told, but he's just a picker, not a foreman. He lives down the road in the trailer park."

"The same place where María Valdez is staying?"

"I believe so. Why?"

Willie thought that over.

"Did Fernando Ortiz have anything to do with Mendoza being fired?"

"No, he had nothing to do with that. It was me who fired Mendoza."

"Are you sure there was no bad blood between Mendoza and Fernando?"

"Not as far as I know, but I can transfer you to Fernando. He's in the office. I would have fired him by now, but Francisca won't let me."

Moments later Willie heard Fernando on the other end.

"It's Willie Cuesta calling. I have a question for you."

"Yes."

"Have you ever had any problem with Martín Mendoza? Is there any reason he would want to cause you harm? Is he jealous because you kept your job and he didn't?"

The other man hesitated, as if he were reviewing their personal history. It took him longer than expected.

"Are you there?" Willie asked.

"Yes, I'm here. No, I have never had any trouble with Martín Mendoza, nothing at all. He has nothing to do with this. I have to go now. I have to get back to work."

He hung up and left Willie grimacing. He had thought he had a motive for the lies being told about Fernando Ortiz, but his theory seemed to have fallen through.

Willie headed up the road to a rib joint where he took his time and ate a casual dinner. He knew that in the fields, at harvest time, the work would go on into the early evening. When he walked out of the restaurant it was about an hour before sunset. He drove back to the trailer park, but this time he parked near the entrance and walked in. Sitting in a rocking chair outside the first trailer was an old Latin woman in a flowered housedress. Willie had noticed her when he drove in that afternoon, but she had not been in sight when he left. Now she was back.

She tracked him as he entered, and Willie figured there wasn't much that went on there that escaped her attention. She was a kind of unofficial gatekeeper and, if Willie was lucky, a gossip.

She didn't disappoint him. Her name was Mrs. Lara, she had lived in that front trailer for fifteen years and had retired from field work about five years before. Her face was dark and furrowed from all those years in the sun and her hair was white as snow. She told him she was from a tiny village in the Mexican state of Sinaloa, and she obviously had brought to the trailer park that small-town propensity for knowing everything about everybody.

As she spoke to him Mrs. Lara assembled a rosary for the local Altar Society, the beads of which were actually small black beans. She kept her eyes on her holy work, but that didn't keep her from making some very acute observations about others in the trailer park.

Willie asked her about María Valdez, but Mrs. Lara said she knew very little because the young woman had only recently arrived.

"She doesn't work, and I wonder what she lives from. She says she just came here from Mexico, but I don't believe that. The little girl has talked about going to a school over near Orlando last year. But that is all I know."

She knew much more about Martín Mendoza, who had lived in the trailer park for several years.

"I don't think there is anything between him and this Valdez woman, even if she stays with him," she told Willie.

"Why do you think that is?"

She looked around to make sure no one was listening, leaned toward Willie and dropped her voice.

"I don't think he likes women. I've never seen him with a girl-friend. What I know is that for a time a man in a baseball cap would come to see him, but only late at night. I think he worked in the fields, because he always wore layers of clothes. He never said a word to anyone, never looked at anyone. He even wore dark glasses at night. I called out to him one time when he was leaving late at night, but he just hurried away. He would stay awhile in Martín Mendoza's trailer and then leave. That went on for a year or so, but I haven't seen him in some time. Martín was alone until this woman María Valdez arrived with the daughter."

Mrs. Lara went on to give Willie details about other scandalous behavior she had observed from her rocking chair over the past several years while assembling her rosaries. She spoke for a while longer and then looked toward the entrance of the trailer park.

An old school bus had pulled up and workers, both men and women, carrying their plastic buckets and empty lunch sacks, trudged toward their trailers. Wrapped in so many layers of clothing and bandanas, and wearing wide straw hats, they resembled scarecrows. Others arrived in vehicles.

"That's Martín there," Mrs. Lara said. She nodded toward a dented old van that was just passing. At the wheel was a dark, good-looking, long-haired man with a sparse moustache. Mrs. Lara had described him as serious and that's how he looked right then. Willie thanked her and she gave him a bean rosary to take with him.

"Pray for us sinners here at the trailer park."

Willie said he would.

He trotted to the rear of the property, to Mendoza's trailer. The man had already disappeared inside, his bucket sitting next to the stairs, and neither María Valdez nor her daughter was in sight. Willie knocked on the door and waited. He heard low voices inside, but no one responded. Willie knocked again, called out to Mendoza, but again there was no answer.

Then he heard a door creak and footsteps. Willie ducked around the end of the trailer just in time to see that Mendoza had slipped out a back door and was dashing down a trail that cut through the scrub. He took off after him.

The brush gave out quickly and soon they were running down a long, narrow furrow between rows of waist-high tomato plants. Willie hadn't been working in the sweltering fields all day. His legs were also longer and he was faster. He closed ground quickly until

Mendoza stopped, whirled around and confronted him. He was holding a short knife, maybe one he used to trim tomato plants. He looked like he wanted to trim Willie.

Willie stopped about ten feet from him. Enough light still fell on that field for Willie to clearly see the knife. He pulled back the lapel of his sport coat so Mendoza could see the 9mm Browning in his shoulder holster and he wrapped his hand around the grip without removing it.

"I'd stay where you are if I were you," he said.

Mendoza didn't move.

"Why are you trying to ruin the life of Fernando Ortiz? What did he ever do to you?"

Mendoza pursed his sunbaked lips.

"I don't know what you're talking about. Ortiz did nothing to me. What reason could I have to ruin him?"

"Maybe because he still has a job with Fred Camp and you don't."

Mendoza shrugged. "Many people work for Camp. Why would I care about one of them, Fernando Ortiz? Why don't you ask him? He'll tell you, we have no problems."

Of course, Willie had already done that and Fernando had told him exactly that.

Willie pointed back toward the trailer. "That woman staying with you isn't who she says she is."

The other man shook his head. "Then your problem is with her not me, although I don't think she'll speak with you again. You scared her."

"Did I scare you too? Is that why you were running?"

Mendoza's eyes narrowed.

"How do I know who you are? Maybe you're the *migra*."

Suddenly he was just the average undocumented field worker, afraid of getting picked up and deported. Willie didn't believe him for one brief moment, but he wasn't getting anywhere.

He turned and walked back toward his car, leaving Mendoza with the knife in his hand, as if he were doing some after-hours work in the fields. Willie drove out of the trailer park, headed back in the direction he'd come from and then pulled over to the side of the road. He sat there a good twenty minutes, turning over in his mind everything he had seen and heard since he'd arrived that morning. All the possible permutations of desire in the fields and who wanted to hide what.

Then he put the car back in gear. He drove past Fernando Ortiz's cottage, seeing the front door open and the pickup truck outside. But he kept going and pulled into the driveway of the Camps' house instead. One of the two cars parked there earlier was gone. He rang the bell, and after about thirty seconds Susanna answered the door. She glanced at him through the screen.

"My parents are out."

"I'm not here to see your parents. I'm here to talk to you."

"I'm not interested in talking to you."

"Yes, you are. I'm here to discuss Martín Mendoza. . . . Or I can discuss him with your parents."

Her gaze went from warlike to wary and back again and then she opened the door. She led him into the living room and dropped down into a chair with a chagrined look on her beautiful face.

"Okay, talk," she said.

Willie was left standing, looking down at her.

"You had an affair with Martín Mendoza. You used to sneak over to his trailer at night. You wore a baseball cap, hoping no one would see all that auburn hair. You wore layers of field clothes so that no one would even know you were a female. Nobody could know that Fred Camp's daughter was having an affair with one of the help."

She grimaced as if she was about to protest, but Willie held up a hand.

"After a while you walked away from it. I don't know if that happened before Mendoza got fired or after. I figure he probably lost his job because he was trying to be near you in the house and that was why he wasn't doing his job in the fields."

Her face came up and her gaze was combative.

"I didn't break it off because he got fired. The truth is, I was falling in love with Fernando."

Willie took that in.

"I believe you. He's a good fellow, Fernando. It wasn't the same as carrying on a clandestine love affair late at night, complete with disguises, but maybe you were growing up. Fernando is not only hardworking and honest, he's been willing to take the heat—all of it—when things got complicated."

Willie sat on the end of the sofa nearest her.

"It's not Fernando who has a past to hide, it's you. Martín Mendoza was so angry at you for leaving him, he decided to lay waste to your relationship with Fernando. He wasn't angry with Fernando, he hated you. But it's easy to create a fake past for somebody like Fernando Ortiz who comes from far away. I'm sure if I go to the nearest Mexican Consulate I'll find that those documents María Valdez showed your father are forgeries. You can buy counterfeit Social Security cards and work permits just about anywhere undocumented immigrants are found these days. Getting the same counterfeiters to craft bogus Mexican documents is probably a breeze. It should be easy to prove that María Valdez never knew Fernando and that Martín got her to make those accusations, maybe simply by supporting her and her child, maybe through threats. When I do that, your parents will be left posing the question of why this all happened."

Willie paused. Susanna sat staring at the floor, her face the picture of desolation.

"But we don't have to go through all that. I think you have to come clean with your parents. It's your turn to do the right thing and carry the weight for Fernando. You told him about Mendoza, and even then he didn't abandon you. You have to stop letting him take the heat here. He's been willing to sacrifice his reputation, his honor, to hide your history. Along the way, he has lost his good standing with your parents. You can't make him do that anymore."

Her mouth fell open. The thought of telling her mother and father that she had been making love to Martín Mendoza in a ratty trailer down the road was enough to make her die.

Willie shook his head. "You don't even have to tell them who it was but tell them that Fernando was willing to take the fall for you. Then they'll understand who he is. I'll back you up. If you really love Fernando and want a future with him, this is the only way."

It took her a full minute to work her way through it. Finally, she met Willie's gaze and nodded, her eyes now full of fear and sadness because she knew that in her relationship with her folks a degree of innocence would die. Well, if you were ready to get married, maybe it was time.

Minutes later, Fred and Francisca pulled up. Willie started to leave, but Susanna insisted he stay. She sat her parents down and for the next few minutes she bared her soul. She told them about Martín Mendoza, her late-night escapes from the farm to rendezvous with him down the road. She also told them that Fernando had known all along the source of María Valdez's lies but had refused to defend himself in order to protect her.

Willie watched her parents and saw pretty much what he had expected: two adults who understood nascent sexuality and who were relieved that their daughter wasn't marrying a Mexican bigamist, a deceiver who had abandoned his own child. By the end of Susanna's confession they were all standing together in a close family embrace.

Willie left them there, found the nearest motel and headed back to Miami the next morning. He hung the bean rosary Mrs. Lara had given him over his rearview mirror to ensure safe passage.

Two months later, he received a wedding invitation in the mail.

THE MAN FROM SCOTLAND
YARD DANCES SALSA

W illie Cuesta, private investigator, stared at his IRS forms on one side of the desk, his pile of receipts on the other, and he despaired. When they first started doing business, his accountant, Constance Dane, had told him to save every receipt from every assignment he undertook during the year and put them all in an old shoebox. At the end of the year he was to dump out the shoebox and total up all he had spent while on assignment.

"Do you mean for every cup of coffee I drink while staking out a motel in a divorce case?" Willie had asked.

"Every single one," Constance said. "You need the coffee to keep you awake to perform your surveillance, don't you? So, you claim it. And you claim the sandwiches and burritos you eat on the road as well. Keep track of all your mileage on slips of paper with the date. Put them in there too."

The pile of receipts and pieces of paper had to be separated into those categories and several others, totaled up and inserted into the form Constance provided. Every year Willie dreaded the task of doing that and always put it off until that last minute. That minute had arrived, and he was now hunched over his calculator.

At the moment he was having a thought he had every year: that someday, when he had the money, he would invest in Dunkin' Donuts and/or Starbucks stock. Just then his cell phone sounded. Willie answered it on the first ring. Anything to escape the task at hand.

"Cuesta and Associates, Investigations," he intoned.

"Is this Willie speaking?"

The accent on the other end was clipped and very distinctly British. Willie recognized the voice right away.

"Neville, is that you?"

"Right you are, *amigo*. How are you?"

Neville Ashley was the resident representative of Scotland Yard, based at the British Consulate in Miami. He had been working out of South Florida for many years, ever since US authorities discovered that it was much easier to investigate crime links between Miami and the former British possessions in the Caribbean if you had a Scotland Yard detective who lived locally and acted as a liaison between Caribbean police and their American allies. The Yard still had clout in the old colonies.

Over the years, Neville had helped the FBI, US Alcohol, Tobacco, Firearms and Explosives agents and Florida state and local police crack all sorts of crime rings that had Miami and Caribbean branches—including in the fields of drug trafficking, people smuggling, money laundering, insurance scams, etc. During his days as a member of the Miami P.D. Intelligence Unit, Willie had traveled with Neville to Jamaica, the British Virgin Islands and Barbados. Neville not only had great connections with Caribbean law enforcement types, he always knew the best places to stay and eat. Willie was fond of his Scotland Yard partner. In response, Neville had once referred to Willie as "a hail fellow well met," which was apparently high praise from a Brit.

They exchanged a few pleasantries, updates on colleagues and then Neville turned to business.

"Willie, I've called you because I have a very delicate and confidential matter on my plate and I think you are the best man in Miami to help me with it. It concerns the security of British subjects here in South Florida. If you can come to the consulate tomorrow morning, I'll explain it to you. I know you're in business for yourself these days, and Her Majesty the Queen will be glad to pay you your usual day rate."

Willie agreed to be there first thing in the a.m., and they rang off. Glancing at the shoebox, he shoved it to the back of the desk. Only three things in life were inevitable—death, taxes and the fact that Willie would find any reason to not do the latter.

ꙮ ꙮ

The British Consulate in Miami was located in the Brickell Avenue corridor, on Biscayne Bay, just south of downtown. That stretch was lined with tall glass office buildings and residential towers. It played home to various other consulates and also many international banks. Miami had taken very seriously its goal to become the business capital of Latin America, and the gleaming Brickell area was the hub of that ambition. It looked like midtown Manhattan, but with year-round sunshine.

The tower housing the consulate featured palm trees planted out front and a garden of bamboo leading to the glass front doors. Willie took the elevator to the twenty-eighth floor and entered a reception office decorated in tropical colors—in particular lots of Florida orange. The receptionist sat behind bulletproof glass and hanging just behind her was a pastel portrait of Her Majesty Queen Elizabeth in more tropical hues—lemon yellow, aquamarine, sunset pinks—apparently custom-made for the Miami consulate. Instructions for visa applicants and other visitors were displayed in English and Spanish.

Willie stated his business, and moments later Neville emerged to meet him. He was a tall, slim, craggy man, with gray hair, a neat gray moustache and placid blue-gray eyes that disguised a keen investigative intelligence. He preferred three-piece suits—today he wore a dark blue pinstripe—and he always accompanied the suit with a bow tie. On this occasion it was crimson in color.

He shook Willie's hand warmly and then led him to a conference room. There they sat under a photograph of Buckingham Palace, with the red-coated guards peering down at them gravely. Neville reached into a manila folder and handed Willie an eight-by-eleven photograph. It appeared to have been taken by a nightclub photographer and depicted several young people at a table, which they shared with champagne glasses and two bottles in silver buckets. At the very center of the photograph was a particularly attractive young blond woman wearing a low-cut, skimpy black dress and flashing a scintillating smile. Neville tapped that smile.

"This is Ms. Samantha Chesterfield. She is twenty-two years old and the youngest child of Mr. David Chesterfield, the president and

CEO of CTG, Commonwealth Technology Group, one of the largest Internet technology firms in Britain. Four nights ago, she was kidnapped after leaving a nightclub on South Beach. She went there with a woman friend, and when that friend decided to leave at about two a.m. Ms. Chesterfield chose to stay. She was in the company of a couple of local Cuban men whom they had met at the club and those gentlemen offered to give Ms. Chesterfield a ride back to the hotel. She never arrived. While still at the club, the men apparently drugged her drink. She woke up many hours later, tied up at some still-unknown location. The next day, her father received a ransom request for two million dollars and paid it within forty-eight hours. I only learned about it after the girl was released. Luckily, she was unharmed."

Willie took it all in.

"Out of curiosity, what was the name of the club?"

"Nocturne."

Willie nodded. "A very popular spot these days."

Willie knew his nightclubs. His brother Tommy was the owner of one of the oldest and best salsa clubs in Miami—Caliente! Hot!

In fact, Willie was nominal head of security for him, hiring and firing bouncers, filling out security schedules, making sure that the drug dealers, pickpockets, purse snatchers and hookers who gravitated to the club scene gravitated somewhere else. In the usual course of events he didn't have to worry about kidnappers.

"How do you think this happened?" Willie asked. "Do you think that in the nightclub chitchat Ms. Chesterfield dropped information about her family's fortune and these dudes decided to tap the till?"

Neville shook his head. "No, I don't think they did it on the fly. Her name was in a society column in the *Miami Herald* a few days earlier, shortly after she arrived here. I think the kidnappers targeted her and were following her long before she ever stepped into that club. They were just biding their time, these Cuban boys. Ms. Chesterfield wasn't the first of my countrymen targeted by kidnappers here of late."

That made Willie's eyebrows rise. "Really? I hadn't heard of any other snatches, not recently."

"That's because, just as in this instance, the victims and would-be victims didn't want to advertise it."

"Would-be?"

Neville leaned back in his high-backed, black-leather chair.

"About a month ago, a young British man named Joseph Holmes was attacked by some men late at night as he tried to flag down a cab on Collins Avenue. A car pulled up, someone inside called out his name and when he approached two men got out and tried to drag him in. Another man was behind the wheel, ready to take off, but Holmes started to scream at the top of his lungs and luckily was able to fight them off. They jumped back in the car and took off before the coppers came."

"Was he coming out of the same club?"

"No. He'd been to a tango club named Buenos Aires."

"And he tangoed right into the embrace of bad guys. Does Mr. Holmes also come from an affluent family?"

Neville nodded. "Yes, and not only that, his family and that of Ms. Chesterfield have something else in common. Both the family firms do business in Cuba."

"You don't say."

"His family has controlling interest in a firm called Viva Exports. They supply liquor, other beverages and some food products to Cuba, especially to its tourism industry. Like CTG, the firm owned by Ms. Chesterfield's father, they have offices and warehouses in Cuba. And, by the way, he was also mentioned in the society columns after he arrived in town. When you buy a lot of Cristal champagne in clubs at six hundred dollars per bottle, you get mentioned in the celebrity news."

"Which makes it easy for bad guys to get a bead on you."

"Precisely."

Willie thought over what Neville had laid out.

"So, they both came from wealthy families, which explains why they were targeted by kidnappers. The fact that both families have investments in Cuba, could that be a coincidence?"

Neville winced. "I wish it were, but I doubt it. I heard a rumor last week from a friend of mine in the diplomatic corps here. He said the Spaniards may also have had an incident. I didn't act on it at the time, but yesterday, just before calling you, I contacted the Spanish consul general. She spoke to me in confidence, and this has to be kept confidential, but six weeks ago, a middle-aged woman from

Madrid visiting here was kidnapped when she took a walk near her condo on Key Biscayne. The family paid the ransom and the woman was returned, all without a word to the local authorities."

Willie squinted at him hard.

"Let me guess. That woman's family has holdings in Cuba."

Neville nodded. "They are the largest stockholders in a company called CaribTur. They have built hotels in Cuba along prime beach locations right on the Caribbean. I know of her case for sure and who knows who else has been grabbed, given that people don't generally advertise these assaults."

For many years, Miami had been a popular destination for all sorts of celebrities—entertainers, star athletes, political personalities—but you never heard of kidnappings or even attempted kidnappings. Of course, it might have been, as Neville suggested, that the families had hushed up the snatches, and word hadn't leaked out. But Willie had very good contacts in the law enforcement community and if those events were at all frequent, he would have known. With three incidents in a matter of weeks, he was convinced a kidnapping gang had finally set up shop in Miami, but a gang with a very specific set of targets. Many Cuban exiles in Miami, who hated the Castro brothers' government in Cuba, thought no Westerners should have dealings with the island. Despite those attitudes, of late the US government had altered regulations and, after years of trying to isolate Cuba, was making it easier for American companies to do business there. Apparently, a group of the local *cubanos* had decided to take action and dissuade would-be investors from doing that. The question was who those Cubans might be.

"This is going to be like looking for a Cuban needle in a Cuban haystack," Willie told Neville, "but I'll do the best I can."

Neville pulled out a checkbook, handed Willie the equivalent of three days' wages and they shook hands on the deal. As he left the consular offices Willie noticed the queen watching him from where she hung on the wall. He would do his best for Her Majesty as well.

☙ ☙

Willie reached his car again and sat stock still, trying to figure out in which direction to go. After all, in Miami there were Cuban exiles in all directions, hundreds of thousands of them. He was Cuban, had served as a police officer and now a private investigator for a total of twenty years and he knew more than most people. Too many to count. After a half-hour of running through his mental Rolodex, one name emerged from the multitude: Carlos "Papi" Planas. Willie cranked up and headed for Papi's offices in Little Havana.

The truth was that the term "offices" was much too grandiose for the space Papi Planas occupied. His daughter operated a Cuban nostalgia shop on the first floor, where she sold tinted photos of old Havana in the pre-Castro days, copies of old Cuban magazines and replicas of the clothing styles from that era—lots of white linen suits, white shoes and flowered frocks. She even stocked small bags of fine white sand that had allegedly been collected from Cuba's beaches decades earlier. Anything that evoked Cuba before the island became a Communist outpost—and before Cuban exiles had come to Miami—might be found in the shop. It was an oasis of memory.

A staircase at the back of that shop led you to a second-floor cubbyhole where Papi ran a different kind of nostalgia depot. Papi had been born and raised in the old Cuba and had become a civil engineer for the government. In the days just before that government fell, Papi gathered all sorts of property records and blueprints of public works—including railroad lines, port facilities, power stations, bridges, the layouts of the national highway network and sewer systems—and shipped them to Miami. His rationale was that when the war to liberate Cuba came, it would be important for the invading troops to have that information to recapture the island.

Of course, that had never occurred. But over the years, Papi had provided blueprints to exile business people dreaming of returning to Cuba and had also provided old property records to Cuban exiles who had sued the Cuban government demanding reparations for their lost holdings. Key to the current case, exiles had also used Papi's files to find out which foreign companies were now operating out of those old addresses and sued them as well. The legal actions never went anywhere because neither the Cuban government nor the companies paid them attention.

Willie had met Papi when his Uncle Pedro had gone looking for a deed to his old house in Havana in hopes of someday getting it back—or getting the current residents to recompense him for it. Until the end of his life, Uncle Pedro had demanded his due, to no avail. In Miami, those kinds of hopes never died.

Willie parked right in front of the nostalgia shop, entered, walked through the pungent history and stopped at the cash register in the rear. He told the cashier he was there to see Papi and she pointed him up the stairway. Willie took it, reached a plain wooden door, knocked and heard a gravelly male voice speaking Spanish say "Pase." Come in.

Willie had not been in that office in over ten years, but as far as he could tell it hadn't changed one iota. Black filing cabinets lined all four walls. Hanging above them were old photos of industrial installations—sugar refineries, docks with primitive loading cranes, locomotives out of the early twentieth century—and also blueprints that were either big power plants or very complicated kitchen stoves. Willie was no engineer and wouldn't know one from the other.

Papi Planas also didn't look as if he had moved or changed much since the last time Willie had been there. He had to be about eighty-five now, with steel-gray hair combed straight back, maybe a bit sparser than before; deep-set brown eyes; a large, veined, rum-drinker's nose; massive shoulders over a body that was solid as a bridge abutment. He wore a white *guayabera* shirt and steel-gray pants, maybe the exact same ones he had worn the last time. He was smoking a thick dark stogie and the room was hazy with pungent smoke. He squinted through it at Willie, obviously trying to recall who he was.

"Papi, it's Willie Cuesta. The nephew of Pedro Cuesta."

Papi searched the voluminous files he kept in his head and nodded.

"Yes, Willie the detective. Your Uncle Pedro had that very nice house in Havana."

"That's right."

Papi's expression turned sad. "I understand your uncle died sometime back."

"Yes."

He pointed at one of his filing cabinets. "Well, the deed is still there. Someday maybe I can get you or other relatives restitution for what was lost."

Willie thanked him but didn't really think the Cuban government was going to be recompensing the Cuesta family any time soon. Down deep, Papi suspected that too. After all these years he knew that what he was selling weren't documents that might someday be worth real money. What he was peddling were ties to the past—which were so important to exile Cubans—and some wistful, unrealistic dreams about the future. What those file cabinets and computers contained were fantasies.

Willie sized up Papi Planas and decided to take him into his confidence.

"I'm working on a case, Papi, a case that involves some very dangerous people and I'm hoping you can help me."

The old man knitted his bushy eyebrows. "Dangerous how?"

Willie described for him the three kidnappings that had occurred in Miami in recent weeks. Then he told him what all three victims had in common and that made Papi cringe.

"The families all do business in Cuba. You think that's the connection?"

"Yes. And I'm here because I'm playing a hunch, Papi. I'm hoping you'll let me look at your records for the past few months, records of who came to you and what properties they wanted to know about."

Papi stopped swiveling and fixed on Willie. He was no dummy and understood right away what Willie was saying: that one or more of his paying customers might have been involved in kidnappings. The most important word there was "might." How realistic was that theory? Did it warrant divulging confidential information? He was being asked to hand over valuable data for nothing, something Papi was not accustomed to doing. Willie could see the old mind operating, trying to decide. He bore down.

"The next time they target someone, an innocent person could get killed, Papi. Just in case I'm right, you won't want that on your conscience."

The old man who sold dreams was suddenly confronted with a nightmare. Willie could see it in his rheumy eyes. Papi took a deep, despondent breath, turned to his computer and brought up his files. Willie went around behind him to watch. An Excel spreadsheet popped up on the screen

"Here are the customers who have come to me this year."

Names of paying clients were listed on the left. The address of the property they had inquired about was noted next. The current occupants of the property, if known, were also listed. Willie knew that Papi had informants in Cuba who had helped him keep track of who was occupying which properties.

Just like Willie's late Uncle Pedro, most of Papi's clients were individuals who came to him to buy the deeds of their old family homes. And just like Tío Pedro, they did it just in case an accommodation was made some day, or—in the fondest of all Cuban fantasies—the Communist government fell and they could go home. The current residents of those private properties listed in Papi's files were everyday Cuban people Willie had never heard of, not families worth targeting in kidnapping schemes. Not as far as Willie could tell.

But some of the listings involved commercial properties. A number of those addresses housed businesses run by the Cuban Communist government, but others were occupied by foreign corporations. Willie saw one entry for the Hotel Costa de Oro in Havana, owned by CaribTur S.A. That was the company owned by the Spanish family of the woman kidnapped from Key Biscayne.

A bit farther down the list came a reference to the firm Viva Exports, which was cited as occupying two warehouses in Santiago, the second-largest city in Cuba. The family of Joseph Holmes, the boy who had fought off his would-be kidnappers, owned that entity. Just below that Willie found CTG—Commonwealth Technology Group—the firm controlled by the father of Samantha Chesterfield, who had not been so lucky. Its offices were right in downtown Havana.

Willie tapped all three entries, one after the other. "Bingo. Bingo. Bingo. All these foreign firms were targeted by kidnappers in the past three months."

Papi's wide shoulders slumped. "*Dios mío,*" he muttered.

"Who asked you to document these particular properties?"

Papi tapped the keyboard and moved the cursor to the far-right column of the spreadsheet where the clients were listed. The name next to each of the three properties that interested Willie was the same: Robert J. Aguilar.

"Who is this guy, Aguilar?" Willie asked.

Papi shook his head. "I never heard of him before he came in here first time a few months ago. He's from a Cuban family and he told me he was an attorney. He was interested in properties confiscated by the Castro government and said he was going to put in claims for the families who once owned them. What was different about him was he paid me in cash. Most people pay by check or credit card."

Willie told Papi to go into Google and find the website for the Florida Bar Association. Willie then leaned over his shoulder, typed in the name and right away the site responded: "Your search yielded no results." He typed in the address for another site that listed attorneys nationwide—a site he had learned about during his days on the Miami P.D.—but that also came back empty.

"Well, your client ain't no attorney, at least not in this country. Did he ever give you an address or a phone number?"

Papi shook his head. "No, never. He came, put in his order, came back a couple of days later to pick up the information and paid me cash."

"Well, given how much they are asking in ransom, he and his partners can afford to shell out some cash for your data."

Willie grimaced, wondering how he was going to track a phony lawyer who left no tracks. He spent a few moments staring at the motes of dust dancing in the air above Papi.

"When was the last time this Mr. Aguilar was in here?" he asked.

Papi screwed up his fleshy face and then hit on something. "You know, he came here just three or four days ago."

He turned back to the computer, brought up the Excel sheet, ran the cursor to near the bottom and stopped. The name Robert J. Aguilar appeared again. Willie's pulse picked up.

"What property was he asking about?"

Papi ran the cursor to the left and found properties listed in Matanzas province directly east of Havana on the north coast of Cuba. They were now occupied by North Sea Oil, Inc., a British oil-exploration firm. Willie had read about the possibility of petroleum deposits off the coast of the island, and that apparently was what those Brits were looking for.

Willie grabbed a chair, scooted Papi to one side and dug his fingers into the keyboard. During his days on the Intelligence Unit of the Miami P.D., investigating foreign criminals working in South Florida, Willie had learned how to trace the ownership of corporations, including foreign firms. He went into the indicated websites and within three minutes he had the names of the principals in the firm.

He pulled out his cell phone, punched in a number and seconds later the clipped accent of Neville Ashley was in his ear.

"Neville, I need you to reach out to a British firm, North Sea Oil, Inc. The owners are members of a family called Peters. Find out if any of them or their relatives are currently in Miami or are coming to Miami soon." Neville started to ask why, but Willie cut him off. "Do this first and then I'll fill you in. We can't waste any time."

He rang off and thanked the old man.

"If all this works out, I'll make sure you get paid for your time and expertise, Papi."

Willie hurried back to his apartment/office, which was about fifteen blocks west, still in Little Havana. He hadn't eaten, so he opened his refrigerator, retrieved some leftovers from a Cuban Chinese restaurant and zapped them in the microwave. He was about halfway through that hasty lunch—Cuban pork chunks with a side of sesame noodles—when Neville called back.

"I don't know how you knew this, Willie, but . . ."

"Yes."

"You were right. North Sea Oil is privately held by the Peters clan out of Aberdeen. The CEO is one Donald Peters, and he has a granddaughter, named Helen, who is in Miami Beach on her honeymoon. She and her husband, Reginald Stevens, are booked at a boutique hotel called the Cameo, on Collins Avenue."

"Let me guess," Willie said. "Their wedding and their honeymoon plans made the society pages in London so anybody could know they are here."

"Exactly."

Willie was squinting as if trying to see something far away on Miami Beach.

"You have to decide what to do here, Neville. Do you call in the police, or do we handle it on our own?"

Neville already knew what he wanted.

"As I told you, I want this handled as quietly as possible, Willie. If it makes the newspapers, then even if we grab this particular gang, someone else may decide they fancy the business plan. I do have a contact in the FBI here whom I have collaborated with in the past and whom I can trust to be discreet. I also have two security officers attached to the consulate I can call on. Hopefully we can apprehend these individuals and my FBI friend will arrest them, but we have to plot our plan so that Helen Peters and her husband are never at risk of harm."

ꙮ ꙮ

An hour later, the two of them were crossing the Julia Tuttle Causeway to Miami Beach in Neville's Land Rover. At the consulate Neville had introduced Willie to the two security officers, Forster and Graham, both of them attached to the British Army and both built like the Tower of London—tall, square-shouldered, solid. They were on call whenever Neville and Willie might need them.

Neville valet-parked the Land Rover and they entered the Cameo Hotel. The lobby was narrow and about three stories high, with a fountain of sleek, polished black stone in the middle and above it a chandelier made from long, vertical LED lights that resembled sun rays illuminating the arcing water. All very modern. But the most distinctive feature of the lobby was the walls, which were bright white but with cameos everywhere—black heads of different sizes in profile, people looking at each other, but also possibly peeking out of the corners of their eyes at anyone who entered. It was meant to be a modern take on Art Deco, Willie figured. It made him feel like a private eye surrounded by private eyes.

Neville led him across the lobby to the chromed elevator doors. He had called ahead, tracked down Helen and Reginald Stevens and had arranged to meet them in their room, where the conversation couldn't be observed. It turned out that they were both in their mid-twenties, tall, slim, blue-eyed, expensive-looking—and mildly sun-burned.

Neville introduced Willie and then explained the situation, including what had occurred in the previous cases. The couple was more confused than concerned at first. But when he reached the case of Samantha Chesterfield and the two guys who had approached her in the dance joint, the two young people looked at each other with alarm and then back at Neville. Helen Peters did the talking.

"On the beach yesterday two men under the next umbrella chatted us up. We saw them again today and they invited us to go clubbing tonight."

Neville shot Willie a glance and raised his steel-gray eyebrows. Helen's new husband, Reggie, cut in.

"You know, I thought it was strange that they ended up right next to us again today. We didn't get out on the beach until midafternoon, and just minutes after we did, they settled in next to us. To tell the truth, even yesterday they seemed familiar. I'd seen them around here in the past few days. You think they were watching and waiting for us?"

Neville nodded. "If they are who we think they are. What did they look like?"

Helen did the describing. "Thirties, Latin, ladies' men."

Again, Neville glanced at Willie.

"Bingo!" Willie said.

"What plans were proposed for tonight?" Neville asked.

"We're to meet them at midnight tonight at a club called Havana Nights, which is just down Collins Avenue," Helen said.

Willie nodded. "Yes, I know it."

Neville took over at that point. The newlyweds were seated on the bed and he stood over them.

"We want to catch these criminals and we would like you to help us. I assure you we will avoid putting either of you at any serious risk, but it's still up to you if you want to involve yourselves."

The young people glanced at each other, and Willie saw their lips purse, their jaws set and then a frisson of excitement exchanged between them. Helen looked up and nodded at Neville.

"It will give us a tale to tell our children."

Willie and Neville stepped out onto the balcony overlooking the aquamarine sea and put their heads together. It was as if their plan was slowly coming toward them over the horizon. After a while they reentered the room and laid out the operation for the couple. Neville asked them to order from room service instead of going out for dinner that night, just to keep them under wraps. He told them that since the club, Havana Nights, was only a few blocks from the hotel, they should walk. The two security officers from the consulate would be tailing them all the way, but not to look for them. At that point, he took out his cell phone and shot a photo of the couple so his operatives would know who to tail.

"Once you get in the club, Mr. Cuesta, plus my FBI contact and I, will be there. Don't look for us; we'll look for you. If we need to communicate with you, we'll text you. Keep your phone on, Ms. Peters. If and when a confrontation occurs, follow our verbal commands."

Neville and Willie then headed for the door. After all, the two young people were on their honeymoon.

ॐ ॐ

Nightclubs on South Beach don't come alive until midnight. That is when the restaurants both on the beach and on the mainland tend to empty and people who have been putting on calories for the past few hours look for clubs where they can dance off the weight. Many of them will dance till dawn—some of them with the help of illegal substances and others only on the strength of the carbohydrates they've consumed. South Beach offers a variety of choices for all-night dancers—rock-'n'-roll, thumping techno, tango, reggae and also a slew of Latin lounges where you can move to salsa, *merengue* or other tropical rhythms to your liking. If by dawn whatever you swallowed hasn't worn off, you can move on to after-hours venues where the music goes until at least midafternoon. The experience sold by the South Beach entrepreneurs can be summed up easily: excess 24/7.

Willie was to pick up Neville and his FBI contact outside the British Consulate at eleven. When he arrived at the door, he was surprised to find the Brit standing next to a statuesque, raven-haired

Latina woman, about thirty-five, who wore a black dress that was both high-hemmed and low-cut.

"This is FBI Special Agent Esperanza Alves," Neville said by way of introduction. "She has been assigned to help us."

Willie knew a number of local FBI agents but had never had the pleasure of meeting Agent Alves. He gave her a warm hello and was ready to be helped by her any way she pleased.

By eleven-thirty they had crossed the bay to Miami Beach and were at Havana Nights. Lots of the doormen at South Beach clubs had danced at Willie's brother's place over the years and he knew them all, so he and his companions were ushered in like royalty. Part of that special treatment was that they weren't checked for weapons, which was a good thing because they were all carrying.

The three of them crossed the dance floor, and Willie took the opportunity to look around as they did. Havana Nights was a slice of heaven for salsa dancers. It was a big place with amphitheater seating surrounding the sunken, circular dance floor, allowing everyone to study attendees of the opposite sex everywhere in the arena and shop for potential dance partners. At the center of the room hung a mirrored globe which revolved constantly and sent lasers of reflected light all around the room. At the far end stood a stage where music stands and very large speakers were propped, awaiting the house orchestra. Willie had heard them play numerous times, a twelve-piece ensemble that included both Cuban and Puerto Rican musicians decked out in tropical shirts and white linen pants, who played killer salsa and even broke into some coordinated dance steps during choruses.

The layout was good for Willie and crew because it would allow them to keep an eye on Helen and her husband no matter where they sat. Willie found a table as centrally located as possible on the far side. They ordered drinks and settled in.

The place filled up quickly. Just after midnight, it was packed. Willie sipped a margarita and searched the crowd for two men matching the description of the would-be kidnappers but didn't spot any obvious suspects. A few minutes later, he saw Helen and Reggie walk in and they were ushered to a table right on the edge of the dance floor almost directly across from where Willie and his party were seated—clearly visible. Forster and Graham, the two big consular security agents, were right behind them. They took a table across the way, a bit higher up but also with a clear view of the would-be victims. The couple's table was for four, but no one sat with them, not at first.

A few minutes later, the orchestra came through the curtains at the back of the stage and began to play—leading off with a beautifully orchestrated, brassy salsa number. The eager clientele rushed to the floor and fell right into the intricate rhythms of the dance. Many Latinos could trace back their parentage to chance meetings on dance floors in Latin dance joints between Mama and Papa, and the rhythms were in the blood. The dance floor became dense with bodies.

Willie was just about to suggest to Esperanza that they dance— Why waste good dance music?—when Neville beat him to it. He took the lady's hand in his.

"Excuse us while we take a turn and let the honeymooners know we're here," he said.

Willie watched them as they walked down the stairs to the floor, saw Neville take the special agent in his arms and they fell effortlessly into the three-beat rhythm of the music. In his three-piece suit, and with his craggy face and slight stoop, Neville was no Cuban club boy. He didn't have any flamboyant moves, and his style was stiff, but his rhythm was precise, his turns cleanly executed and his direction of his partner was authoritative. Willie's Scotland Yard colleague could salsa, by Jove!

Willie watched as Neville and Esperanza expertly edged their way through the crowd to a point where they were visible from Helen's table. After a minute or so, he saw Helen fix on Neville and eye contact was made. Neville gave the slightest of nods and so did the girl. She was discreet, Helen, like a good British lady. After a couple of tunes Neville and Esperanza returned to the table to sip on their drinks.

"I never knew you had it in you, Neville."

Neville sipped his Scotch and shrugged.

"I've been stationed all around the world, Willie. I always try to be in step with the locals."

They were still sipping their drinks a few minutes later when two Latin men dressed in *guayabera* shirts—one white, one black—

showed up at the couple's table and it was handshakes and kisses all around. They sat on either side of the couple and quickly fell into lively banter. Helen and Reggie were just a touch rigid, given what they suspected about their new acquaintances, but they kept smiles on their faces and the Cubans apparently didn't notice.

Over the next couple of hours, the party ordered several rounds of drinks. The "amigo" in the white shirt asked Reggie for permission and then escorted Helen out onto the dance floor. Awhile later, his partner in black did the same. Neville, Esperanza and Willie tried to keep sight of them in the crowd, to make sure that one *amigo* or the other didn't try to simply dance Helen out the door. At one point, Helen and the man in black disappeared behind a bobbing wall of revelers and for several fraught moments didn't emerge. Fearing Helen might be halfway to a getaway car, Willie jumped up, sprinted down the aisle and snaked his way, not at all delicately, through the couples on the floor, with his hand on the butt of his gun in his shoulder holster. He finally saw them on the far side of the floor, still dancing. Helen caught sight of him over the shoulder of her partner. Willie gave her a reassuring nod and retreated. He rejoined Esperanza and Neville and all together they kept their eyes glued to the table across the floor for any sign of trouble.

The two bad guys made their move at about two-thirty a.m. At that point, the *amigos* goaded Reggie to take his bride for a spin on the floor, literally pushing him up out of his chair. They were all laughter and joshing until Reggie and Helen were engulfed by the crowd—and at least momentarily out of sight. At that point, the man in black immediately lost his smile, reached quickly into his top pocket, pulled out a small white envelope, poured powder from it first into Helen's drink and then Reggie's and then threw it to the floor.

"That's it," muttered Neville. "The game is on."

Esperanza, Neville and Willie got up and headed down the stairs. When they reached the dance floor, Willie took Esperanza in his arms and danced her in the direction of the two men. Willie bided his time for about a minute while Neville and his two operatives assumed their positions behind the table in question. Then Willie spun Esperanza into a particularly energetic double-axel salsa turn that made her short skirt flair provocatively. When she came out of the turn, she was standing right over the two men at the table, plucked her FBI credential out of her décolletage and held it near their faces.

"FBI. You are under arrest and coming with me."

Willie had his hand on the butt of his gun again. For several moments it wasn't clear if the Cubans would comply, try to make a run for it or—if they had managed to smuggle weapons in—turn the club into a shooting gallery. While they decided, Neville came up behind them and, with a nifty move, took custody of the two tainted drinks. As he did, the Cubans leapt to their feet and attempted to bolt, one in each direction. By that time, the two British commandos were right behind them. Graham was able to grab "Mr. White" and wrap him in a headlock before he could travel two steps.

"Mr. Black" was a bit faster. Forster tried to grab him, but the other man darted away and headed in the only direction he could, onto the teeming dance floor, knocking couples out of his path. Willie dove in after him, ricocheted off a number of bodies and finally caught him by the collar in the very center of the crowd. Women screamed, and all the dancers fled toward the edges of the floor, creating space for the two fighters. The band, inured to occasional and inevitable conflicts in the crowd, never stopped playing.

It was over quickly. Mr. Black managed to break the hold on his collar, but Willie was able to grab him by one arm. In the approximation of a salsa turn, he swung the other man around, got him off balance and then, in perfect rhythm to the music, hit him three times, twice in the gut and once on the jaw. When he still didn't go down, Willie did it again. One-two-three. One-two-three. Mr. Black hit the floor hard, exactly on the downbeat.

Moments later, Forster, the commando and several club security folks swarmed the dance floor, clapping the fallen kidnapper into handcuffs. Neville appeared, still holding the two drinks containing the evidence.

"I must say, you have very good rhythm, my friend."

Willie shrugged.

"I'll take that as a compliment, Neville, even though you're British."

꣓ ꣓

Papi Planas later identified the man in white as the fellow who had visited his shop claiming to be attorney Robert J. Aguilar. His real name was Sergio Veras, and the man in black was his brother, Bernardo. The powder in the drinks tested positive for Rohypnol, a powerful sedative. The other victims were sent photos and identified them as their assailants. It turned out the brothers' own family had lost land that was now in the hands of the Cuban government and they were out for revenge. They were locked up without bail, awaiting trial.

The honeymooners returned to their honeymooning.

A few days later, Neville phoned Willie.

"Helen tells me when the time comes someday, they'll name their first son after us," he said.

"Willie Neville Stevens," Willie offered. "It has a ring to it."

Neville cleared his throat. "We'll see, Willie. We'll see."

ALSO BY JOHN LANTIGUA

Burn Season

Heat Lightning

The Lady from Buenos Aires: A Willie Cuesta Mystery

On Hallowed Ground: A Willie Cuesta Mystery

Remember My Face: A Willie Cuesta Mystery

The Ultimate Havana